RULES FOR PE

Peter Swanson's novels include *The Girl With a Clock for a Heart*, nominated for an *LA Times* book award, *The Kind Worth Killing*, a Richard and Judy pick and the iBooks store's thriller of the year in 2015, and, most recently, *Before She Knew Him*. He lives with his wife and cat in Somerville, Massachusetts.

PRAISE FOR PETER SWANSON

'Deliciously good – dry, intelligent, perfectly paced, there is more than a touch of the Barbara Vines.' *Observer*

'Neatly knotted suspense.' *New York Times*

'He's the real deal . . . in the ranks of the killer elite alongside Tana French, Gillian Flynn and Lauren Beukes.' Joe Hill

'Another read in one sitting from the bestselling Swanson.' *Metro*

'A brilliantly original premise, delivered with panache.'
Clare Mackintosh

'His writing is meticulous and alert.' *Daily Mail*

'Gripping, elegantly and stylishly written, and extremely hard to put down!' Sophie Hannah

'Chilling and hypnotically suspenseful . . . could be an instant classic.'
Lee Child

'*The Girl with a Clock for a Heart* is a twisty, sexy, electric thrill ride and an absolute blast from start to finish.' Dennis Lehane

'As good as they come. Contemporary noir with twists that you won't see coming.' Mark Billingham

ALSO BY PETER SWANSON

RULES
FOR
PERFECT
MURDERS

A NOVEL

PETER
SWANSON

FABER & FABER

First published in the UK in 2020
by Faber & Faber Ltd Bloomsbury
House
74–77 Great Russell Street
London WC1B 3DA

First published in the USA in 2019
by HarperCollins Publishers
195 Broadway, New York
NY 10007

Printed and bound by CPI Group (UK) Ltd, Croydon CR0 4YY

Photograph on title page by Koldunuv/Shutterstock, Inc.

A CIP record for this book
is available from the British Library

ISBN 978–0–571–34235–8

2 4 6 8 10 9 7 5 3 1

[TK]

a memoir

Disclaimer: While what you are about to read is largely true, I have re-created some events and conversations from memory. A few names and identifying characteristics have been changed to protect the innocent.

RULES FOR

PERFECT

MURDERS

CHAPTER 1

The front door opened, and I heard the stamp of the FBI agent's feet on the doormat. It had just begun to snow, and the air that rushed into the store was heavy and brimming with energy. The door shut behind the agent. She must have been just outside when she'd called because it had only been about five minutes since I'd agreed to meet with her.

Except for me, the store was empty. I don't know exactly why I'd opened it that day. A storm was forecast to drop over two feet of snow, beginning in the morning and continuing through until the following afternoon. Boston Public Schools had already announced they were closing early, and they'd canceled all classes for the following day. I'd called the two employees who were scheduled to come in—Emily for the morning shift and early afternoon, and Brandon for the afternoon and evening—and told them both to stay home. I logged on to the Old Devils Bookstore Twitter account and was about to send out a tweet saying that we were closed for the duration of the storm, but something stopped me. Maybe it was the thought of spending all day in my apartment alone. And besides, I lived less than half a mile from the store.

I decided to go in; at the very least I'd be able to spend some time with Nero, straighten up some shelves, maybe even pack up some online orders.

A sky the color of granite was threatening snow as I unlocked the front doors on Bury Street in Beacon Hill. Old Devils Bookstore is not in a high-traffic area, but we're a specialty bookstore—mystery books, used and new—and most of our customers seek us out or simply order directly from our website. On a typical Thursday in February I wouldn't be surprised if the total number of customers barely reached double digits, unless of course we had an event planned. Still, there was always work to do. And there was Nero, the store cat, who hated spending the day alone. Also, I couldn't remember if I'd fed him extra food the night before. It turned out I probably hadn't because when I stepped through the front door, he came racing along the hardwood floor to greet me. He was a ginger cat of indeterminate age, perfect for the store because of his willingness (his eagerness, really) to put up with the affections of strangers. I turned on the store lights, fed Nero, then brewed myself a pot of coffee. At eleven, Margaret Lumm, a regular, entered.

"What are you doing open?" she asked.

"What are you doing out?"

She held up two grocery bags from an upscale grocery store on Charles Street. "Provisions," she said, in her patrician voice.

We talked about the latest Louise Penny novel. She talked, mostly. I pretended I'd read it. These days I pretend I've read many books. I *do* read the reviews from the major trade publications, of course, and I go to a few blogs. One of them is called *The Armchair Spoiler* and it includes reviews of recent titles that discuss endings. I no longer have the stomach for contemporary mystery novels—sometimes I reread a particular favorite from my childhood—and I find the book blogs indispensable. I suppose I could be honest, tell people that I've lost interest in mystery novels, that I primarily read history these days, poetry before I go to bed, but I prefer to lie. The few people I've told the truth to always want to know why I've given up reading crime, and it's not something I can talk about.

I sent Margaret Lumm away with a used copy of Ruth Rendell's *Shake Hands Forever* that she was 90 percent sure she'd never read. Then I ate the lunch I'd packed—a chicken salad sandwich—and was just about thinking of calling it a day when the phone rang.

"Old Devils Bookstore," I answered.

"Is Malcolm Kershaw available?" A woman's voice.

"Speaking," I said.

"Oh, good. This is Special Agent Gwen Mulvey of the FBI. I'd love a little bit of your time to ask you a few questions."

"Okay," I said.

"Is now good?"

"Sure," I said, thinking she wanted to talk on the phone, but instead she told me she'd be right over and disconnected the line. I stood for a moment, phone in hand, imagining what an FBI agent named Gwen would look like. Her voice on the phone had been raspy, so I imagined her to be nearing retirement, an imposing, humorless woman in a tan raincoat.

A few minutes later Agent Mulvey pushed through the door, looking very different from how I'd imagined her. She was in her thirties, if that, and wearing jeans that were tucked into forest green boots, plus a puffy winter coat and a white knit hat with a pompom on it. She stomped her boots on the welcome mat, removed her hat, and came across to the checkout counter. I came around to meet her, and she reached out a hand. She had a firm handshake, but her hand was clammy.

"Agent Mulvey?" I asked.

"Yes, hi." Snowflakes were melting on her green coat, leaving behind dark spots. She briefly shook her head—the ends of her thin, blond hair were wet. "I'm surprised you're still open," she said.

"I'm just about to close up, actually."

"Oh," she said. She had a leather bag slung over one shoulder and she lifted the strap over her head, then unzipped her jacket. "You have some time, though?"

"I do. And I'm curious. Should we talk back in my office?"

She turned back and glanced at the front door. The tendons in her neck popped out against her white skin. "Will you be able to hear if a customer comes in?" she said.

"I don't think that'll happen, but, yes, I'll be able to hear. It's this way."

My office was more of a nook at the back of the store. I got Agent Mulvey a chair and went around the desk and sat in my leather recliner, its stuffing bulging out from the seams. I positioned myself so that I could see her between two stacks of books. "I'm sorry," I said. "I forgot to ask you if you wanted anything? There's still some coffee in the pot."

"No, I'm fine," she said, removing her jacket, and putting her leather bag, more of a briefcase, really, on the floor by her side. She wore a black crewneck sweater under the coat. Now that I could really see her, I realized it wasn't just her skin that was pale. It was all of her: the color of her hair; her lips; her eyelids, almost translucent; even her glasses with their thin wire rims almost disappeared into her face. It was hard to know exactly what she looked like, almost like some artist had rubbed a thumb across her features to blur them. "Before we start, I'd like to ask you to please not discuss anything we are about to talk about with anyone. Some of it is public record but some of it is not."

"Now I'm really curious," I said, aware that my heart rate had accelerated. "And, yes, absolutely, I won't tell anyone."

"Great, thank you," she said, and she seemed to settle in her chair, her shoulders dropping, her head squaring with mine.

"Have you heard about Robin Callahan?" she asked.

Robin Callahan was a local news anchor who, a year and a half ago, had been found shot in her home in Concord, about twenty-five miles northwest of Boston. It had been the leading local news story since it had happened, and despite a suspicious ex-husband, no arrests had been made. "About the murder?" I said. "Of course."

"And what about Jay Bradshaw?"

I thought for a moment, then shook my head. "I don't think so."

"He lived in Dennis on the Cape. In August he was found beaten to death in his garage."

"No," I said.

"You sure?"

"I'm sure."

"Then what about Ethan Byrd?"

"That name rings a bell."

"He was a college student from U Mass Lowell who went missing over a year ago."

"Okay, right." I did remember this case, although I couldn't remember any of the details.

"He was found buried in a state park in Ashland, where he was from, about three weeks after he'd gone missing."

"Yeah, of course. It was big news. Are those three murders connected?"

She leaned forward on her wooden chair, reached a hand down to her bag, then brought it back suddenly, as though she'd changed her mind about something. "We didn't think so, at first, except that they're all unsolved. But someone noticed their names." She paused, as though giving me a chance to interrupt her. Then she said, "Robin Callahan. Jay Bradshaw. Ethan Byrd."

I thought for a moment. "I feel like I'm failing a test," I said.

"You can take your time," she said. "Or I can just tell you."

"Are their names related to birds?" I said.

She nodded. "Right. A Robin, a Jay, and then the last name of Byrd. It's kind of a stretch, I realize, but . . . without going into too much detail, after each murder the local police station closest to the crime received . . . what appeared to be a message from the killer."

"So they are connected?"

"It seems that way, yes. But they might be connected in another way, as well. Do the murders remind you of anything? I'm asking you because you are someone who is an expert on detective fiction."

I looked at the ceiling of my office for a moment, then said, "I mean, it sounds like something fictional, like something from a serial killer novel, or something from an Agatha Christie."

She sat up a little straighter. "Any particular Agatha Christie novel?"

"The one that's jumping to my mind is *A Pocket Full of Rye* for some reason. Did that have birds?"

"I don't know. But that's not the one I was thinking of."

"I guess it's similar to *The A.B.C. Murders* as well," I said.

Agent Mulvey smiled, like she'd just won a prize. "Right. That's the one I'm thinking of."

"Because nothing connects the victims except for their names."

"Exactly. And not just that, but the deliveries to the police station. In the book Poirot gets letters from the killer signed A. B. C."

"You've read it, then?"

"When I was fourteen, definitely. I read almost all of Agatha Christie's books, so I probably read that one, too."

"It's one of her best," I said, after a brief pause. I'd never forgotten that particular Christie plot line. There are a series of murders and what connects them are the victims' names. First, someone with the initials A. A. is killed in a town that begins with the letter A, then someone with the initials B. B. is killed in a B town. You get the idea. It turns out that the perpetrator really only wanted to kill one of the victims, but he made it look like a series of crimes done by a deranged serial killer.

"You think so?" the agent said.

"I do. One of her best plots, for sure."

"I'm planning on reading it again, but I did just Wikipedia it to remind myself of the story. There was a fourth murder in the book, as well."

"I think so, yes," I said. "Someone with a D name was the last person killed. And it turned out that the killer was making it look like a madman was doing it when all along he just wanted to kill one person. So the other murders are basically cover."

"That's what the plot summary on Wikipedia said. In the book it was the person with the double C name who was the intended victim all along."

"Okay," I said. I was starting to wonder why she had come to me. Was it just because I owned a mystery bookstore? Did she need a copy of the book? But if that were the case, then why did she ask for me, specifically, on the phone? If she just wanted someone who worked in a mystery bookstore, then she could have come inside and talked with anyone.

"Can you tell me anything else about the book?" she asked, then added, after a moment, "You're the expert."

"Am I?" I said. "Not really, but what is it you want to know?"

"I don't know. Anything. I was hoping you'd tell me."

"Well, besides the fact that a strange man comes into the store every day and buys a new copy of *The A.B.C. Murders*, I don't know what else to tell you." Her eyes raised for a moment before she realized I'd made a joke, or an attempt at one, then she smiled a little in acknowledgment. I asked her, "You think these murders are related to the book?"

"*I* do," she said. "It's too fantastical for it not to be."

"Is it that you think someone's copying the books in order to get away with a murder? That someone wanted to murder Robin Callahan, for example, but then murdered the other people to make it look like a serial killer obsessed with birds?"

"Maybe," Agent Mulvey said, and she rubbed a finger along the edge of her nose, up near her left eye. Even her small hands were pale, the fingernails unpainted. She was quiet again. It was a strange interview, full of pauses. She was hoping I'd fill in the silence, I guess. I decided to not say anything.

Eventually, she said, "You must be wondering why I came to talk with you."

"I am," I said.

"Before I tell you I'd like to ask you about one other recent case."

"Okay."

"You probably haven't heard of it. A man named Bill Manso. He was found near the train tracks in Norwalk, Connecticut, back in the spring. He was a regular commuter on a particular train, and initially it looked as though he'd jumped, but now it looks as though he was killed elsewhere and brought to the tracks."

"No," I said, shaking my head. "I didn't hear about it."

"Does it remind you of anything?"

"Does *what* remind me of anything?"

"The nature of his death."

"No," I said, but that wasn't entirely true. It did remind me of something, but I couldn't remember exactly what it was. "I don't think so," I added.

She waited again, and I said, "Do you want to tell me why you're questioning me?"

She unzipped her leather bag and removed a single sheet of paper. "Do you remember a list you wrote for this store's blog, back in 2004? A list called 'Eight Perfect Murders'?"

'd worked in bookstores ever since graduating from college in 1999. First briefly at a Borders in downtown Boston, then both as an assistant and a senior manager at one of the few remaining independents in Harvard Square. Amazon had just won its war for total domination and most of the indies were folding up like flimsy tents in a hurricane. But the Redline Bookstore was sticking it out, partly due to an older clientele not yet savvy enough to figure out online shopping, but mostly because its owner, Mort Abrams, outright owned the two-story brick building the store was housed in and didn't have to pay rent. I was at Redline five years, two as an assistant manager, then three as senior manager and part-time book buyer. My specialty was fiction, and in particular, crime fiction.

During my time at the store I also met my future wife, Claire Mallory, who was hired as a bookseller shortly after she'd dropped out of Boston University. We got married the same year that Mort Abrams lost his wife of thirty-five years to breast cancer. Mort and Sharon, who lived two streets over from the bookstore, had become close friends, substitute parents really, and Sharon's death was hard, especially since it robbed Mort of any remaining zest for life. A year after her death he told me that he was shutting down the store, unless, of course, I wanted to buy him out, take it over myself. I considered it, but at that point Claire had already left Redline, going to work at the local cable access station, and I didn't necessarily want to take on the hours, or the financial risk, of running my own store. I contacted Old Devils, a mystery bookstore in Boston, and John Haley, the owner at the time, created a job for me. I would be the events manager, but also create content for the store's burgeoning blog, a site for mystery lovers. My last day at Redline was the store's last day in business, as well. Mort and I locked the front doors together, then I followed him back to his office where we drank from a dusty bottle of single malt that had been given to him by Robert Parker. I remember thinking that Mort, without his wife, and now without the store, wouldn't make it through the winter. I was wrong. He lived through the winter and spring, but he did manage to die the following summer at his lake house at Winnipesaukee, a week before Claire and I were planning to visit.

"Eight Perfect Murders" was the first piece I wrote for the Old Devils blog. John Haley, my new boss, had asked me to write a list of my favorite mystery novels, but instead I pitched the idea of writing a list of perfect murders in crime fiction. I don't exactly know why I was reluctant to share my favorite books yet, but I remember thinking that writing about perfect murders might generate more traffic. This was right around the time that several blogs were taking off, making their authors rich and famous. I remember someone doing a blog about making one of Julia Child's recipes every day that was turned into a book, and maybe even a movie. I think I must have had some delusions of grandeur that my blog platform might turn me into a public and trusted aficionado of crime fiction. Claire added fuel to the fire by telling me repeatedly that she thought this blog could really blow up, that I'd find my calling—a literary critic of crime fiction. The truth was that I'd already found my calling, at least I thought I had, and I was a bookseller, content with the hundreds of minute interactions that make up a bookseller's daily life. And what I loved most of all was to read—that was my true calling.

Despite this, I somehow began to see my "Perfect Murders" piece—not yet written—as more important than it really was. I'd be setting the tone for the blog, announcing myself to the world. I wanted it to be flawless, not just the writing, but the list itself. The books should be a mix of the well known and the obscure. The golden age should be represented, but there should also be a contemporary novel. For days on end, I sweated it out, tinkering with the list, adding titles, subtracting titles, researching books I hadn't yet read. I think the only reason I ever actually finished was because John started to grumble that I hadn't published anything on the blog yet. "It's a blog," he'd said. "Just write a list of goddamn books and post it. You're not getting graded."

The post went up, appropriately enough, on Halloween. Reading it now makes me cringe a little. It's overwritten, even pretentious at times. I can practically taste the need for approval. This is what was eventually posted:

EIGHT PERFECT MURDERS
by Malcolm Kershaw

In the immortal words of Teddy Lewis in *Body Heat*, Lawrence Kasdan's underrated neo-noir from 1981: "Any time you try a decent crime, you got fifty ways you're gonna fuck up. If you think of twenty-five of them, then you're a genius . . . and you ain't no genius." True words, yet the history of crime fiction is littered with criminals, mostly dead or incarcerated, who all attempted the near impossible: the perfect crime. And many of them attempted the ultimate perfect crime, that being murder.

The following are my choices for the cleverest, the most ingenious, the most foolproof (if there is such a thing) murders in crime fiction history. These are not my favorite books in the genre, nor do I claim these are the best. They are simply the ones in which the murderer comes closest to realizing that platonic ideal of a perfect murder.

So here it is, a personal list of "perfect murders." I'll warn you in advance that while I try to avoid major spoilers, I wasn't one hundred percent successful. If you haven't read one of these books, and want to go in cold, I suggest reading the book first, and my list second.

The Red House Mystery (1922) by A. A. Milne

Long before Alan Alexander Milne created his lasting legacy—Winnie-the-Pooh, in case you hadn't heard—he wrote one perfect crime novel. It's a country house mystery; a long-lost brother suddenly appears to ask Mark Ablett for money. A gun goes off in a locked room, and the brother is killed. Mark Ablett disappears. There is some preposterous trickery in this book—including characters in disguise, and a secret passage—but the basic fundamentals behind the murderer's plan are extremely shrewd.

Malice Aforethought (1931) by Anthony Berkeley Cox

Famous for being the first "inverted" crime novel (we know who the murderer and victim are on the very first page), this is essentially a case study in how to poison your wife and get away with it. It helps, of course, that the murderer is a country physician with access to lethal drugs. His insufferable wife is merely his first victim, because once you commit a perfect murder, the temptation is to try another one.

The A.B.C. Murders (1936) by Agatha Christie

Poirot is investigating a "madman" who, it appears, is alphabetically obsessed, killing off Alice Ascher in Andover followed by Betty

Barnard in Bexhill. You get the idea. This is the textbook example of hiding one specific premeditated murder among a host of others, hoping that the detectives will suspect the work of a lunatic.

Double Indemnity (1943) by James M. Cain

This is my favorite Cain, mostly because of the grim fatalistic ending. But the murder at the center of the book—an insurance agent plots with femme fatale Phyllis Nirdlinger to off her husband—is brilliantly executed. It's a classic staged murder; the husband is killed in a car then placed on the train tracks to make it look as though he fell off the smoking car at the rear of the train. Walter Huff, her insurance agent lover, impersonates the husband on the train, ensuring that witnesses will attest to the murdered man's presence.

Strangers on a Train (1950) by Patricia Highsmith

My pick for the most ingenious of them all. Two men, each with someone they want dead, plan to swap murders, ensuring that the other has an alibi at the time of the murder. Because there is zero connection between the two men—they briefly talk on a train—the murders become unsolvable. In theory, of course. And Highsmith, despite the brilliance of the plot, was more interested in the ideas of coercion and guilt, of one man exerting his will on the other. The finished novel is both fascinating and rotten to the core, like most of Highsmith's oeuvre.

The Drowner (1963) by John D. MacDonald

MacDonald, my choice for underrated master of midcentury crime fiction, rarely dabbled in whodunits. He was far too interested in the criminal mind to keep his villains hidden until the end. *The Drowner* is an outlier, then, and a good one. The killer devises a way to drown his or her victims so that it looks exactly like an accident.

Deathtrap (1978) by Ira Levin

Not a novel, of course, but a play, although I highly recommend reading it, along with seeking out the excellent 1982 film. You'll never
look at Christopher Reeve in the same way again. It's a brilliant, funny
stage thriller that manages to be both the genuine article, and a sa-
tirical one, at the same time. The first murder—a wife with a weak
heart—is clever in its construction, but also foolproof. Heart attacks
are a natural death, even when they aren't.

The Secret History (1992) by Donna Tartt

Like *Malice Aforethought*, another "inverted" murder mystery, in
which a small cadre of classics students at a New England University
kill one of their own. We know the who long before we know the why.
The murder itself is simple in its execution; Bunny Corcoran is pushed
into a ravine during his traditional Sunday hike. What makes it stand
out is ringleader Henry Winter's explanation of the crime—that they
are "allowing Bunny to choose the circumstances of his own death."
They are not even sure of his planned route for that day but wait at
a likely spot, wanting to make the death seem random instead of
designed. What follows is a chilling exploration of remorse and guilt.

Truth is, it was a hard list to put together. I thought it would be
easier to come up with examples of perfect murders in fiction, but
it just wasn't. That's why I included *Deathtrap*, even though it's a
play and not a book. I'd actually never even read Ira Levin's original script or even seen it onstage. I was just a fan of the film. Also,
looking back on the list now, it's clear that *The Drowner*, a book I
really do love, doesn't quite belong here. The murderer lurks at the
bottom of a pond with an oxygen tank, then pulls her victim down
into the depths. It's a fun concept, but highly unlikely, and hardly

foolproof. How does she know where to wait? What if someone else is at the pond? I suppose that, once pulled off, it is a crime that truly looks like an accident, but I think I just put the book on the list because of how much I love John D. MacDonald. I suppose I also wanted something slightly obscure, something that hadn't been turned into a movie.

After I posted it, Claire told me she loved the writing, and John, my boss, was just relieved that the blog had been started. I waited for comments to appear, allowing myself brief fantasies in which the piece would start an online frenzy, blog readers chiming in to argue about their own favorite murders. NPR would call and ask me to come on-air to discuss the very topic. In the end, the blog piece got two comments. The first came from a SueSnowden who wrote, Wow!! Now I have so many new books to add to my pile!! and the second came from ffolliot123 who wrote Anyone who writes a list of perfect murders that doesn't have at least one John Dickson Carr on it obviously knows nothing about anything.

The thing about John Dickson Carr is that I just can't get into those books, even though the commenter was probably right in calling out their absence. Carr specialized in locked-room murder mysteries, impossible crimes. It seems ridiculous now but at the time I was bothered by the opinion, probably because I agreed with it to a certain degree. I even considered a follow-up post— maybe something like "Eight More Perfect Murders." Instead, my next post was a list of my favorite mystery novels from the previous year, and I wrote the entire thing in about an hour. I also figured out how to link the titles of the books to our online store, and, for that, John was extremely grateful. "We're just trying to sell books here, Mal," he'd said. "Not trying to start arguments."

CHAPTER 3

Agent Mulvey was holding out a printed-out sheet of paper. I took it from her, glanced down at the list I'd written, then said, "I remember this, but it was a long time ago."

"Do you remember the books you picked?"

I glanced down at the printout again, my eyes going immediately to *Double Indemnity*, and suddenly I knew why she was here. "Oh," I said. "The man on the train tracks. You think that's based on *Double Indemnity*?"

"I think it could be, sure. He was a regular commuter. Even though he'd been killed elsewhere, it was made to look like he'd jumped off the train. When I heard about it, it made me immediately think of *Double Indemnity*. The movie, anyway. I haven't read the book."

"And you're coming to me because I've read the book?" I said.

She blinked rapidly, then shook her head. "No, I'm coming to you because when I realized that maybe this crime was mimicking a movie, or a book, I did a Google search that included *Double Indemnity* and *The A.B.C. Murders* together. And that's how I found your list."

She was watching me expectantly, making eye contact, and I felt my own eyes skidding away from hers, taking in the large expanse of her forehead, her nearly invisible eyebrows. "Am I a suspect?" I said, then laughed.

She leaned back a little in her chair. "You're not an official suspect, no. If that were the case, then it wouldn't just be me here questioning you. But I *am* investigating the possibility that all these crimes were committed by the same perpetrator, and that that perpetrator is purposefully mimicking crimes from your list."

"Mine can't be the only list that includes both *Double Indemnity* and *The A.B.C. Murders*?"

"To tell the truth, it pretty much is. Well, yours is the shortest list that contains them both. Both books were on other lists together, but those lists were all much longer, like there was one called 'a hundred mysteries you need to read before you die,' that sort of thing, but yours jumped out. It's about committing the perfect murder. Eight books are mentioned. You work at a mystery bookstore in Boston. All the crimes have happened in New England. Look, I know it's probably all a coincidence, but I thought it was worth following up."

"I get that it's somewhat clear someone is copycatting *The A.B.C. Murders*, but a body found near the train tracks? That seems a stretch to say that's from *Double Indemnity*."

"Do you remember the book well?"

"I do. It's one of my favorites." This was true. I'd read *Double Indemnity* around the age of thirteen and was so thrilled by it that I sought out the film version with Fred MacMurray and Barbara Stanwyck that was made in 1944. That film led me down a rabbit hole of film noirs, my teenage years spent seeking out video stores that stocked classic film. Of all the noirs I saw because of *Double Indemnity*, none of them topped that first viewing experience. Sometimes I think the Miklos Rosza score to that movie is permanently embedded in my brain.

"On the day that Bill Manso's body was found on the tracks, one of the emergency windows on the train had been busted open, near to where the body was found."

"So, is it possible he really did jump?"

"Not a chance. The scene-of-crime officers could tell that he'd been killed in a separate location and driven to the tracks. And the coroner confirmed that he'd died from blunt force trauma to the head, probably from some kind of weapon."

"Okay," I said.

"That means that someone, probably the person who killed him, or an accomplice, was on the train, and smashed the emergency window to make it look like he'd jumped."

For the first time since we'd started talking, I felt a little jolt of alarm. In the book, and the movie as well, an insurance agent falls for the wife of an oil executive and, together, they plot to murder him. They do it for each other, but also for the money. The insurance agent, Walter Huff, fakes an accident policy on Nirdlinger, the man they plan to murder. Included in the policy is a "double indemnity" clause that doubles the amount of the payoff if death occurs on a train. Walter and Phyllis, the unfaithful wife, break the husband's neck in a car, then Walter poses as Nirdlinger and goes onto the train, himself. He wears a fake cast on his leg, and has crutches, since the real Nirdlinger had recently broken his leg. He figures that the cast is perfect because other passengers will remember seeing him, but not necessarily remember seeing his face. He goes to the smoking car at the back of the train and jumps off. Then Walter and Phyllis leave the dead man by the tracks, so it looks as though he fell.

"So, you're saying it was definitely made to look like the murder from *Double Indemnity*?" I said.

"*I* am," she responded. "I'm the only one, though, the only one who's convinced of the connection."

"What were these people like?" I asked. "The people who were killed."

Agent Mulvey glanced toward the drop ceiling of the book-store's back room, then said, "As far as we can tell, there's no way to connect them, besides the fact that all the deaths happened in New England, and besides the fact that they seem to be copycat murders from fictional sources."

"From my list," I said.

"Right. Your list is one possible connection. But there's also a connection . . . it's not really a connection, more of a gut feeling on my part, that all the victims . . . weren't bad, exactly, but weren't good people. I'm not sure any of them were really well liked."

I thought for a moment. It was getting darker in the back room of the bookstore, and I instinctively checked my watch, but it was still early afternoon. I looked back toward the stockroom, where two windows looked out onto the back alley. Snow had begun to pile in both of them and the portion of outside that I could make out through the windows was as dark as dusk. I turned on my desk lamp.

"For example," she continued. "Bill Manso was a divorced investment broker. The detectives who interviewed his grown children said they hadn't seen him in over two years, that he wasn't exactly the paternal type. It was clear that they disliked him. And Robin Callahan, as you've probably read, had been pretty controversial."

"Remind me," I said.

"I guess a number of years ago she broke up a marriage of one of her co-workers. And, subsequently, her own marriage. Then she wrote a book against monogamy—this was a while ago. A lot of people don't like her. If you google her name . . ."

"Well . . ." I said.

"Right. Everyone has enemies now. But to answer your question, I think it's a possibility that everyone who has been killed so far was a less–than–stellar person."

"You think that someone read my list of murders," I said, "then decided to copy the methods in them? And they wanted to make sure that the people they were killing somehow deserved to die? Is that your theory?"

She pushed her lips together, making them even more colorless than they already were, then she said, "I know it sounds ridiculous—"

"Or you think that I wrote this list, and then decided to test out the murders for myself?"

"Equally ridiculous," she said. "I know it is. But it's also unlikely, isn't it, that someone would copy a plot line from an Agatha Christie novel, and at the same time someone would stage a train murder from a . . ."

"From a James Cain novel," I said.

"Right," she said. My desk lamp has a yellow-tinged bulb and in the glow from it she looked like she hadn't slept in about three days.

"When did you make the connection between these crimes?" I asked.

"You mean, when did I find your list?"

"I guess so. Yes."

"Yesterday. I've already ordered all the books, and I've read all their plot summaries, but then I decided I'd come directly to you. I was hoping you might have some insight, that maybe you'd be able to connect some other unsolved recent crimes to your list. I know it's a long shot . . ."

I was looking down at the printout she'd given me, reminding myself of the eight books I'd picked. "Some of these," I said, "you couldn't exactly copy the murders from them. Or you could, but they'd be hard to spot."

"What do you mean?" she said.

I scanned the list. "*Deathtrap*, the play by Ira Levin. Do you know that one?"

"I do but remind me."

"The way the wife gets killed is that she's scared to death and has a heart attack. It's set up by the husband and his boyfriend. It's a perfect murder, of course, because you could never prove that someone who's had a heart attack was actually murdered. But let's say someone wanted to replicate it. First of all, it's pretty hard to give someone a heart attack, and it would be even harder for you to figure it out. I don't suppose you've found a suspicious heart attack victim, have you?"

"I actually have," she said, and for the first time since she'd arrived at the store, I saw a gleam of self-satisfaction in her eye. She really did believe she was on to something.

"I don't know much about it," she continued, "but there was a woman named Elaine Johnson from Rockland, Maine, who died of a heart attack in her home last September. She had a heart condition, so it looked like a natural death, but there were signs that her home had been broken into."

I rubbed at my earlobe. "Like a robbery?"

"That's what the police decided. Someone broke into her home to rob it, or to assault her, but she had a heart attack as soon as she saw the housebreaker. So they took off."

"Nothing was taken from the house?"

"Right. Nothing was taken from the house."

"I don't know," I said.

"Think about it, though," she said, moving a little forward in her chair. "Let's say you wanted to murder someone by causing a heart attack. First of all, you pick a victim who's already had one, which, in this case, Elaine Johnson had. Then you sneak into her house, where she lives alone, put on some sort of horrifying disguise, and leap out at her from a closet. She drops dead, and you've committed murder, just like in your book."

"And if it doesn't work?"

"Then the murderer bolts from the house and she can't identify them."

"But she'd report it?"

"Of course."

"Did anyone report something like that happening to them?"

"No. At least not that I know of. But that only means that it worked the first time."

"Right," I said.

She was quiet for a moment. I heard the ticking sound that meant Nero was coming toward us along the hardwood floor. Agent Mulvey, who heard it as well, turned and looked at the store cat. She let him sniff her hand then expertly rubbed his head. Nero sunk to the floor and flipped onto his side, purring.

"You must have cats?" I said.

"Two. Does this one go home with you or does he just stay in the store?"

"He just stays here. For him the entire universe is two book-lined rooms and a series of strangers, a few of whom feed him."

"Sounds like a good life," she said.

"I think he does all right. Half the people who come in here just come to see him."

Nero stood back up, stretched out his hind legs, one at a time, and walked back toward the front of the store.

"So what is it that you want from me?" I said.

"Well, if someone really is using your list as a guide for committing murders, then you're the expert."

"I don't know about that."

"I mean, you're the expert on the books on your list. They're favorite books of yours."

"I guess," I said. "I wrote that list a long time ago, and some of those books I know a lot better than others."

"Still, it can't hurt to get your opinion. I was hoping you'd look at some cases I put together, a list of unsolved murders in the New England region over the last few years. I threw it together quickly last night, just summaries, really"—she was pulling a stapled sheath of papers from her briefcase—"and was hoping you'd go through them, let me know if any of them seem like they might have something to do with the books on your list."

"Sure," I said, taking the pages from her. "Are these . . . classified, as well?"

"Most of the information I've summarized is public information. If any of the crimes strike you as a possibility, I'll take a closer look. I'm just fishing here, with these ones, honestly. I've already gone over them. It's just that, since you've read the books . . ."

"I'll need to reread some of the books, as well," I said.

"So you'll help me." She sat up a little straighter and half smiled. She had a short upper lip, and I could see her gums when she opened her mouth.

"I'll try," I said.

"Thank you. And there's one more thing. I've ordered all the books, but if you had any copies here, I could get a quicker start on them."

I checked the inventory on the computer; it told me we had several copies each of *Double Indemnity*, *The A.B.C. Murders*, and *The Secret History*, plus one copy of *The Red House Mystery*. We also had one copy of *Strangers on a Train*, but it was a first edition from 1950 in perfect condition that was worth at least $1,000. We had a locked case near the checkout counter that held all our books that were worth fifty dollars or more, but it wasn't there. It was in my office, also in a locked glass case, where I put the editions of books that I wasn't quite ready to part with yet. There was a collector's streak in me, not necessarily a good thing for someone who worked in a bookstore, and for someone whose own bookshelves in my attic apartment were filled to capacity. I nearly told Agent Mulvey that we didn't have the Highsmith book but decided that I shouldn't lie, at least not about something trivial, to an employee of the FBI. I told her what it was worth, and she said she'd wait for her paperback copy to arrive. That left *The Drowner*, which I definitely had at home, and *Malice Aforethought*, which I thought I might have at home, as well. I definitely didn't have a copy of the playscript for *Deathtrap*, either here at the store or at home, but I did know that it existed. I told the agent all this.

"I can't read eight books in a night, anyway," she said.

"Are you going back to . . ."

"I'm staying near here tonight, at the Flat of the Hill Hotel. I was hoping after you looked over the list, maybe in the morning . . . we could meet again, see if you've had any thoughts."

"Of course," I said. "I don't know if I'll be opening the store tomorrow, not if this weather . . ."

"You could come to the hotel. The FBI will pay for your breakfast."

"Sounds fine," I said.

At the front door Agent Mulvey said she'd pay for the books she was taking home with her.

"Don't worry about it," I said. "You can return them to me when you're done."

"Thank you," she said.

She opened the door just as a gust of wind ricocheted down Bury Street. The snow was piling up, the wind causing drifts, obliterating all the sharp angles of the city street.

"Be careful out there," I said.

"It's not far," she said. "Tomorrow at ten, right?" she added, confirming the time for our breakfast meeting.

"Right," I said, and stood in the doorway, watching her disappear into the enveloping snow.

CHAPTER 4

I lived alone on the other side of Charles Street, up the hill in a brownstone attic apartment that was rented to me by a ninety-year-old Boston Brahmin who had no idea of the actual worth of her property. I paid a scandalously low rent and fretted selfishly about the day my landlady would die and pass her property on to one of her more financially astute sons.

It normally took me less than ten minutes to get from the bookstore to my apartment, but I was walking against the storm in a pair of shoes with worn-out treads. The snow stung my face, and the wind was bending trees and singing down the empty streets. On Charles I considered checking to see if the Sevens was open for a drink but decided to pop into the cheese and wine shop instead, where I bought myself a six-pack of Old Speckled Hen and a premade ham-and-cheese baguette for my dinner. I had been planning on cooking the pork chop that I'd taken out to defrost that morning, but I was anxious to read through Agent Mulvey's list that night.

At my apartment building I climbed the unshoveled steps to the heavy front door, made from walnut and with cast-iron door handles. I let myself in after knocking the snow from my shoes. Another tenant, probably Mary Ann, had already sorted the mail and left it on the side table in the foyer. I picked up my damp credit card solicitations while I dripped onto the cracked tile floor, then climbed the three flights of stairs to my converted attic space.

As always, during the winter months, it was stiflingly hot inside my place. I removed my jacket and sweater, then opened both my windows, one on either side of the slanted walls, just enough so that cold air could seep in. I put five of the beers into my fridge and cracked the sixth. Even though my apartment was a studio, there was enough space for a clearly delineated living room, and I stretched out on the sofa, put my feet up on the coffee table, and began to read through Agent Mulvey's list.

It was organized chronologically, every entry formatted the same way, the header specifying the date, the location, and the name of the victim. Even though it was a summary, dashed off at the last minute, it was composed of complete sentences and read like textbook journalism. Agent Mulvey had probably never received less than an A in her entire academic career. I wondered what had attracted her to the FBI. She came across as someone more suited to academia, an English professor maybe, or a researcher. She reminded me a little of Emily Barsamian, my extremely bookish employee, who couldn't look me in the eye when we talked. Agent Mulvey wasn't quite that awkward, just young and inexperienced, maybe. It was impossible for me to not think of Clarice Starling (another bird name) from *The Silence of the Lambs*. It was where my mind almost always went, to books and movies. It had been that way since I first began to read. And Mulvey, like her fictional counterpart, seemed too tame for the job. It was hard to imagine her whipping a gun from a holster, or aggressively questioning a suspect.

She did question a suspect, though. She questioned you.

I pushed that particular thought out of my head, drank some beer, and looked at her list, scanning the items before settling down to read the details. I knew right away that there wasn't much here; at least nothing obvious was jumping out. Many of the unsolved murders were gun crimes. Young people in cities, mostly. One of the victims of gun violence sounded like a possibility but there wasn't much detail in the description. A man named Daniel Gonzalez had been gunned down while taking his dog for a walk in the Middlesex Fells. It had happened early in the morning the previous September, and Agent Mulvey made a note that there were currently no leads in the case. The only reason this particular crime jumped out at me was because of the murder in *The Secret History*. The college-aged murderers in Donna Tartt's book decide that they need to get rid of their friend Bunny Corcoran, fearful that he will reveal what he knows about a previous murder when the classics students had emulated a Dionysian bacchanal in the woods and accidentally (or not) killed a farmer. Bunny had not been part of the ritual, but he finds out about it and begins to leverage this information to get things—dinners out, trips to Italy—from his wealthy friends. They also worry he'll drunkenly tell someone about what took place. Because of this, they plot to murder him. Henry Winter, the smartest of the group of students, finalizes their plan. They know that Bunny takes long walks on Sunday afternoon, and they lie in wait at a place where they think he might wind up, a trail above a deep ravine. When he arrives, they shove him off the edge, hoping it will look like an accident, hoping that the randomness of Bunny's walk will hide the design of the murder.

Could the case of Daniel Gonzalez, killed while on his morning run, possibly be related? The fact that he was shot made it seem unlikely, but maybe the idea behind this copycat murder was to take someone out while he was doing a predictable activity. I got my laptop and looked up his obituary. He had been an adjunct professor at a local community college, teaching Spanish. While it wasn't Latin or Greek, he was a languages professor. It was a possibility, and I decided to tell Agent Mulvey about it the following morning.

I went through the rest of the crimes. I was particularly look-ing for a drowning, thinking of John D. MacDonald's book *The Drowner*. But, of course, if someone were drowned in such a way as to make it look like an accident, then it probably wouldn't exactly make a list of unsolved murders.

There were also no listings for accidental overdoses. That was the method of killing in *Malice Aforethought*. The murderer, a doc-tor, turns his wife into a morphine addict. Then it is simply a matter of making sure other people know about her addiction, that it becomes local gossip. Then he kills her with an overdose. Of course, there must have been hundreds, if not thousands, of drug overdoses in New England the past few years. Could one of those have been an intentional murder? The thing about my list was that, when I originally created it, I really was trying to come up with murders that were so clever that the perpetrator would never be caught. With that in mind, if someone successfully copycatted some of these murders, they'd be undetectable.

I ate two bites of my sandwich then had another beer. The apartment was too quiet, and I didn't want to turn on the televi-sion, so I played music instead. Max Richter's *24 Postcards in Full Colour*. I lay back on my sofa and looked up at the high ceiling, at a thin crack that zigzagged out from under the molding; it was a familiar sight, that ceiling. I thought about what I'd tell Agent Mulvey the next morning at breakfast. I'd tell her about Daniel Gonzalez, of course, and how it might be related to *The Secret His-tory*. I'd suggest that she research accidental drownings, especially ones that happened in ponds or lakes, and I would also suggest that she look into overdose deaths, especially ones in which the deceased used a syringe.

The album ended, and I restarted it, lying back down on the

sofa. My mind was going in many different directions, so I decided to slow down and make a mental list. I told myself to list assumptions first. Assumption number one was that someone was using my list to murder random people. Well, maybe not random. Maybe the victims somehow deserved to die, at least according to the murderer. Assumption number two was that, while I was probably a suspect, I was in no way a serious suspect. As Agent Mulvey herself pointed out, she wouldn't have come alone had that been the case. The purpose of her interview that afternoon had been to feel me out, try to get a sense of me. If she thought I was involved, I decided that the next time we met—breakfast tomorrow, or sometime after that—she would be with another FBI agent. Assumption number three: Whoever is doing this isn't just using my list. The killer knows me. Maybe not a lot, but a little.

The reason I thought that—the reason I *knew* that—is because the fifth victim that Agent Mulvey mentioned, the woman who had the heart attack at her house in Rockland, Elaine Johnson— thing is, I actually knew her. Not well, but as soon as I heard the name, I knew that it was the same Elaine Johnson who used to live in Beacon Hill, a frequent customer at the bookstore, and a woman who came to every author reading we ever hosted. I knew I should have told Agent Mulvey this at the time, but I didn't, and until I felt I had to, I didn't plan on telling her.

I'm sure she's withholding information from me, so I plan on withholding this information from her.

I have to begin to protect myself.

CHAPTER 5

I was beginning to fall asleep on the sofa, so I got up, rinsed out the beer bottles, threw away the remainder of my sandwich, brushed my teeth, and changed into my pajamas. Then I went to my bookshelf and found the book I was looking for. *The Drowner.* I had the original Gold Medal paperback, printed in 1963. It had one of those lurid illustrated covers that adorn pretty much all of John D. MacDonald's midcentury paperbacks. On this one, a dark-haired woman in a white bikini is being pulled down through the murky green depths by a pair of hands gripping one of her pretty legs. It promised, like all these covers, two things: sex and death. I ran my thumb along the edge of the book, riffling the pages, and that musty, prickly smell of an old paperback reached my nostrils. I've always loved that smell, even though the book collector side of me knew that it was a sign of a book that had been improperly maintained over the years, a book that had probably sat in a cardboard box on the floor of a damp cellar for too many seasons. But to me the smell took me instantly back to the Annie's Book Swap where I began to buy books when I was in the sixth grade. I grew up in Middleham, about forty-five minutes west of Boston. The year that I turned eleven was also the year that I was allowed to ride my bike the mile and a half along Dartford Road into Middleham's town center. There were only three stores: a convenience store that called itself Middleham General, in an attempt to sound like something quainter than what it was, an antiques shop located in the old post office building, and an Annie's Book Swap, a franchised used bookstore run by an English man named Anthony Blake. It sold primarily mass markets—those paperbacks that could just about fit in a back pocket—and it was there that I bought the Ian Fleming novels, and the Peter Benchleys, and the Agatha Christies that got me through my younger years. It was there that I almost definitely bought *The Drowner*, having already purchased every available Travis McGee book, John D. MacDonald's famous series. It was rare to find MacDonald standalones, but some devoted crime reader in my part of Massachusetts must have died around the time I started riding my bike to the town center, because Annie's was suddenly swamped with stacks of pulp novels, not just John D. MacDonald but Mickey Spillane books, and Alistair MacLeans, and Ed McBain's 87th Precinct novels. I allowed myself three books per shopping expedition, which just about used up my allowance. In those days it took me less than a week to read those three books—sometimes it took me just three days—but I was always happy to reread books I already owned. I probably hadn't read *The Drowner* since then, since I was a preteen, but the basic plot had stuck with me.

The villain—and she was a good one—was a highly religious secretary who sublimated all her repressed sexual energy into physical exercise. She murdered the sinful people around her, including a married woman having an affair with her boss. She drowned her by lurking, in scuba gear, at the bottom of the pond where this woman swam. Then she got hold of one of her legs and pulled her down under the water. That particular murder I never forgot. When I made up my perfect murders list, it had jumped into my mind. I didn't reread the book, but I familiarized myself with it.

I brought *The Drowner* into bed with me. I read the first paragraph, its words hauntingly familiar. Books are time travel. True readers all know this. But books don't just take you back to the time in which they were written, they can take you back to different versions of yourself. The last time I'd cracked this particular paperback I was probably eleven or twelve. I like to think it was summertime and I was up late in my cramped bedroom under a single sheet, a mosquito probably whining in one of the corners of the room. My father was playing his records in the living room, too loudly, depending on how drunk he was. Most nights ended the same, with my mother turning down his music—jazz usually, although sometimes he'd listen to fusion stuff like Frank Zappa or Weather Report—and my father berating her for not understanding him. But this was simply background noise. Because I wasn't really there in that bedroom. I was actually in Florida, in 1963, hanging out with shady real estate developers, and sexy divorcées, and drinking bourbon highballs. And now here I was again—almost forty years old—and my eyes were running over the same words, holding the same book I held twenty-eight years ago, the same book some businessman or housewife held sixty years ago. Time travel.

I finished the book at about four in the morning. I almost got out of bed to get another book from the list but decided to try and sleep instead. I rolled onto my stomach, thinking about the book, about what it must feel like to be swimming along in a pond when something grabs you from below, pulls you down to your death. Then, because I was starting to get sleepy, my wife's face came into my mind, as it always did. But I didn't dream of her, and I didn't dream about *The Drowner*. I dreamed about running, about people coming after me.

The same dream I have every night of my life.

IT WAS STILL SNOWING when I left my apartment in the morning, but it was a light, drifting snow, half of it kicked up by a wind that was still gusting. There was about two feet already on the

ground. The roads had been plowed but no one had been out yet
to shovel the sidewalks, so I walked in the middle of the street,
careful going down the steep hill to Charles. Even though the skies
were blanketed in clouds, the day was bright, maybe from all that
pristine snow. I carried my old bike messenger bag, its strap over
my shoulder.

I got to the hotel early. The Flat of the Hill was a recent addition
to my part of Boston, a boutique hotel inside a refurbished ware-
house just off Charles. It had a high-end restaurant and a pretty bar
that I occasionally went to on Monday nights when oysters were a
dollar each.

"I'm meeting someone for breakfast," I said to the lone employee, a sad-eyed woman behind the check-in desk, and she directed me past the bar into a small dining area with about eight
tables. There was no one there to seat me so I sat myself at a corner
table by a large window that looked out onto a wall of brick. I
was the only one in the room, and I wondered if anyone was actually working there, or if all the staff were unable to make it to
work because of the snowstorm. Then, simultaneously, a man in a
crisp white shirt and black pants pushed through a pair of swinging
doors, while Agent Mulvey appeared at the entrance to the dining
room. She spotted me and came over, just as the waiter was dropping off menus. We both ordered coffee and juice.

"The FBI has a decent travel budget," I said.

She looked confused for a moment, then said, "Oh. I booked
this place myself because it was close to your store. Who knows if
they'll reimburse me."

"How'd you sleep?" I asked. She had dark purple shadows under her eyes.

"Very little. I was reading."

"Me, too. What book did you read?"

"*The Red House Mystery.* I thought I'd start at the beginning."

"What did you think?" I said and took a sip of my coffee, scalding the tip of my tongue.

"It was good. Clever, I guess, and I didn't guess the ending." She touched the side of her porcelain coffee cup then leaned down, pursing her lips, and sipped a little bit from the top. The maneuver made me think of a bird.

"Honestly," I said. "I know I included it on my list, but I don't remember the exact details. I read it a long time ago."

"It's pretty much how you described it. It's a country house mystery that is kind of ludicrous. I kept thinking about Clue, the game—"

"Colonel Mustard in the library."

"Exactly. But it was better than that." She described to me the basic plot, and it started to come back. There's a rich man named Mark Ablett who lives in a country house, the kind of English one that seems specifically designed to have a murder occur in it. He gets a letter from his estranged no-good brother, saying he's coming to visit from Australia. When the brother arrives, he's told to wait in the study for Mark Ablett. Then a shot is heard. The brother from Australia is dead and Mark Ablett is missing. It seems clear that Mark has killed his own brother and fled.

The detective in the story is actually just a passing acquaintance of one of the country estate's guests. His name is Tony Gillingham and together with his friend Bill they begin to investigate. It turns out that there is a secret tunnel that runs from the study underneath the house and all the way out to a golf course, and there are, of course, multiple suspects.

"There's no brother, right?" I said, interrupting her.

"Right, exactly. The real brother died years ago and isn't part of the present action. Mark Ablett had been talked into impersonating him, and then he's killed. But that wasn't the part of the murder that I found clever. Did you?" She was talking fast and only after she paused did I realize that she was expecting an answer.

"I think I put it on the list because the murderer had basically provided a corpse and a killer at the same time. They were the same person, but only the killer knew that. So, there are two people murdered, but only one body found."

"Can I read a section I underlined last night?"

"Sure," I said, and she pulled the paperback from her bag and began flipping through pages. I could see from where I was seated that she'd underlined several passages. I thought of my wife, the way she would always read with a pen in her hand, ready to write in whatever book she was reading. I was suddenly glad I hadn't given Agent Mulvey the expensive first edition of *Strangers on a Train*.

"Okay. Got it," she said, flattening the book on the table and leaning forward to read. "'The inspector had arrived in it,' the house I think he's talking about, 'to find a man dead and a man missing'" she began. "'It was extremely probable, no doubt, that the missing man had shot the dead man. But it was more than extremely probable, it was almost certain that the Inspector would start with the idea that this extremely probable solution was the one true solution, and that, in consequence, he would be less disposed to consider without prejudice any other solution.'" She finished reading and closed the book. "It's got me thinking," she continued. "If you were going to commit a murder based on this book, how would you do it?"

I must have looked confused, because she added, "Would you shoot someone in the study of a country house?"

"No," I said. "I guess I would kill two people, then hide one of the bodies, and make it look as though the killer has gone on the run."

"Exactly," she said.

The waiter was hovering, so we both ordered. Agent Mulvey got the eggs Florentine. I wasn't hungry but ordered two poached eggs on toast, with fresh fruit on the side. After we ordered, she said, "This has me thinking about rules."

"What do you mean, rules?"

"Okay," she said, and thought for a moment. "If I was the one who had set myself this task . . . this goal of committing the eight murders that you described in your list, then it would be helpful to set some guidelines. Some rules. Do you copy the murders exactly? Or the *idea* behind the murders? How similar do they have to be?"

"So, you think the rules dictate that the murderer adheres as closely as possible to the actual murders in the book?"

"No, not the details of the murders, but the philosophies behind them. It's almost as though the murderer is testing these books in real life. If the idea was simply to mimic the books, then you could just shoot someone in a country house library and call it a day. Or, for the *A.B.C. Murders*, you'd actually copy them exactly. You know, find someone named Abby Adams who lived in Acton and kill her first, et cetera. But it's not just about that, it's about doing them right. There are rules."

"So, for *The Red House Mystery*, it's all about pointing the police toward a suspect that they will never find, and never get to question."

"Yes, exactly," Agent Mulvey said. "It actually is clever. I was thinking about it all last night. Let's say I wanted to kill someone . . . my ex-boyfriend, for example."

"Okay," I said.

"If I just killed him, then I would be a suspect. But let's say I killed two people—like my ex-boyfriend, and my ex-boyfriend's new girlfriend, say—and made sure that the body of the new girl-friend wasn't found. That way I could make it look like the killer had run away. The police wouldn't be looking for the identity of the killer; they'd think they already knew it."

"It wouldn't be easy, you know," I said.

"Ha," she said. "I wasn't really considering it."

"Because the killer would have to be willing to kill two people."

"Right."

"And hiding a body is not easy."

"You're not speaking from experience, are you?" she said.

"I've read a lot of mystery novels."

"I think I need to look for a crime in which the prime suspect has disappeared."

"Is that common?" I asked.

"It isn't, really. It's not so easy to disappear these days. Most people leave pretty obvious trails. But it happens."

"I think you're on to something," I said. "It might be a matter of looking for two deserving victims—criminals, maybe—one of whom died and one who disappeared. That is, if your theory's correct that—what should we call our suspect? We should have a name."

"Why don't we call him . . . ?" She paused.

"Something with a bird."

"No, that's confusing. Let's call him Charlie," she said.

"Why Charlie?"

"It just popped into my head. No, that's not true. I was trying to think of a name, and I thought of copycat, which made me think of a cat, which made me think of my first cat, when I was young, and his name was Charlie."

"Poor Charlie. Does he deserve to have his name used this

way?"

"He does, actually. He was a total killer. Brought us a mouse or a bird every day."

"Perfect," I said.

"Charlie it is."

"So what was I saying? Right, look for deserving pairs of victims. Charlie doesn't like to kill innocent people."

"We don't know that for a fact, but it's a possibility," she said, pushing herself a little back from the table to allow her food to be put in front of her. "Thank you," she said to the waiter, then picked up a fork. "Mind if I eat and talk? I skipped dinner last night and I'm starving."

"No, that's fine," I said. My poached eggs had arrived, and the sight of them, the edges of the whites slightly translucent, made my stomach flip. I speared a cube of cantaloupe on the end of my fork.

"And maybe I'm wrong," Agent Mulvey said, when she was done chewing her first bite of breakfast. "This could have something to do with *you*, of course. Someone trying to get your attention, maybe someone trying to frame you." She opened her eyes a little wider as she said this. I jutted out my lower lip, as though thinking about the possibility.

"And if that's the case," I finally said, "then it makes sense to ensure that the murders have obviously been based on the books on the list."

"Right," she said. "That's why I want to look more closely at what happened to Elaine Johnson, the heart attack victim—"

"Who might or might not have been killed by Charlie," I said.

"But if she was, then I need to go to the crime scene. There might be something that connects it to *Deathtrap*."

"I have a confession to make," I said and watched as Agent Mulvey's cheeks reddened in anticipation. "I haven't actually ever seen the play, or even read it. But I have seen the movie and I'm pretty sure that it's very faithful. Anyway, I'm embarrassed."

"You should be," she said, but laughed. Her face was no longer red.

"So, *in the movie*, all I can actually talk about," I said, "the victim dies of a heart attack when she sees a man she thinks is dead loom up in her bedroom and murder her husband. Was Elaine Johnson found dead in her bedroom?"

"I'll have to check," she said. "I can't remember offhand. You know, when you said you had a confession, I thought you were going to say something else."

"You thought I was going to confess to being Charlie," I said, in what I hoped was a flippant way.

"No," she said. "I thought you were going to confess to me that you knew Elaine Johnson."

hesitated, then said, "Is she the same Elaine Johnson who used to live in Boston?"

"Uh-huh."

"Then I did know her. Not well, but she used to come into the bookstore all the time, and she used to come to author readings."

"You didn't want to tell me this yesterday afternoon?"

"Honestly, it didn't occur to me that it was the same person. The name rang a bell but it's a common name."

"Okay," she said, but her eyes didn't quite meet mine. "What was she like, Elaine Johnson?"

I pretended to think, just to buy a little time, but the truth was, Elaine was memorable. She had seriously thick glasses—I think you'd call them coke bottles—and thinning hair, and she always wore what appeared to be handmade sweaters, even in summertime, but none of that was what had made her memorable. She was memorable because she was one of those people who take advantage of the vulnerable nature of retail employees, by cornering them and subjecting them to endless monologues, more like diatribes, on her favorite subjects. Elaine's favorite subject was crime writers—who was a genius, who was merely good, and who was bad ("fucking atrocious" was the phrase she generally used), and she used to come into the store every day and corner whatever employee she encountered first. It was exhausting, and annoying, but we all figured out the best way to deal with her, which was

to continue working while she talked, give her about ten minutes, then tell her, in no uncertain terms, that her time was up.
It sounds rude, but the thing is, Elaine Johnson was rude, herself.
She said outrageous things about the authors she didn't like. She
was casually racist, openly homophobic, and, surprisingly, loved to
comment on other people's appearances, despite her own. I think
anyone who works in a bookstore, or any store probably, is used to
dealing with difficult customers, including difficult customers who
come in every day. The thing about Elaine Johnson was that she
also showed up at all our author readings, and she was always the
first to raise her hand, asking a question that subtly, or not so subtly, insulted the poor author onstage. We would always warn the
authors in advance, but we'd also mention that she always bought
a copy of the book to get it autographed, even when they were,
according to her, "a no-talent fraud." Most authors, I find, are
willing to put up with an asshole if it means a book sale, especially
a hardcover book sale.

I knew that Elaine Johnson had moved to Rockland, Maine,
because she told us about the move on a daily basis for about a year
before it happened. Her sister had died and left her a house. On the
day she finally left, my employees and I went out for a celebratory
drink.

"She was pretty abrasive," I said to Agent Mulvey. "She came to
the store every day and cornered one of us to talk about the book
she was reading. I remember now that she did move to Maine, but
but I didn't connect the name when you said it. I just knew her as
Elaine, not Elaine Johnson."

"Did she deserve to die?" she asked.

I raised my eyebrows. "Did she deserve to die? Are you asking
me personally? No, of course not."

"No, sorry. I mean, you said she was an abrasive personality. It's clear, at least to me, that all the victims so far have been less than likable people. Did she fall into the category?"

"She was definitely not likable. She told me once that lesbians made terrible writers because they didn't spend enough time with men, who had superior intellects."

"Oh."

"She used to say stuff just to get a rise, I think. Ultimately, she was sad and lonely, more so than a terrible person."

"Did you know she had a weak heart?"

After her surgery, I remember her pulling down the neck of her pilly sweater to show me the puckered scar on her wrinkled chest. I remember saying, "Please don't ever show that to me again," which got a laugh. Sometimes I thought that Elaine Johnson's act was just that, an act, and what she really craved was people being rude to her back.

"It rings a bell," I said to Agent Mulvey. "I remember there was a time when she didn't come in to the store—we were all thrilled—but then she started to come back. I remember it was medical."

The waiter had sidled over. Agent Mulvey's plate was spotless, and my eggs were untouched. He asked if everything was okay.

"Sorry," I said. "It's fine. I'm still working on these."

He cleared the agent's plate, and she ordered more coffee. I decided to make an attempt on my eggs, thinking it would look strange if I didn't. Agent Mulvey looked at her watch and asked me if I was going in to work.

"I'll go in," I said, "I doubt I'll have any customers, but I'll check on Nero."

"Oh, Nero," she said, with affection in her voice.

I remembered that she had cats of her own and asked her, "Who's looking after your cats?" As soon as I said it, I realized that it was a very personal question. It also sounded as though I was try-ing to figure out if she were single. I wondered if she thought I was hitting on her. I wasn't a whole lot older than she was—ten years maybe—although I did know that my hair, prematurely white, made me look a little older.

"They're fine," she said, avoiding the question. "They have each other."

I continued to eat, and she glanced at her phone, then put it facedown back on the table.

"I do have to ask you where you were the night of September thirteenth, the night that Elaine Johnson died."

"Of course," I said. "What night was it?"

"It was the thirteenth."

"No, the day of the week."

"Let me check." She picked her phone back up, scrolled for ten seconds, then said, "It was a Friday night. Unlucky, I guess." I must have looked confused because she added, "Friday the thirteenth."

"I was away," I said. "In London." I take the same vacation every year, two weeks in London, usually at the beginning of Sep-tember. It's low tourist season because the kids are back in school, but the weather is usually still good. Plus, it's an okay time to be away from the store.

"Do you know the exact dates you were away?" she asked.

"If the thirteenth was Friday then I flew back the next day, on Saturday, the fourteenth. I can send you the flights I was on, if you'd like. I know it was basically the first two weeks in Septem-ber."

"Okay, thanks," she said, which I took to mean that she wanted me to send her my exact flights.

"If Elaine Johnson was killed by Charlie . . ." I said.

"Yes?"

"Then it makes it much more likely that Charlie is definitely using my list."

"Yes, it does. And it means that he not only knows who you are, but that he knows people around you. I'm assuming it can't be a coincidence that one of the victims is someone you knew personally."

"I don't think so," I said.

"Is there anyone who has a grudge against you, maybe an ex-employee, someone who might have known that Elaine Johnson was a regular at Old Devils?"

"Not that I know of," I said. "There aren't that many ex-employees from the store, actually. I only need two extra people, and the two I have now have both been with me for over two years."

"Can you tell me their names?" she said, pulling a notebook out from her bag.

I gave her Emily's and Brandon's full names and she wrote them down.

"What can you tell me about them?" she said.

I told her what I knew. It wasn't much. Emily Barsamian had graduated from Winslow College, outside of Boston, about four years ago, and gotten an internship at the Boston Athenaeum, a prestigious and historic independent library. She'd supplemented her income by coming to work at Old Devils for twenty hours a week. When the internship was finished, she upped her hours and had been with me ever since. I knew hardly anything about her personal life because she rarely talked, and when she did, it was only about books, or sometimes movies. I suspected that she was a secret writer but hadn't confirmed it. Brandon Weeks was my gregarious employee. He still lived with his mom and his sisters in Roxbury, and both Emily and I probably knew everything about him, certainly everything about his family, and about his current girlfriend. When I'd hired him, as extra help during the holiday season two years ago, I admit that I had doubts about whether he'd show up with any kind of regularity. But he stayed on, and as far as I remembered, had never missed a single day or even been late.

"And that's it?" Agent Mulvey asked.

"For current employees? Yes. I go in every day, myself. And when I go on vacation, either we hire a temp, or Brian, my co-owner, comes in and does a few shifts. If you want, I'll put together a list of past employees and send it to you."

"Brian is Brian Murray?" she said.

"Yes, you know him?"

"I saw his name on your website. I've heard of him, yes."

Brian is a semifamous writer who lives in the South End, and who writes the Ellis Fitzgerald series. He's easily up to about twenty-five books by now; they don't sell as well as they used to, but Brian writes them anyway, keeping his female detective Ellis at a perpetual thirty-five years old, and keeping both fashion and technology advancements out of his narratives. The books are set sometime in late '80s Boston, as was the TV series called *Ellis* that ran for two years and provided Brian with the town house he bought in the South End, his lake house in the far north of Maine, and enough extra money to invest in Old Devils.

"Include other people on your list, if you think of them. Pissed-off customers? Any exes of yours we should know about?"

"It's going to be a short list," I said. "My only ex is my wife, and she's dead."

"Oh, I'm sorry," she said, but it was clear from her expression she already had that information.

"And I'll keep thinking about the books on the list."

"Thank you," she said. "Don't hold back. Let me know any thoughts you have, even if they seem insignificant or unlikely. It can't hurt."

"Okay," I said, folding my napkin and putting it over the un-eaten portion of my breakfast. "Are you checking out, or are you staying here?"

"Checking out," she said. "Unless for some reason the train is canceled, then I guess I'll spend one more night here. But I'm not leaving right now. You haven't told me if you looked at the un-solved crimes I gave you last night."

I told her that none of them had jumped out at me, except for possibly Daniel Gonzalez, the man who'd been shot while jogging.

"How does it relate to your list?" she asked.

"It probably doesn't, but it made me think of the Donna Tartt book, *The Secret History*. In that book the killers wait for their vic-tim at a place they think he might be hiking."

"I read that book, in college," she said.

"So you remember?"

"Sort of. I thought they killed someone doing a sex ritual in the woods."

"That's the first murder; they kill a farmer. The second murder is the one I reference in the list. They push their friend off a cliff."

"Daniel Gonzalez was shot."

"I know. It's a long shot. It has more to do with the fact that he was out walking his dog. Maybe it's a walk he does every day, or once a week. It probably has nothing to do—"

"No, it's helpful. I'll look into it further. There were several persons of interest in the Daniel Gonzalez case, including a former student who is still under investigation. But it does seem like a possibility."

"Was Daniel Gonzalez . . . an asshole?" I said. "For lack of a better word."

"That I don't know, but I'll check it out. It seems likely, though, if there were several persons of interest in his killing. So that was the only case, the Gonzalez one . . . ?"

"Yes," I said. "I did think that you should look outside of unsolved homicides, though. Look at accidental drownings and, also, accidental overdoses. Oh, that reminds me." I opened my bike messenger bag and pulled out the two books I'd brought with me, the paperback copy of *The Drowner* that I'd reread the night before, plus a paperback copy of *Malice Aforethought* that I'd found in my personal collection that morning. It was a Pan Books paperback in very poor condition, the cover almost falling off. I slid both across to Agent Mulvey. "Thanks," she said. "I'll make sure they get returned to you."

"Don't worry too much about it," I said. "Neither is irreplaceable. And I read *The Drowner* last night. Read it again, I mean, because it had been a while since I last read it."

"Oh, yeah," she said. "Any insights?"

"There are two murders in it. There's the woman who gets killed while swimming. She's pulled down from below, basically what the cover is showing you. But there's a second murder, a really disturbing one. The killer, who's this very physically strong woman, almost supernaturally strong, kills a man by giving him a heart attack with her hand. She holds it rigid like this," I demonstrated by holding up my hand, fingers extended, "and pushes it slowly up under his rib cage until she can feel his heart and then she wrenches it."

"Ugh," the agent said and made a face.

"I don't know if it's even possible," I said. "And even if it was, I'm pretty sure an autopsy would show what happened."

"I'd think so, too," she said. "I still think we should look for drownings. I think our Charlie would want to copy the drowning killing, especially since it's the title of the book."

"Right," I said.

"Did you get anything else from the book?"

I didn't tell her how I hadn't remembered just how sexualized the killings were. That Angie, the insane murderer, imagined two personalities for herself, a Joan of Arc side in which her purity made her impervious to pain, but then there was a side to her that she called her "red mare" feeling, her back arched, her nipples erect, and how she experienced both of these personalities when she committed a murder. It made me wonder if all murderers needed to do this, needed to disassociate during the act, become someone else. Was Charlie like this?

But what I said to Agent Mulvey was, "It's actually not a great book. I love John D. MacDonald but, except for the Angie character, this wasn't one of his best."

She shrugged and put both the books in her own bag. I realized that my critical assessment of the book was not exactly relevant. Still, she looked up and said, "You've been incredibly helpful. Do you mind if I send you anything I might have for your opinion? And if you'd keep rereading the books . . ."

"Of course," I said.

We exchanged emails, then stood, and she walked me to the entrance of the hotel. "I want to look at the weather," she said, stepping outside with me. The snow was barely falling now, but the city was transformed, drifts of snow gathered in corners, the trees bent over, even the brick walls of nearby buildings coated with a scrim of white.

"Good luck getting home," I said.

We shook hands. I called her Agent Mulvey, and she asked me to call her Gwen. As I walked slowly away, through the shin-high snow, I decided it was a good sign, her asking me to call her by her first name.

When I got to the store, twenty minutes later, Emily
Barsamian was under the awning, looking at her
phone.

"How long have you been here?" I asked.

"Twenty minutes. When I didn't hear from you, I just figured
we'd be open for regular hours."

"Sorry. You should have sent me a text message." I said this
knowing that in four years she had never sent me a text message,
and that she probably never would.

"I didn't mind waiting," she said, as I opened the door, then
followed her in. "It was my fault for forgetting my keys."

Nero came over to greet us, meowing, and Emily crouched
down to scratch his chin. I went behind the checkout desk and
turned on the lights. Emily stood and removed her long green coat.
Underneath she wore what I had come to think of as her work
uniform, a midlength dark skirt, chunky boots, a vintage sweater
over a button-up shirt, or, occasionally a T-shirt. The T-shirts she
wore provided rare clues as to Emily's likes and dislikes. Some of
the shirts were book related—she had one with a vintage cover of
Shirley Jackson's *We Have Always Lived in the Castle* with an illus-
tration of a black cat in tall green grass—and several T-shirts for a
band called The Decemberists. The previous summer she wore a
T-shirt that advertised SUMMERISLE MAY DAY 1973 and I spent all
day with a nagging feeling that it sounded familiar. I finally asked

her, and she told me it was referencing *The Wicker Man*, a horror film from the 1970s I hadn't seen in many years. "You're a horror fan?" I asked.

As usual when we spoke she was either looking at my forehead or my chin. "I guess," she said.

"What are your top five?" I said, hoping to continue the conversation.

She frowned briefly, thinking, then said, "*Rosemary's Baby*, *The Exorcist*, *Black Christmas*—the original one—*Heavenly Creatures*, and, um, *The Cabin in the Woods*, I guess."

"I've seen two out of five. What about *The Shining*?"

"Uh-uh." She shook her head rapidly, and I thought she might elaborate, but that was the end of the conversation. I didn't mind that she was a private person. I was, as well. And being a private person is a rare trait these days. Still, I did wonder about her interior life. And I wondered if she had ambitions beside being a bookseller.

As she hung up her damp coat, I asked her if it had been hard getting to the store. "I took the bus. It was fine," she said. She lived on the other side of the river, near Inman Square in Cambridge. All I knew about her living situation was that she shared a three-bedroom apartment with two other Winslow College graduates.

Emily went to the back, to the table where I stacked the new arrivals. Her primary job was updating and monitoring our online stores. We sold used books through eBay, and Amazon, and a site called Alibris, and a few more that I didn't even know about. I used to do some of it myself, filling orders, but Emily had taken over completely. That was one of the reasons I was anxious about her future plans. If she ever left here, I'd be in big trouble.

I stayed behind the counter and checked the phone for messages—there were none—then logged on to the Old Devils blog, something I rarely did these days, but the visit from Gwen Mulvey made me interested in taking a look. There were 211 total blog entries, the last one entered two months ago. It was called "Staff Picks" and it was something I periodically forced Emily and Brandon to do; write two sentences on the last book they'd read and loved. Brandon had picked Lee Child's last Jack Reacher novel, and Emily had written a quick blurb on Dorothy B. Hughes's *In a Lonely Place*. My pick had been *Started Early, Took My Dog* by Kate Atkinson. I hadn't read it, of course, but I'd read enough reviews and summaries to feel as though I had; also, I was fond of the title.

I spent the next hour or so scrolling backward through blog entries, and it was like living the past ten years of my life in reverse. There was John Haley's first and last entry, posted on the week he left the store, leaving me in charge. He'd sold Old Devils, and all its stock, to Brian Murray and me in 2012. Brian had put up most of the capital, but given me 50 percent ownership share, since I'd be the one running it. So far, it had worked out. I thought at first that Brian would want to be more involved than he was, but that hadn't been the case. He came to the store for our annual holiday party, along with attending almost all our readings, but, other than that, he has left me in charge, except for those two weeks a year when I take my annual my trip to London. I did see Brian frequently, though. It took him about two months to write an entry in his Ellis Fitzgerald series. The rest of the year he called his "drinking vacation," most of which he spent on a leather-padded stool at the small bar of the Beacon Hill Hotel. I stopped in often to have a drink with him, although I tried to do it early in the evening. If I arrived too late, Brian, a habitual storyteller, would play his greatest hits for me, stories I'd heard a hundred times already.

I scrolled farther back through the posts, noting the absence of posts from five years ago, the year my wife died. The last entry before that event had been a list I'd written called "Mysteries for a Cold Winter Night," posted on December 22, 2009. My wife died in the early morning hours of January 1, 2010; she'd been in a car accident, sliding off an overpass on Route 2 while inebriated. They'd shown me pictures for identification purposes, a white sheet covering her head from the eyebrows up. Her face looked unmarked even though I imagined her skull had completely collapsed from the impact.

I read the list of mysteries I'd selected, all ones that took place in wintertime time or during a storm. At this point in my blog-writing career I was happy to just list books, and not describe them. This was my post:

The Sittaford Mystery (1931) by Agatha Christie
The Nine Tailors (1934) by Dorothy L. Sayers
The Corpse in the Snowman (1941) by Nicholas Blake
Tied Up in Tinsel (1972) by Ngaio Marsh
The Shining (1977) by Stephen King
Gorky Park (1981) by Martin Cruz Smith
Smilla's Sense of Snow (1992) by Peter Hoeg
A Simple Plan (1993) by Scott Smith
The Ice Harvest (2000) by Scott Phillips
Raven Black (2006) by Ann Cleeves

I remembered putting it together, remembered worrying about including *The Shining*, because it was a horror novel and not at all a mystery, but included it anyway because it was a book I loved. It was strange to remember such minutiae, these insignificant thoughts I'd had less than two weeks before my world would change forever. If I could go back to late December of that year, then I would never have written this list. I would have spent all my time fighting tooth and nail for my wife, telling her that I knew about her affair, that I knew she was doing drugs again, telling her I forgave her, and that she could come back to me. Who knows if any of it would have made a difference? But at least I would have tried.

I scrolled back some more, found another list, "Crime Novels About Cheating," and quickly checked the date. I didn't officially know about my wife at that point, but I must have guessed, must have known something was going on at a gut level. I kept scrolling backward, the blog posts coming more and more frequently as I reached the years when I'd been better at keeping the blog updated. I thought, not for the first time: *Why does everything need to be a list? What compels us to do that?* It was something I'd been doing ever since I became an obsessed reader, ever since I started spending all my money at Annie's Book Swap. Ten favorite books. Ten scariest books. Best James Bond novels. Best Roald Dahl. I suppose I know why I did it back then. It doesn't take a psychology degree to understand that it was a way of giving myself an identity. Because if I wasn't a twelve-year-old who'd already read every single Dick Francis novel (and could name the five best), then I was just a lonely kid without friends, with a distant mother and a father who drank too much. That was my identity, and who wants that? So I guess the question is, Why keep doing it, making lists, even after I was living in Boston, had a good job, was married and in love? Why wasn't all that enough?

Eventually I made it all the way back to the start of the blog, to "Eight Perfect Murders." I'd read it so many times in the past twenty-four hours that I didn't need to read it again.

The front door opened, and I lifted my head. It was a middle-aged couple, both encased in puffy winter coats with hoods. They were probably already large under their coats, but the added layers rendered them almost spherical. They had to walk single file through the door. When their hoods were down and their parkas unzipped they approached me, smiling, introduced themselves as Mike and Becky Swenson from Minnesota. I recognized them immediately as a certain kind of customer we occasionally get, fanatical mystery readers who make a point to visit us during their trip to Boston. Old Devils is not a famous store, but we are famous to a certain kind of reader.

"You brought your weather with you," I said, and they both laughed, told me how they'd been planning on coming to Boston for years.

"Got to see Cheers, got to try some clam chowder, and definitely got to come to Old Devils," the man said.

"Where's Nero?" his wife said, and as if on cue, Nero rounded the New Releases shelf and visited the pair. We all had to chip in, I guess.

Mike and Becky left an hour and a half later. It was 90 percent talking and 10 percent shopping, although they did buy a hundred dollars' worth of signed hardcovers, giving me their address in East Grand Forks so that we could mail them to them. "We forgot to leave any room in our suitcases," Becky said.

It had stopped snowing when they left. They had taken several of our bookmarks with them as souvenirs, plus I'd steered them to a few restaurants in the nearby area that were better than Cheers. As I held the door for them, Brandon arrived, dressed only in a hooded sweatshirt, although he was wearing gloves and a wooly hat under the hood. I'd forgotten he was scheduled to come in today. "You look surprised," he said. "It's Friday."

"I know," I said.

"Thank God it's Friday," he added, in his booming voice, stretching the vowel sound on the word *God* to an impressive length. "And thank God I've got work to go to, so I don't have to be home all day."

"Your class was canceled?" I asked.

"Oh, yeah," he said. He was taking business classes, mostly in the mornings, and had been since he'd started working at the bookstore. Last I checked he would graduate soon, and I knew I'd most likely lose him. It was going to be fine, but I was going to miss his nonstop chatter. It was a nice counterpoint to Emily's silence. My silence, as well, I guess.

He pulled a paperback—Richard Stark's *The Hunter*—from the pouch at the front of the hoodie, and handed it to me. "Effing awesome," he said. When he'd first started at the store, I had to keep reminding him not to swear, because of the customers, so he'd amended his ways. He'd borrowed the book from the store at my suggestion just two days earlier. Between working full-time and going to school *and* maintaining (according to him) a pretty active social life, he also managed to read about three books a week. I looked at the paperback, one in which the name of the book had been changed to *Point Blank!* in order to reflect the Lee Marvin movie that was made in 1967.

"That's the way I got it, Mal," he said, meaning the condition of the book. The borrow policy for employees meant they could take any book home to read just so long as they didn't add any extra wear to it.

"No, it looks fine," I said.

"Yeah, it does," Brandon said, then shouted, "Emily," in three equally accented syllables. She came out from the back, and Brandon hugged her, something he occasionally did if he had been more than a day since he'd last been in the store. He only hugged me at the holiday party, and at the few occasions when we'd close up the shop then grab a quick beer at the Sevens. I am not a natural hugger, even though it is now standard greeting protocol among men of my generation. I can't get the movements down, especially if the hug involves one of those manly backslaps. Claire, my wife, when I told her about this particular anxiety, started to practice with me. For a while there we'd greet each other at home with a man hug.

Brandon followed Emily into the back room where he took the mail order list and began to assemble piles of books for shipping. A huge advantage of having the same employees here for so long is that I hardly ever have to tell them what to do. Because of their loyalty, I pay them far more than I suspect other retail places offer. I don't need the store to make a big profit, and I don't think Brian Murray cares that much, either. He's just happy to be able to call a mystery bookstore his own, or half his own.

I listened to Brandon tell Emily the entire plot of *The Hunter* while I updated New Releases. Four more customers came in, all alone: a Japanese tourist, a regular named Joe Stailey, a twenty-something guy I knew by sight who always browsed through the horror section and never bought anything, plus a woman who had clearly come in only to escape the cold outside. I checked my phone for the weather. The snow was done now, but temperatures were dropping over the next few days into the teens. All the snow that had fallen was going to harden into piles of ice, black with city grime.

I went back to my computer to check on emails again, then glanced again at the blog site, still on the "Eight Perfect Murders" list. A sort of byline at the bottom of the list said that it was posted by MALCOLM KERSHAW, then gave the date and time of the post, then indicated that there were three comments. I remembered there only being two, so I clicked through to read them. The latest comment was posted less than twenty-four hours earlier, at three

A.M., from a user named Doctor Sheppard, that read, I am halfway through your list. STRANGERS ON A TRAIN, done. THE ABC MURDERS, finally finished. DOUBLE INDEMNITY, kaput. DEATHTRAP, saw the film. When I'm finished with the list (it won't be long now) I'll get in touch. Or do you already know who I am?

CHAPTER 8

That night I cooked myself the pork chop that was in the refrigerator, although I was still shaken, and I overcooked it. Its sides curled up, and it was as tough as jerky.

Since late afternoon, and through until our closing time of seven, I hadn't been able to stop thinking about that third comment on the "Perfect Murders" blog post. I must have read it thirty times now, parsing every word. The name used by whoever had written the post—"Doctor Sheppard"—nagged at me until I finally googled it. It was the name of the narrator in Agatha Christie's famous novel, *The Murder of Roger Ackroyd*. That was the book that put Christie on the map, so to speak. Written in 1926, it is most famous for a very clever plot twist. The book is told in first person, from the point of view of Sheppard, a country village doctor, and a neighbor of Hercule Poirot's. Honestly, I don't remember anything about the crime itself, except for the name of the victim, obviously. What I do remember is that at the end of the novel it is revealed the narrator is the actual murderer.

When I got home, I went immediately to my bookshelf and found my copy of Christie's book. I owned the Penguin paperback edition, one from the 1950s, with the simple green cover, and no artwork. I flipped through to see if it would somehow jog my memory as to the actual plot, but it didn't, and I decided I'd read it that night.

Was it possible that whoever posted the comment was really

only a reader, working his or her way through my list? I'd think it was a possibility, a very slim one, except for the fact of the books mentioned as having been read. They were the books for which there had already been a crime. *The A.B.C. Murders*, *Double Indemnity*, and *Deathtrap*. *Strangers on a Train*, as well, although Gwen Mulvey doesn't know all about that one yet. I do. And someone else does, as well.

If these words are ever read, then I am sure that the reader might have already guessed that I have more to do with these crimes than I've been letting on. It's not as though there haven't been clues. For instance, why did my heart beat faster when Gwen Mulvey first began interviewing me?

Why didn't I immediately tell her that I knew who Elaine Johnson was?

Why did I only eat two bites of my sandwich the night after I was visited by the FBI agent?

Why do I dream of being chased?

Why did I not immediately tell Gwen about the comment from Doctor Sheppard?

And a really astute reader might even have noticed that my name, shortened, is Mal—French, of course, for bad. That's taking it too far, though, because that really is my name. I've changed some names for the purposes of this narrative, but not my own.

It is time to tell the truth.

It is time to speak of Claire.

That was her real name, as well. Claire Mallory, who grew up in a wealthy town in Fairfield County, Connecticut, one of three sisters. Her parents were not particularly good people, but they weren't bad enough to really figure into this story. They were well-off, and shallow; her mother, in particular, was obsessed with all three of her daughters' attractiveness and weight, and because she obsessed about it, that meant their father—devoid of any independent thoughts, himself—agreed with her. They sent their children to summer camps in Maine and to fancy private schools, and Claire, who was the oldest, chose to go to Boston University, because she wanted to be in a city, and both New York City and Hartford felt too close to where she'd grown up

At BU she majored in film and television, wanting to be a documentary filmmaker. Her first year was okay, but in her second year, prompted by a boyfriend majoring in theater arts, she got heavily into drugs, particularly cocaine. As her habit grew, she began to have panic attacks, and that caused her to drink more. She stopped going to classes, was put on academic probation, briefly rebounded, then failed out her junior year. Her parents tried hard to get her to come home, but she stayed in Boston, instead, renting an apartment in Allston, and getting a job at the Redline Bookstore, where I'd just been promoted to manager.

It was love at first sight, really. At least for me. When she came in to interview it was clear that she was nervous, her hands trembling slightly, and she kept yawning, which seemed weird, but I was able to recognize it as a sign of extreme anxiety. She sat on a swivel chair in Mort's office, her hands resting on her thighs. She wore a corduroy skirt and dark leggings, plus a turtleneck. She was thin, noticeably so, and with a long neck. Her head seemed too big for her body, her face almost perfectly round. She had dark brown eyes, a thin nose, and lips that looked puffy and bitten. Her hair was very dark, cut in what I thought of as a bob. It looked like a dated style to me, something an intrepid amateur detective might wear in a 1930s film. She was so pretty that a dull throb had taken up residence in my solar plexus.

I asked her about work experience. She had very little, but

during the past few summers she'd worked at a Waldenbooks at her local mall down in Connecticut.

"Who are your favorite writers?" I'd asked, and she'd looked surprised at the question.

"Janet Frame," she said. "Virginia Woolf. Jeanette Winterson." She thought for a while. "I read poetry, as well. Adrienne Rich. Robert Lowell. Ann Sexton."

"Sylvia Plath?" I'd asked, and inwardly cringed. It sounded stupid, mentioning the most famous confessional female poet, as though I were somehow reminding her of the name.

"Sure," she said, then asked me who my favorite writers were.

I told her. They were all crime writers, for the most part, but I read enough that I'd gotten through most of the classics. We kept talking this way, about writers, for the next hour, and I realized I'd only asked her one question about the actual job.

"What hours will you be available?" I said.

"Oh." She touched her cheek when she thought. I noticed it right away, not aware in that moment of how many times I'd see her make that gesture, and how eventually I would see it not just as something endearing and individual, but as something worrying. "I don't know why I'm thinking about it," she said, laughing. "Any hours."

It was six weeks before I got up the nerve to actually ask her out.

Even then, I'd framed it as a work outing. Ruth Rendell was doing an event at the Boston Public Library and I asked Claire if she wanted to join me. She'd said yes, then added, "I haven't read her books, but if you like them, I should," a sentence that I analyzed in the following days the way a graduate student might pick apart a Shakespeare sonnet. "Maybe we can get a drink afterward?" I said, and my own voice in my head sounded relatively calm.

"Sure," she said.

It was a November night, dark by the time we were diagonally crossing Copley Square to get to the library, and the park was littered with brittle leaves. We sat toward the back of the small auditorium. Ruth Rendell was interviewed by a local radio personality, who was far too interested in himself. Still, it was an interesting conversation, and afterward, Claire and I walked to the Pour House for a drink, sitting in a corner booth until closing time. We talked about books, of course, and the other employees at the bookstore. Nothing personal. But when we were standing in front of her apartment building in Allston at two in the morning, the wind causing us both to shiver, she said, before we'd even kissed, "I'm a bad idea."

"What do you mean?" I laughed.

"I mean, whatever ideas you're having about me are bad ones. I've got issues."

"I don't care," I said.

"Okay," she said, and I followed her inside.

I'd had two girlfriends in college, one of whom was a German exchange student studying for a year in Amherst, and the other a freshman when I was a senior, a girl from Houlton, Maine, who joined the literary magazine that I was then editing. I'd had roughly the same feelings toward both of them. What drew me to them was the fact that they were drawn to me. Both were nervous talkers, and since I tended on the quiet side, it had worked out. When Petra returned to Germany, I told her that I'd be visiting her as soon as possible. Her response, that she never expected our relationship to last beyond her time in America, was both confusing and somehow an enormous relief. I had been under the impression that she was in love with me. Two years later, when I'd graduated, I'd told Ruth Porter, my freshman girlfriend, that now that I was moving to Boston, and she was staying in Amherst, we should end the relationship. I'd expected a happy indifference on her part, but she looked as though I'd shot her in the stomach. Through a series of wrenching conversations, I did finally manage to break up with her, realizing that I'd also broken her heart. I decided then that I was not good at reading women, or maybe just people in general.

So when I stepped into Claire Mallory's apartment, and when we began to kiss before we'd even gotten our jackets off, I told her, "Just so you know, I think I'm terrible at nonverbal cues. I need you to tell me everything."

She laughed. "Are you sure?"

"Yes, please," I said, and it was all I could do to not tell her I was already in love with her.

"Okay. I'll tell you everything."

She started that night. In bed, with the dawn light filling her two dusty bedroom windows, she told me how her middle-school science teacher had molested her over the course of two years.

"You didn't tell anyone?" I said.

"No," she said. "It's a cliché, but I was ashamed. I thought it was my fault, and I kept telling myself that he wasn't having sex with me, at least. We'd never even kiss. In fact, he was nice to me in a way, both him and his wife. But when he got me alone, he'd always manage to somehow get behind me, pull me in for a hug, put one hand in my shirt, and the other down my jeans. I think he used to come that way. But he never took my clothes off, or his, and afterward he'd always look a little sheepish, say something like, 'That was nice,' and then he'd change the subject."

"Jesus," I'd said.

"It wasn't a huge deal," she said. "Other shitty things have happened to me and that was just one of them. I sometimes think my mom fucked me up even more than my molester did."

She had tattoos on the insides of her arms, and along her rib cages. Just straight lines, dark and thin. I asked her about them, and she told me she loved the feeling of getting a tattoo but could never pick any image that she'd want on her body forever. So she just got lines, one at a time. I thought they were beautiful, just as I thought her body, unhealthily thin, probably, was also beautiful. I think our relationship worked so well for a time because I never judged her, never questioned what she told me. I knew she had issues, that she drank too much (although she hadn't taken drugs in close to a year), and that she ate too little, and that, sometimes, when we had sex, I could feel her wanting me to objectify her, that it wasn't always enough to have normal, loving sex, that she wanted more. When she was drunk, she'd turn her back to me, pull my hands around to her front, grind herself up against me, and it was impossible for me to not think of her teacher in middle school and wonder if she was thinking of him, as well.

But all this darkness, if that's what it's even called, was only part of what we had for the first three years we were together. Most of what we had was an incredible closeness, the happiness that comes with finding someone who seems to fit inside of you like a key in a lock. That's the best metaphor I can come up with. I know it's trite, but it's also true. And it was the only time that this type of connection ever happened with me, then or since.

We got married in Las Vegas, our witness a blackjack dealer we'd met five minutes earlier. The major reason we eloped was because Claire could not deal with the prospect of her mother hijacking her own wedding. It was fine with me. My own mother had died three years prior from lung cancer. She'd never smoked a day in her life, but my father, the chain smoker, was still alive, of course, now living in Fort Myers, Florida, and still, as far as I knew, an alcoholic, and a three-packs-a-day Winston man. After Claire and I were married, we moved to Somerville together, rented the middle floor of a triple decker near Union Square. Claire had left Redline Bookstore by this point, getting an administrative job at Somerville's cable access station, where she had begun to make short documentary films. And a year later, after Redline shuttered its doors, I got the job at Old Devils. I was twenty-nine years old and felt as though I'd found the job that I would have for the rest of my life.

It wasn't so easy for Claire. She hated her job at the cable station, but she didn't have a college degree and every position she was interested in required one. She decided to go back to school part-time at Emerson College and finish an undergraduate degree; and she got work as a bartender at a divey club in Central Square. I used to visit her there, sitting long hours at the bar, suffering through overamplified punk bands, drinking Guinness, and watching my wife get ogled by hipsters in dark-rimmed glasses and skinny jeans. I developed the ability to read entire novels while ignoring the thunderous amateurs onstage. Even though I wasn't older than the other patrons of the bar, I felt older, what with my book, and my graying hair. The other bartenders referred to me as Claire's old man, and Claire started calling me Old Man as well. I think that, for a time, my wife loved my presence at her bar. At the end of her shift, she'd join me in having a beer, and then we'd walk back home together, arm in arm, through the dark, cluttered streets of Somerville. But something changed in 2007. Claire's sister Julie was getting married, and Claire was suddenly embroiled back with her family, recruited in to serve as a buffer between her youngest sister and her mother. She lost the weight she'd gained over the last few years and added several new tattooed lines to the inside of her left thigh.

Also, she fell in love with a new bartender named Patrick Yates.

CHAPTER 9

After my bad dinner, I got into bed early with my Penguin edition of *The Murder of Roger Ackroyd*, but I couldn't concentrate. I kept rereading the first page, my mind skipping around between thoughts of my wife and wondering who had written the comment on my blog post. I filled my lungs with the stale air of my apartment, then slowly exhaled. Why did he call himself Doctor Sheppard? Because he was the killer, right? Still, that didn't mean I needed to try and read the book. I put it on my nightstand, where I kept a stack of poetry collections. That's what I read at night now, before I go to sleep. Even if I'm currently into a literary biography (even though I rarely read crime, I do read biographies of crime writers), or something on European history, the last words I read before I try and fall asleep are the words of poets. All poems—all works of art, really—seem like cries of help to me, but especially poetry. When they are good, and I do believe there are very few good poems, reading them is like having a long-dead stranger whisper in your ear, trying to be heard.

I got out of bed and went to my bookshelf to find an anthology of poems that contained one of my favorites, "Winter Nightfall" by Sir John Squire. I could probably recite it by heart, but I wanted to see the words. When I found a poem I loved, I would read it again and again. For one entire year I must have read Sylvia Plath's "Black Rook in Rainy Weather" every night before I fell asleep. Lately I'd been reading Peter Porter's "An Exequy" even though

I understood less than half of it. I do not have a critical mind for poetry, but I react to them.

Back in bed I read the Squire poem, then shut my eyes and let the final words gallop over me—"and the slop of my footsteps in this desolate country's cadaverous clay"—again and again like a mantra. I thought some more of my wife, and the decisions that I made. When Patrick Yates came into her life, and I actually remember the date because it was March 31, my birthday, I knew right away that something momentous had occurred. Claire had done the afternoon shift that day at the bar, so as to get out early and take me to the East Coast Grill for my birthday dinner. "We finally hired a new bartender," she said.

"Oh."

"Patrick. I started training him today. He seems okay."

The way she said his name, a combination of hesitancy and boldness, and I knew right away that he had made an impression on her. My body felt as though an almost imperceptible electric current had coursed through it.

"Does he have experience?" I asked, as I tipped an oyster back.

"He worked at a pub in Australia for a year, so that's something. I thought of you because he has a tattoo of Edgar Allan Poe on his right shoulder."

I was not a jealous husband, but I was also aware that Claire, unlike myself, was never going to go through life content with just me. She'd been with numerous men in college, and she'd admitted, more than once, that she'd go through periods when every time she met a man, or every time she'd pass a man on the street, she'd wonder if that man wanted her, and then she'd obsess over what these men might think about doing to her. I'd listen to these confessions and tell myself that it was better that she told me. Better than the alternative. Better than secrets.

She did have a therapist, a woman she referred to as Doctor Martha, whom she saw once every two weeks, but after her appointments she'd be in a dark mood, sometimes for days, and I wondered if it was worth it.

Part of me had always told myself that one day Claire would cheat, or maybe not cheat, but that she would fall for someone else. And I'd accepted that. And hearing about Patrick I knew that day had come. It scared me, but I had already decided what to do. Claire was my wife. She would always be my wife, and I would stand by her no matter what. It provided a sense of comfort, knowing that I was in it for the long haul, no matter what.

She did have an affair with Patrick, at least an emotional one, although I suspect it tipped over into the physical on at least a couple of occasions. I waited patiently, like the wife of a sea captain, hoping that she'd make it alive through the storm. I wonder sometimes if I should have fought more, threatened to leave, berated her when she came home two hours after the bar had closed, her clothes smelling of the American Spirits that he smoked, her breath sharp with gin. But I didn't. That wasn't my choice. I waited for her to come back to me, and one night, a hot summer night in August, she did. I had just arrived home from the bookstore, and she was sitting on our sofa, head bowed, tears in her eyes.

"I've been such an asshole," she said.

"A little bit."

"Will you ever forgive me?"

"I will always forgive you," I said.

Later that night she asked me if I wanted details, and I said only if she needed to say them out loud.

"God, no," she said. "I'm done with it."

I found out later, but not from Claire, that Patrick Yates had disappeared after cleaning out the till on a Saturday night, and that at least three other female bartenders at the club had all been devastated by his departure.

After that incident, it got better between Claire and me, although things were worse with her. She quit the club and dropped out of Emerson College. For a while she did a few shifts at Old Devils, but then she got another job as a bartender at an upscale restaurant in the Back Bay. The money was good, but she felt frustrated with the lack of creativity in her life. "I don't want to be a bartender for the rest of my life. I want to make films, but I need to go to school to do that."

"You don't *have* to go to school," I said. "You could just make a film."

And that's what she did. There were her evening shifts at the restaurants and during the daytime she made short documentary films. One about tattoo artists, one about the polyamory community in Davis Square, even one about the Old Devils Bookstore. She posted them on YouTube, and that was where Eric Atwell found her. Atwell ran what he called "an innovation incubator" outside of Boston in a renovated farmhouse in Southwell. He offered free workspace (and occasional bedrooms) to young creatives, in return for a percentage of their final product's profits. He contacted Claire, told her he liked her tattoo documentary, and asked if she'd film a promotional video for his incubator. Unlike with Patrick Yates, I didn't get a bad feeling about Eric Atwell when Claire first started telling me about him. She said he was a cliché, a fifty-year-old who acted thirty, someone who clearly liked to surround himself with young people, preferably sycophants.

"Sounds like a creep," I said.

"I don't know. More like a con man. I think he's just really hoping to stumble into the next big thing and make a quick buck."

She spent a weekend at the farmhouse—the name of his

company was Black Barn Enterprises—and when she returned, I sensed that something had changed in her. She was jumpy, a little irritated, but also somewhat more affectionate with me. A few days after the weekend, Claire woke me up in the middle of the night and asked me, "Why do you love me?"

"I don't know," I said. "I just do."

"You must have reasons."

"If I had reasons to love you, then there'd be reasons for me to not love you."

"What do you mean?"

"I don't know. I'm tired."

"No, tell me, I'm curious."

"Okay. So if I loved you because you're beautiful, then that would mean I wouldn't love you anymore if you had some kind of accident that disfigured your face—"

"Or simply grew old."

"Right, or grew old. And if I loved you because you're a good person, then that would mean I would stop loving you if you did something bad. And that wouldn't happen."

"You're way too good for me," she said, but she laughed.

"What do you love about me?" I said.

"Your youthful good looks," she said, laughing some more. "Actually, I love you because you're an old soul in a young man."

"And one day I'll be an old soul in an old man."

"I can't wait," she said.

Because I worked mostly during the daytime and she tended to work night shifts at the restaurant, it took me a while to find out that she had kept going back out to Southwell during the daytime hours. I started keeping track of the mileage on her Subaru; I felt bad spying in that way, but my suspicions turned out to be correct. It was clear that she was going out to Southwell two or three times a week. I assumed she was having an affair either with Atwell, or maybe with one of Atwell's tenants. It didn't occur to me, at least not in those first few weeks, that she'd been going to Black Barn Enterprises for another reason, until I realized that the normally skintight jeans she wore to work were beginning to look baggy around her waist. I found her cocaine, plus a small pillbox filled with an assortment of pills, in one of the compartments of the jewelry box she'd inherited from her grandmother.

Later, after I'd confronted her, she told me how that first weekend at Black Barn Atwell had thrown a dinner party with a ton of great wine. When she'd told him she was ready for bed, he'd talked her into a small amount of coke just to keep the party going. The next day, after she'd finished getting footage for her film, he'd thanked her by giving her a bottle of the Sancerre they'd been drinking the night before, plus a half gram of the cocaine. He'd also explained to Claire that he had devised a system for his drug use, spreading it out, so as to not get addicted. He convinced her it was okay, so long as you followed his scientific schedule.

If I'd initially known that Claire's trips out to Southwell were for drugs and not for sex, I might have tried to intervene sooner. As it was, by the time I was hearing about it, Claire was a full-blown addict again. I decided to do what I always did. I decided to wait it out in hopes that she would eventually agree to quit, or to go to rehab. I know how it sounds. I know that maybe if I'd done something—given her an ultimatum, contacted her parents, gotten her friends involved, anything—that maybe the outcome would have been different. I still think about this all the time.

When I was a teenager, I remember asking my mom why she put up with my father's drinking.

She'd frowned, not because she was upset, but because she was confused. "What choice do I have?" she'd finally said.

"You could leave him."

She shook her head. "I'd rather wait for him."

"Even if you have to wait forever?" I said.

She nodded in response.

That was how I felt about Claire during those moments when she wasn't fully mine. I was waiting for her.

When the two uniformed officers knocked on my apartment door early on the first day of 2010, I knew that she was dead before either of them spoke.

"Okay," I remember saying after they'd delivered the news that she'd been in a car accident at three in the morning, and that she'd been killed instantly.

"Was anyone else hurt?" I asked.

"No, she was alone, and no other vehicles were involved in the accident."

"Okay," I said again and went to shut the door, figuring that the police were done with me. But they stopped me from closing the door, explained that I needed to come down to the station for identification purposes.

THREE MONTHS LATER I found a journal she'd been keeping. It was hidden behind a number of larger hardcovers in the section of our bookshelf that she had claimed for herself. I almost burned it without reading it, but curiosity got the better of me, and one wet spring evening I bought myself a six-pack of Newcastle Brown, settled in, and read the entire contents.

CHAPTER 10

E ven though I don't read contemporary mysteries anymore, I keep up with the trends. I am well aware that *Gone Girl* by Gillian Flynn has changed the industry, that unreliable narrators are suddenly popular, along with domestic suspense, with books that posit the question of whether we can really trust anyone, especially the ones closest to us. Some of the reviews I read make it sound as though this is a recent phenomenon, as though the idea of discovering a spouse's secrets constituted something new, or that the omission of facts from a narrative hadn't been the bedrock upon which psychological thrillers have been built for over a century. The narrator of *Rebecca*, a novel published in 1938, never even gave the readers her name.

The thing is, and maybe I'm biased by all those years I've spent in fictional realms built on deceit, I don't trust narrators any more than I trust the actual people in my life. We never get the whole truth, not from anybody. When we first meet someone, before words are ever spoken, there are already lies and half-truths. The clothes we wear cover the truth of our bodies, but they also present who we want to be to the world. They are fabrications, figuratively and literally.

So I wasn't surprised when I found my wife's secret journal, and I wasn't surprised that there were things inside it that she'd never told me. Many things. For the purposes of this story—of *my* story—I won't go into everything that I discovered from reading the journal. She didn't want the world to know, and I don't either.

But I do need to record what happened between Claire and Eric Atwell. Not surprisingly, they had been sexually involved. It wasn't a romantic liaison. Claire had become addicted to cocaine, and after a time during which Atwell had been furnishing it free of charge, he began to ask for money. She and I had shared one bank account together—for rent, for household expenses, for vacations—but we each had separate accounts as well. And hers had been emptied in about the space of three weeks. After that she had paid Atwell in sexual favors. It was his idea. Without going into detail, some of what he asked her to do was truly demeaning. At one point she'd told him about her bad experience with Mr. Clifton, the middle-school teacher; "I could see the excitement in his eyes," she wrote.

I read the rest of the journal, then the following weekend, I drove out to Walden Pond in Concord, passing through Southwell. The lot was nearly empty—it was ten degrees outside, the pond frozen, the skies above a chalky white. I walked along a trail that climbed a ridge above the pond, then doused the journal in kerosene and burned it in a clearing, stomping on the remains until the book was nothing more than a crater of black soot in the snow and ashes in the air.

I never regretted destroying Claire's journal although sometimes, to this day, I regret having read it. When I moved from our apartment in Somerville to the studio in Beacon Hill, I got rid of everything else that remained of Claire—her clothes, the furniture she'd bought for our place, her school yearbooks. I kept a few of her books, her childhood copy of *A Wrinkle in Time*, an annotated paperback of Ann Sexton's collected poetry that she'd bought for a class during her freshman year at Boston University. That book is on my bedside table, always. Sometimes I read the poems inside, but mostly I look at Claire's notes and doodles, the lines and the words she'd underlined. Sometimes I touch the indentations that her ballpoint pen made on the page.

Mostly, these days, I just like that the book is there, within easy reach. It's been five years since she died, but I talk to her more now, in my head, than I did immediately after she died. I talked to her the night I got into bed with Agatha Christie's *The Murder of Roger Ackroyd*, told her all about the list, and the visit from Agent Mulvey, and what it felt like to be reading these books again.

I WOKE AROUND EIGHT thirty in the morning, surprised that I'd gotten any sleep at all. I'd forgotten to pull the curtains in my apartment and bright, hard sunlight was flooding in. At the window I looked outside toward the irregular roofline across the street, now covered with snow, icicles decorating the gutters. There were spidery lines of frost on the outside of the windows, and the street below had the grayish pallor that meant it was incredibly cold outside. I checked my phone, and it was currently registering one degree above zero. I almost considered sending emails to Emily and Brandon, letting them know that they could take the day off, that it was too cold to ask them to come in, but changed my mind.

I bundled up and walked down to Charles Street to a café that served oatmeal. I was sitting at a corner table reading a copy of yesterday's *Globe* that had been sitting on the table when my cell phone rang.

"Malcolm, it's Gwen."

"Hi," I said.

"Were you sleeping?"

"Oh, no. I'm getting breakfast. I'm about to go into the store. Are you still in Boston?"

"No, I got home yesterday afternoon, and all the books I'd

ordered had arrived, so last night I read *Strangers on a Train*."

"Yeah, and?"

"I'd love to talk with you about it. Is there a good time?"

"Can I call you back when I get to the store?" I said. My oatmeal had just arrived, steam pouring from the bowl.

"Sure," she said. "Call me back."

After finishing breakfast, I went to Old Devils. Emily was already there, and Nero had been fed.

"You're here early," I said.

"Remember that I'm leaving early."

"Oh, right," I said, although I hadn't remembered that.

"Mr. Popovitch complained again," she said, rubbing her hands together. "He wants to return his last shipment."

"The whole shipment?"

"Yep. He says they were all improperly graded."

David Popovich was a collector who lived in New Mexico but all of us at the bookstore felt like he might as well live next door. He bought a ton of books from us and returned half of them, at least. He occasionally called to complain but mostly he sent us snide emails.

"Cut him off," I said.

"What?"

"Write him back and tell him that we'll accept whatever returns he has but that he can't order through us, anymore. I'm done with him."

"You serious?"

"Yes. Would you rather I write the email?"

"No, I'm happy to do it. Should I cc you?"

"Sure," I said. Banishing Popovich would probably hurt our bottom line in the end, but for the moment I didn't care. And it felt good.

Before calling Gwen back I sent an email to a publicist at Random House that I'd been ignoring and confirmed a date for her author to come and give a reading in March. Then I opened up the glass case and got our first edition copy of *Strangers on a Train*, bringing it back with me to the phone. Its cover was deep blue, garishly illustrated with a close-up of a man's face and a sickly-looking woman with red hair.

Gwen picked up after one ring.

"Hi, Gwen," I said, and her first name sounded strange coming out of my mouth.

"Thanks for calling me back. So, this book."

"What did you think?"

"Bleak. I knew the story, because of the movie. But the book was different. Darker, I thought, and do both the men commit murders in the movie?"

I tried to remember. "I don't think so," I said. "No, definitely not. I think the main character in the movie—the tennis player—almost kills the father but doesn't. That probably had a lot more to do with the production code than with what Hitchcock actually wanted to do. I don't think they were allowed to have characters get away with murder." I hadn't read the book in many years, or seen the movie, but I remembered both of them pretty well.

"The Hayes code," she said. "If only it was that way in real life."

"Right."

"And he's not a tennis player in the book."

"Who?"

"Guy. The main character. He's an architect."

"Oh, right," I said. "Was reading the book helpful?"

"You mentioned in your list that you thought it was the very best example of a perfect murder," she said, ignoring my question. "What exactly did you mean?"

"It's a perfect crime," I said, "because when you swap murders with someone else, a stranger basically, then there is no connection between the murderer and their victim. That's what makes it foolproof."

"That's what I've been thinking about," she said, "What's clever about the murder in the book," she continued, "is that the person committing it can't be connected to the crime. It has nothing to do with the method."

"What do you mean?" I said.

"Bruno kills Guy's wife at an amusement park. He strangles her to death. But there's nothing clever about that. I've been thinking about Charlie's rules again. So, if you were Charlie, just humor me, then how would you commit a murder based on *Strangers on a Train*?"

"I see what you mean. It would be very hard."

"Right. You could just go strangle someone at an amusement park but that wouldn't be following the philosophy of the crime."

"He'd have to find someone else to commit a murder with him."

"That's what I thought, but not necessarily, really," she said. "If I were Charlie, if I were trying to copy *Strangers on a Train*, then I would select as a victim someone who is already likely to be murdered. My mind is going blank right now, but suppose someone just went through a bitter divorce, or . . ."

"Who's the guy in New York, who stole everyone's money?" I said.

"Bernie Madoff?"

"Right, him."

"He'd work, but there are maybe too many people who want him dead. I would pick one-half of a bad divorce, I think. Something slightly public, then I would wait until the spurned spouse was away, and I would commit the murder. I think that would be the best way to honor the book."

"That makes sense," I said.

"I think so too. Worth looking into. How about you, did you have any new thoughts last night?"

"I was pretty tired last night, after staying up the night before. So, no. But I'll keep thinking about it."

"Thanks," she said. "You've been helpful." Then she added, in a slightly different tone of voice, "Don't forget to send me your flight information for the trip you took to London this past fall."

"I'll do that today," I said.

After I hung up, Nero came clicking along the hardwood floor to settle himself down by my legs. I watched him, in a slight daze, thinking about the phone conversation I'd just had.

"I did it," came Emily's voice, and I turned around; she was coming toward me, a rare grin on her face.

"Did what?"

"Sent the email to Popovich. He's going to be in shock."

"You seem very pleased."

"No, I'm . . . you know how much he drives me crazy."

"It's fine. Honestly, I think he needs us more than we need him. The customer isn't always right, you know."

Emily grinned again, then said, "Are you feeling okay?"

"I'm fine. Why?"

"Oh, nothing. You seem distracted, that's all. I didn't know if there was anything going on."

It was so out of character for her to express this much interest in me that I realized that I must be acting noticeably different. I think of myself as stoic, as someone who never reveals too much of themselves, and it worried me that that might not be the case.

"Would it be okay if I go for a walk?" I said. "You can cover the store?"

"Sure."

"It'll be a quick walk," I said.

Outside it was still bitterly cold, but the sun was out, the sky a hard, unforgiving blue. The sidewalks had been cleared and I walked toward Charles Street, thinking I'd cut up to the Public Garden. I kept thinking about the conversation with Gwen about *Strangers on a Train*, a book that I'd worked hard at not thinking about for many years.

There were more people in the park than I thought there would be, considering the temperature. A father was wiping snow off one of the *Make Way for Ducklings* bronze figures so that he could put his toddler on top of it and take a picture. I must have walked past those ducklings a thousand times and there was always a parent, or a set of parents, posing their child for a photograph. In summertime there was often a line. And I always wondered what the parents got out of it, their insistence to document a particular moment. Not being a parent, I don't really know. It was actually something that Claire and I had never talked about, having children. I had told myself it was up to her, but maybe she'd been waiting for me to broach the subject.

I walked around the frozen pond, the wind now spinning dead leaves, and started to make my way back to the store. I was not innocent, even though sometimes I allowed myself the luxury of thinking that I was. And if Gwen Mulvey discovered the truth, then I would have to accept it.

CHAPTER 11

I knew that I was going to kill Eric Atwell the moment I'd finished reading Claire's diary. But it took me many more months to work up the courage to admit that to myself.

I also knew that when Atwell was dead, I was going to be an immediate suspect. My wife had been coming from his home on the night she died in a car accident. Atwell had even confessed to providing the drugs that were found in her system, and the police, no doubt, had also determined that Claire Kershaw née Mallory had been having an affair with the wealthy owner of Black Barn Enterprises.

I thought of hiring someone to kill Atwell, then making sure that I was far away (out of the country?) when it happened. But there were so many reasons this wouldn't work. For one, I doubted I had the kind of money it would take to hire a professional hit man, and even if I could scrape it together somehow, it would be obvious to anyone looking at my suddenly depleted bank account. I also had no idea how to go about hiring a killer. Nor did I even want to support such a profession. Anyone who killed people for money was not someone I wanted to be involved with; besides, it would be giving someone far too much power over my own life.

So I decided that I couldn't hire a killer. But I did like the idea of being far away when Eric Atwell was killed.

A year earlier, sometime in 2009, a young woman had come into Old Devils with a stack of incredibly valuable first editions.

They weren't primarily mystery novels, although there had been an 1892 Harper & Brothers edition of *The Adventures of Sherlock Holmes* that had made me ache with longing. There were about ten books in all—including two Mark Twain firsts that must have been worth thousands—and the woman, who had stringy hair and scabbed lips, had been carrying the books in a grocery bag. I asked her where she got them.

"Don't you want them?" she said.

"Not if you can't tell me where you got them from."

She'd left the store, as quickly as she'd come in. In retrospect I began to wish I'd simply bought them from her with whatever money was in the register. And then I'd have been able to find the owner—she must have robbed someone's home—and returned the books. As it was, I did call the police to report the incident, and they told me they'd keep an eye and an ear out for reports of stolen books. I never heard anything back from them, and I never saw the young woman again. At that time, Old Devils had an employee named Rick Murphy, who worked weekend shifts. Rick was a collector, primarily interested in anything horror related.

I told Rick about the woman who'd come in with the rare first editions.

"She might try and sell them online," Rick had said.

"She didn't look like the type who goes online."

"Worth checking, though," he said. "There's this pretty tasty little site, more of a dark web place, where people sell collectibles under the table."

Rick, who worked in IT at an insurance company during the week, showed me a site called Duckburg. To me it looked nearly incomprehensible, like message boards from the early internet days, but Rick pulled up a section where rare collectibles were offered for sale. It was all anonymous. We did searches for some of the books that had been brought into the stores, but nothing popped up.

"What else is on here?" I said.

"Ah, the gentleman is intrigued. A lot of it is just a place to chat anonymously. To tell the truth, this isn't the true dark web, but it's darkish enough."

Rick went to get his gigantic soda and I quickly bookmarked the page. I thought I might check it out later, but never did.

After deciding in late 2010 to kill Eric Atwell, I went to my bookmarks and discovered I still had that link. I spent a few hours one night after closing time, exploring the different portals, and creating a fake identity, calling myself "Bert Kling." Then I logged on to a portal called "Swaps," that didn't specify exactly what it was for but primarily seemed to be sexual in nature. Sixtyyearold man wants to buy a you a 1000dollars in clothes. Young and sexy only. Won't mind me accompanying you into changing room. No touching, just looking. But there were also offers such as Looking for cleaning ladies that want to be paid in oxy.

I opened up a dialogue box and wrote, Any Strangers on a Train fans out there? Would love to suggest a mutually beneficial swap. I posted it and logged off.

I told myself to wait for twenty-four hours before *getting* back on, but only managed about twelve. It was a quiet day at the store, and I logged back on to Duckburg under my alias. I'd gotten a response. Big fan of that book. Would love to discuss. Go to private chat?

Okay, I responded, clicking the box that made the chat only visible to the two parties involved. Two hours later there was a new message: What did you have in mind?

I wrote, There's someone who deserves to disappear from the face of the earth. Can't do it myself, though. I somehow couldn't bring myself to actually write the word *die*.

I have the same problem, came back almost immediately.

Let's help each other out, okay?

Okay.

My heart was beating, and my ears had gone warm. Was I being trapped? It was possible, but all I had to give up was Eric Atwell's information, not my own. I decided, after about five minutes, that it was worth it.

I wrote: Eric Atwell, 255 Elsinore Street, Southwell, Mass. Anytime from February 6 through February 12. I was going to be at an antiquarian bookseller's conference in Sarasota, Florida, during that week. My ticket was already bought.

I watched the screen for what seemed like an hour but was probably only ten minutes. Finally, a message appeared. Norman Chaney, 42 Community Road, Tickhill, New Hampshire. Anytime from March 12 through 19. After that message another one popped up thirty seconds later. We should never message again.

I wrote, Agreed. Then I copied down Norman Chaney's address on the back of an Old Devils bookmark and logged out. From what I understood of Duckburg's policy, the conversation would now disappear forever. It was a comforting thought, even though I doubted its veracity.

Taking a deep breath, I realized that I'd been barely breathing for the past twenty minutes. I stared at the name and address I'd written down and was just about to punch it into the computer when I stopped myself. I needed to be more careful than that. There were other ways to find out about this person. Right now, the name was enough. I was glad, I had to admit, that it was a man I was supposed to kill. And I was very glad that I was going second.

Obviously, I would only have to go through my half of the bargain if Eric Atwell died while I was in Sarasota.

IN FEBRUARY 2011 I attended the conference. I'd never been to Sarasota before and I fell in love with its old brick downtown. I made a pilgrimage to what had been John D. MacDonald's house on Siesta Key, peering through the locked gates at a midcentury modern structure surrounded by lush vegetation. I even attended some presentations and had dinner with one of my few friends in the antiquarian world, Shelly Bingham, who had owned a used bookstore in Harvard Square before "retiring" to Bradenton, Florida, and selling used books at Anna Maria Island's weekly flea market. We drank martinis at the Gator Club, and after our second Shelly said, "Mal, I was so gutted to hear about Claire last year. How are you doing?"

I opened my mouth to speak, but began to cry instead, loudly enough that several heads swiveled toward me. The suddenness and force of the tears was shocking. I stood up and walked to the restroom at the back of the dark bar, where I composed myself, then returned to the bar, and said, "Sorry about that, Shel."

"No, please. I'm sorry I brought it up. Let's have another drink and talk about the books we're reading."

It was later that night, back alone in my hotel room, that I got onto my laptop and checked out the *Boston Globe*'s online site. The top story was related to an off-season trade the Red Sox had just made, but the second story was about a homicide in Southwell. The name of the victim had not yet been disclosed by the police. I was tempted to sit with my laptop, refreshing the site until Eric Atwell was named as the victim, but I forced myself to try and sleep instead. I opened the window of my hotel room, lay on the bed under a single sheet, and listened to the breeze, plus the occasional truck rumbling by on the nearby highway. Sometime near dawn I fell asleep, waking up a few hours later, skin damp with sweat, the sheet twisted around my body. I logged back on to the *Globe* website. The body that had been found had been identified as Eric Atwell, a prominent local entrepreneur and angel investor. After throwing up in the hotel bathroom, I lay back down on the bed and savored, for a moment, the fact that Atwell had gotten what he deserved.

By the time I was back in Boston, I'd learned that Eric Atwell had been reported missing on Tuesday night by one of his house-mates. He had gone out on one of his daily walks earlier in the day and had never returned. The following morning the police conducted a search and Atwell's body was found near a walking path on conservation land about a mile from his house. He had been shot several times; his wallet had been taken, along with an expensive set of headphones, and his cell phone. The police were investigating the possibility of a robbery and asking for help from nearby residents. Had anyone seen someone suspicious? Had any-one heard the gunshots?

The article went on to mention that Atwell was a renowned philanthropist, someone with a keen interest in the local arts scene, who frequently hosted gatherings and fund raisers at his restored farm in Southwell. The article didn't mention drugs, or extortion, or anything about Atwell's role in the vehicular death of Claire Mallory. For that, I was glad. A week passed, and I had begun to believe that no one had made any connection between me and Atwell. Then, on a Sunday afternoon, nursing a cold, I was sur-prised by the sound of the door buzzer. Before I even answered it, I was sure it was the police, come to take me away. I braced myself. And it *was* the police—a tall, sorrowful-looking detective named James—but she did not have the look of a police officer preparing to make an arrest. She said she had a few quick questions. I let her in, and she explained to me that she was a Boston Police detective following up on some leads on an unsolved homicide in Southwell.

"Did you know Eric Atwell?" she asked, after she'd taken a seat on the edge of the sofa.

"I didn't, but my wife knew him. Unfortunately."

"Why unfortunately?"

"I'm sure you know this already, because it's why you're here. My wife produced a video for Eric Atwell, and after that they became friends. She . . . Claire . . . my wife died in a car accident coming home from his house in Southwell."

"And did you blame Eric Atwell for this accident?"

"I did, partly, at least. I know that my wife started doing drugs again after she met him."

The detective nodded slowly. "Did he provide those drugs?"

"He did. Look, I know where this is going. I hate . . . hated . . . Eric Atwell. But I didn't have anything to do with his death. The truth is, my wife had on-again, off-again problems with drugs and alcohol. He didn't force her to start taking drugs. He didn't introduce her to them. Ultimately, it was my wife's decision. I forgave him. It took a lot, but after what happened, I did finally make a decision to forgive him."

"So how do you feel now that you know he's been murdered?"

I stared at the ceiling, as though I were thinking. "Honestly, I don't really know. I'm telling the truth when I say that I forgave him, but that doesn't mean that I liked him. I'm not sad, and I'm not exactly happy. It is what it is. If I'm honest about it, I think he probably got what was coming to him."

"So you think he was murdered by someone from a sense of . . . out of revenge, maybe?"

"You mean do I think he was intentionally murdered . . . as

opposed to just being mugged?"

"Right, that's what I mean." The detective was very still, barely moving in the sofa.

"It occurred to me. Sure. I can't imagine that my wife is the only one he gave drugs to. And she probably wasn't the only one he started charging after she became addicted. He must have done that to other people." As soon as I spoke the words, I realized it was more than I had wanted to tell the detective. There was something about her calm presence that was making me want to talk.

She was nodding again, and when she realized that I had stopped speaking, she said, "Did your wife end up giving a lot of money to Atwell? Money you didn't have?"

"My wife and I had separate accounts so I wasn't aware of it at the time. But, yes, she started giving money to Atwell for drugs."

"I'm sorry to have to ask you this, Mr. Kershaw, but as far as you knew, was there any sexual relationship between your wife and Atwell?"

I hesitated. Part of me just wanted to tell this detective everything I had learned from Claire's diary, but I also knew that the more I spoke, the more it became obvious that I had a very serious motive for Atwell's death. I said, "I don't know, to tell the truth. I suspect they might have." Saying the words made my throat start to close a little, as though I were about to cry, and I pressed the heel of my hand against an eye.

"Okay," the detective said.

"She wasn't herself," I said, unable to stop myself. "I mean, because of the drugs." I wiped a tear from my cheek.

"I understand. I'm sorry to come out here and make you go through all this again, Mr. Kershaw. I hate to have to do this, but investigations of this kind are often all about the elimination of possible suspects. Do you remember where you were on the afternoon of February eighth?"

"I was in Florida, actually. At a conference."

"Oh," Detective James said, almost looking pleased. "What kind of conference was that?"

"Antiquarian booksellers. I run a used bookstore here in Boston."

"Old Devils, right. I've been there."

"Really? Are you a mystery fan?"

"Sometimes," the detective said and fully smiled for the first time since she'd stepped inside of my apartment. "I went to see Sara Paretsky read. About a year ago?"

"That sounds right," I said. "She was good, I thought."

"She was. Were you the one who introduced her?"

"I was. You'll be forgiven if you don't remember me. Public speaking is not my forte."

"I think I remember you being fine," she said.

"Thank you for that," I said.

Detective James put her hands on her knees, and said, "Unless you have anything to add, I think we're probably done here."

"I don't," I said, and we stood up at the same time. She was almost exactly my height.

"I will need some corroboration about the conference in Florida," she said.

I promised to send her flight details, and I also gave her Shelly Bingham's name and address.

The detective left a card. Her first name was Roberta.

CHAPTER 12

The sign that welcomed me to Tickhill, New Hampshire, also informed me that the total population was 730 inhabitants.

It was March 14, 2011, a Monday. I had left Boston at just after five in the morning and it was now eight thirty. The village of Tickhill was just north of the White Mountains. I'd done some research on the town, and some on Norman Chaney, the man I was there to kill, but not too much. And what research I'd been able to do I did at a library computer, jumping onto one of the desktops after a patron had left without logging off. I'd had my notebook with me and was able to take notes. What I learned about Tickhill was that it had one diner, and two bed-and-breakfasts, both popular because of their proximity to several ski areas. I pulled up a map and got an exact location for Norman Chaney on Community Road. The house, at least according to the map, looked fairly isolated. After sketching the location in my notebook, I began to research Norman Chaney, who had purchased the Tickhill house three years earlier for 225 thousand dollars. The only other possible hit I got on Norman Chaney was an obituary from 2007 for Margaret Chaney, a schoolteacher from Holyoke, in western Massachusetts, who had died in a house fire. Margaret Chaney, forty-seven years old when she died, had left behind two children, twenty-two-year-old Finn and nineteen-year-old Darcy, and her husband of twenty-three years, Norman Chaney. It wasn't much, but it made me wonder. Could Norman Chaney have been re-sponsible for the death of his own wife, and, if so, was that why he'd been marked for death? And was that why he'd left Holyoke to live in a town of less than a thousand residents?

It had occurred to me that I didn't really need to kill Norman Chaney. If Duckburg, the site where I'd arranged the murder swap, was as anonymous as it promised, then there was no way that the stranger I'd communicated with would ever find out who I was. Well, that wasn't entirely true. Even if this stranger—this shadow version of myself—knew nothing about me, he did know one thing. He knew that I wanted Eric Atwell to die. That might put me on a long list, but it also might not. I had decided to go through with my half of the bargain; it seemed the safest thing to do, but also maybe the right thing to do, in a twisted way.

Before shutting down the library computer, I quickly looked up both Finn Chaney and Darcy Chaney. Unlike their father, they each had online presences. If I'd found the right people, then Finn Chaney was currently working at a small bank in Pittsfield, where he was also a trivia host at a local pub. Darcy Chaney now lived outside of Boston, attending graduate school at Lesley University in Cambridge. There were pictures of them both, and they were undoubtedly brother and sister. Jet-black hair, heavy eyebrows, blue eyes, small mouths. Neither of them seemed to live with their father, and that was the most important piece of information that I got. If Norman Chaney lived alone, then my job became substan-tially easier.

It had just begun to snow as I entered Tickhill, light flakes that filled the air without seeming to land. I found Community Road, a sparsely populated and poorly paved road that wound up a hill. I slowed down as I approached number 42; the mailbox, painted black with white letters, was the only indication that a property

even existed. Driving slowly by, I peered down the dirt driveway but couldn't make out the house in the woods. At the end of
Community Road, I U-turned, then made a decision. This time I
turned down the driveway. It twisted to the left and then I could
see the house. It was an A-frame construction, more windows than
wood, made to look like a miniature ski chalet. I was very happy to
see that there was no garage and that only one vehicle—some kind
of SUV—was parked out front. The chances that Norman Chaney
was alone just went up significantly.

Wearing gloves, and with a balaclava on my head but not pulled
all the way down over my face, I stepped out of the car, holding a
crowbar down near my leg. I approached the house, stepping up
the two steps to the front door. It was solid wood, but there was
a strip of beveled glass on either side. After ringing the doorbell,
I peered into the dark interior of the house, made wonky by the
ripple effect of the glass. I'd decided that if anyone other than a
middle-aged man came toward the door, I would pull down my
balaclava and make my way back to the car. I'd already smeared
enough mud on the license plate so that both the number and the
state were obscured.

No one answered the door. I rang the bell again—a four-note
chime—then saw a large, heavyset man lumbering slowly down
the stairs. Even through the glass I could see he was wearing gray
sweatpants and a flannel shirt. His face was ruddy, and his thick
dark hair was sticking up in tufts, as though it was unwashed.

The man pulled the door open. There was no fear in his expression, not even any hesitation. "Uh-huh," he said.

"Are you Norman Chaney?" I asked.

"Uh-huh," he said again. He was over six feet tall, even though
he stooped slightly, one shoulder noticeably higher than the other.

I swung the crowbar, aiming for the side of his head, but Chaney reared back, and the tip of the bar connected with the bridge of his nose. There was a splintery crack as he staggered back, blood falling in a sheet down over his chin. He raised his hands to his face and wetly said, "the fuck."

Stepping into the house I swung the crowbar again, but Chaney easily blocked it with his meaty left arm, then swung at me with his right, batting me in the shoulder with a fist. It didn't hurt but it knocked me off balance for a moment, and Chaney charged, grabbing me by my tracksuit in both fists, shoving me up against a wall. Something, probably a coat hook, jabbed me high up in my back. Warm blood was spraying from Chaney's nose, hitting me in the face. Some memory, probably from an Ian Fleming novel, went through my panicked mind, and I raised my right foot, bringing my heavy boot down hard on Chaney's instep. Chaney grunted and loosened his grip, and I pushed forward as he stumbled backward, both of us falling after a few steps, me landing on top of him, hard, hearing something snap. Chaney's face contorted, and his mouth opened and closed like a fish pulled from the water. I pushed myself off his body, then put a knee on his chest and leaned on top of him again. He struggled to breathe, and I put my gloved hands around his thick neck, and squeezed, pressing as hard as I could with my thumbs. He tried to pull my hands loose, but he was already weakening. I closed my eyes and kept squeezing. After about a minute, or it might have been longer, I stopped and rolled off to the side, breathing heavily and aware that my mouth was salty and thick with blood. I ran my tongue around my teeth, but it was the tip of my tongue that was ragged and painful. I must have bit it during the fight. Blood was filling my mouth, and I swallowed it. It seemed a bad idea to spit a mouthful of my own blood onto the scene of a crime, even though I knew I'd probably left all sorts of DNA traces already.

Crouching in front of Chaney, and without directly looking at him, I felt for a pulse in both his neck and his wrist. There was none.

I stood, the word wobbling around me for a moment, then bent to pick up the crowbar. I had decided earlier that I would need to go through the house, take a few valuables, after Chaney was dead, but I didn't know if I had it in me. I just wanted to be back in the car, heading as far away from what had just happened as possible.

I was about to turn when movement from the corner of my eye made me look across the foyer toward the open-plan living room with floor-to-ceiling windows. A ginger cat was making its way slowly toward me, its unclipped nails clicking on the hardwood floor. The cat stopped and sniffed at Chaney's body, then looked again at me and meowed loudly, taking two steps closer, then flopping onto its side, and stretching out to show his white tufted stomach. A wave of almost paralyzing cold swept through my body, a premonition that for the rest of my life this one image, this cat asking for love while its owner lay murdered on the floor, would haunt me forever. Without thinking, I bent down and scooped up the cat, bringing it with me out to my car, and driving away.

The snow had picked up and had now begun to stick to the roads. I drove slowly, reversing my route back through Tickhill's town center then picking up the highway that would lead me through the White Mountains and south to Massachusetts. My movements in the car felt slow and deliberate, and even the car itself felt like it was moving through air that had turned into something close to solid. Time had slowed down, and everything was suffused with a sense of unreality. I looked down at the passenger seat where I'd put the docile cat. Some part of my brain was yelling that you never take anything from the scene of a crime, telling me I'd just signed my death warrant, but I kept driving. The cat was now looking up toward the window, at the snowflakes flying by the car. There was no collar. I reached a hand out and rubbed the cat along its spine; it was thinner than I thought, most of its bulk coming from its thick orange fur. I thought I could detect a tiny purr vibrating through my fingertips.

Once I was through the mountains, and my mind had started to clear a little, I made the decision that I would pull over into some random town, look for a store, or an inn, someplace with an unlocked door, and slide the cat inside. He or she would be found and taken to a shelter. There was a risk, a huge risk, that someone would see me, but I had to try. I should never have taken the cat, and I couldn't even remember now why I had done it. But now that the cat was in the car, I couldn't bring myself to simply push it out onto the side of the road. That would be the prudent thing to do, but the cat's chances of survival would be so slim.

I kept driving, and somewhere in southern New Hampshire the cat put its head down and went to sleep. I hadn't pulled over in any random town, and I suddenly knew that I wasn't going to. When I arrived back in Beacon Hill and found a parking spot right in front of my building, the cat was still with me. I scooped it up and took it with me upstairs. It was ten thirty in the morning.

While the cat padded around my small apartment, sniffing and rubbing its cheek along every piece of furniture, I stripped off all my clothes and put them, along with the crowbar, into a heavy-duty garbage bag. Then I showered, soaping up and rinsing off at least three times, until the hot water began run out.

In my original plan for the day, I was going to leave Chaney's house, then drive slightly north to a used bookstore I knew that was in an old refurbished barn. I'd been there multiple times, and in the past had had luck finding rare editions of crime novels. If for some reason I wound up being a suspect in Chaney's death, if my car had been spotted by someone, then at least I'd have had some reason for being in New Hampshire on that particular Monday. It was a very thin alibi, but it was better than nothing. I supposed that now I could say that I was planning on driving to a favorite bookstore but turned back because of the snow.

Of course, none of that would explain the presence of a murdered man's cat in my apartment, a cat that was now rubbing its chin up against my ankle. I found a can of tuna, tipped it into a bowl, then filled a second bowl with water. I also found the lid from a cardboard box, and scattered some dirt from one of my spider plants into it, hoping it would work as a litter box. While the cat ate, I went onto my computer and did a Google search to find out how to know if a cat was male or female. After some poking around, I decided that the cat was male. I spent the day inside with him, at one point both of us sleeping together on the sofa, the cat down by my feet. Toward nightfall, he'd found his way onto the bed, and he curled up on my current book, a paperback copy of Rex Stout's *Too Many Cooks*. I named the cat Nero.

ONE MONTH LATER—ONE MONTH after I had left Norman Chaney's corpse in Tickhill, New Hampshire—two things were clear. One, the police weren't coming for me. Even though I hadn't gone online to look up anything about the Chaney murder case, I felt, deep in my bones, that I'd gotten away with it. The second realization was that Nero, who'd taken to his new home pretty happily, needed more people around him. I was often gone for twelve hours at a time, and when I returned home, Nero was right at the door desperate for affection. Mary Anne, my downstairs neighbor, told me she could hear him crying during the day.

I was beginning to think that Nero would make an excellent store cat at Old Devils.

CHAPTER 13

Being an avid mystery reader as an adolescent does not prepare you for real life. I truly imagined that my adult existence would be far more booklike than it turned out to be. I thought, for example, that there would be several moments in which I got into a cab to follow someone. I thought I'd attend far more readings of someone's will, and that I'd need to know how to pick a lock, and that any time I went on vacation (especially to old creaky inns or rented lake houses) that something mysterious would happen. I thought train rides would inevitably involve a murder, that sinister occurrences would plague wedding weekends, and that old friends would constantly be getting in touch to ask for help, to tell me that their lives were in danger. I even thought quicksand would be an issue.

I was prepared for all this in the same way that I wasn't prepared for the soul-crushing minutiae of life. The bills. The food preparation. The slow dawning realization that adults live in uninteresting bubbles of their own making. Life is neither mysterious nor is it adventurous. Of course, I came to these conclusions before I became a murderer. Not that my criminal career satisfied the fantasy life I had as a kid. In my fantasies I was never the murderer. I was the good guy, the detective (amateur, usually), who solved the crime. I was never the villain.

Another skill set I thought I'd utilize more in my adult years was the ability to follow someone. And conversely, the ability to know when I was being followed. Again, these things never really came up. But on that Saturday night, after closing up Old Devils, I walked across the Boston Common, wind cutting through my clothes, and wound up at the bar at Jacob Wirth, drinking German beer and eating Wiener schnitzel. It was the middle of February but there were still Christmas lights strung up along the high ceilings of the beer hall, and, somehow, this place made me feel okay about eating alone. That was how I judged restaurants near me; there were the ones that made you feel lonely when you ate alone, like some of the higher-end haunts that clutter Back Bay, and then there were those places—Jacob Wirth, a restaurant called Stoddards—that were boisterous enough, and dark enough, that being alone didn't seem to matter so much.

It was when I left Jacob Wirth, and began the cold walk home, that I felt sure I was being watched. Maybe I really *have* read too many books, but I felt it in my neck, an almost physical sensation that eyes were on me. I turned back, scanned the heavily bundled residents and tourists, but saw no one who seemed suspicious. But the feeling continued all the way to Charles Street, and when I turned up Revere toward my apartment, I looked back and saw a man, in the hazy light of the gas lamps, walking slowly across the intersection, his gaze in my direction, his face in shadow. The only distinguishing characteristic that I could make out was that he wore a hat, something with a narrow brim. He kept walking, a slow, rolling gait, and for a moment I almost considered turning around to confront him. But then he disappeared behind a building, and I changed my mind. Everyone walking along Charles Street glances up the residential side streets, especially in wintertime when they are at their prettiest.

When I was inside, I thought some more about the man on the street and decided that I was being paranoid. No one was literally following me. But that didn't mean that I wasn't being watched, somehow, that I wasn't being toyed with.

Ever since Gwen Mulvey had arrived at Old Devils, asking me about the list of perfect murders, I'd been thinking about my shadow, the man (I always thought of him as a man) whom I'd met when he answered an anonymous message about *Strangers on a Train*. The man who killed Eric Atwell for me. The man who wanted Norman Chaney dead.

What if he'd figured out who I was? It wouldn't have been too hard. Maybe he found me by doing some research into Eric Atwell. If he'd done just a little looking, he would have found out about Claire's car accident, and the husband left behind, a man who worked at a mystery bookstore. Not only that, but a man who had once published a blog post about his eight favorite perfect murders, one of them being *Strangers on a Train*. It would have been easy to find me. And once he did, then what? Maybe he'd enjoyed killing Eric Atwell, and he wanted to keep on doing it? What if he decided to use my list as a blueprint for further murders? It would be a way to get my attention. It had, hadn't it? Was it all some kind of game?

The more I thought about it, the more I became convinced that Charlie, who'd staged the A.B.C. murders, and the train murder from *Double Indemnity*, and probably scared Elaine Johnson to death up in Rockland, Maine, was the same man who'd shot Eric Atwell for me.

He knew me.

And his actions had brought the FBI to my door. Maybe that was his intention, as well.

Charlie, what is it that you want?

I thought some more about *Strangers on a Train*. The book wasn't about the people who were murdered. It was about Bruno and

Guy, the murderers, and their relationship with each other. Maybe whoever I contacted through that website felt as though we were in a relationship, as well. I remembered the commenter on my blog post, Doctor Sheppard. It was clear he wanted to know me, and that he wanted me to know him.

My cell phone rang. I looked and saw it was Gwen.

"Hello," I said.

"Sorry I'm calling you so late. Were you up?"

"It's fine," I said. "I'm up."

"Great. A couple of things. I did some more poking around in the case of Elaine Johnson, the heart attack victim."

"Right."

"I spoke with the police detective who attended the scene, and she told me that the house was absolutely packed with books."

"I'm not surprised."

Gwen paused, then said, "I have a request of you. I know it's strange, but I think it would be helpful. I'm driving to Rockland tomorrow afternoon. Could you come with me?"

"I suppose I could," I said, "but I'm not sure I'd be any help. What would I be able to see that you wouldn't be able to?"

"I've already thought about this," Gwen said. "Maybe you'd see nothing, but maybe you'd see a lot. You knew her. I'm not sure it would be helpful, but I don't think it could hurt. Does that make any sense to you?"

"A little bit," I said.

"So you'll come?"

"Sure, I guess. When are you leaving?"

"Excellent. I have to be here in New Haven all morning, and then I thought I could leave around noon. I'll swing through Boston and pick you up one-thirtyish and we'll get to Rockland about five in the afternoon. Will that work?"

"Okay," I said. "I can get coverage at the store. Will we be there overnight?"

"I hadn't even thought of that. I just decided five minutes ago to make this trip." She thought for a moment. "Let's plan on spending the night. The detective said she'd meet us there at five, but we might want to take more than one look at the house, and there might be other witnesses I can interview the next day. Is an overnight okay?"

"Sure," I said.

"Perfect. I'll text you when I'm leaving New Haven. Should I pick you up at the store, or at your apartment?"

I told her I'd be at the store, and we ended the call.

I stood for a moment, then went and grabbed a beer from the fridge. I didn't really know why Gwen wanted me to come along with her to Elaine Johnson's house. She was grasping at straws. Maybe she was ambitious and thought I'd help her take down a serial killer. Maybe she wanted me there because she was hoping I'd tip my hand, that confronted with a crime scene I'd give myself away. Of course, her impulse was correct. Elaine Johnson was one of the murders on the list. The same man, my shadow, who killed Eric Atwell, had decided to keep killing people, and to use my list. And he was reaching out to me; that was made clear by choosing Elaine as one of the victims. But how exactly did he know about her, know that she used to frequent the bookstore? How close was he to me?

I didn't have the answers to those questions, but I did know, in my gut, that Gwen Mulvey was going to figure it out. She'd put it all together so far and she was going to continue to put it together. And it was going to lead back to me, to the murder of Eric Atwell, and to what I'd done to Norman Chaney in New Hampshire. She was going to find me. And that meant I needed to find my shadow first. I needed to beat her to it.

CHAPTER 14

The next day I woke early, packed an overnight bag, and went to Old Devils. I hadn't slept well. I'd been thinking about *him*, of course. I realize that I need to decide on a formal name for this man. I had always thought of him as my shadow, but that sounds a little too much like a comic book character. I think, instead, I'll go with Charlie, the name that Gwen and I came up with together. Charlie works.

After I unlocked the store's front door, Nero came bounding through his cat door that led to the half basement. It was where he sometimes slept, down near the furnace, but he never spent time there if people were around. He dropped and lolled in front of me, and I bent and rubbed his chest, and under his chin. I thought there might be a point in my life when Nero would stretch out to get attention and I wouldn't think of Norman Chaney's bloodied corpse, but it hadn't happened yet.

I went to the store computer and checked emails, then wrote a quick one to Brandon, asking if he'd be willing to close up the shop after his afternoon shift. I knew he'd do it, but I just wanted to make sure. It was Sunday morning, early, so I didn't expect an email back anytime soon.

I drank coffee and thought some more about my plan for that morning. I figured that by nine o'clock, or maybe even eight thirty, it would be a decent time to call Marty Kingship, a former police officer I know who was now working part-time as a security consultant for one of the big downtown hotels. I met Marty three years ago when he came into the store during a Dennis Lehane signing. He stayed long after Lehane left, asking me questions about crime novels, saying that he was thinking of writing one himself since he'd been on the force. Before he left that night, he asked me if I wanted to grab a drink with him sometime. I told him I would and was surprised when he immediately suggested a place and a time: a bar called Marliave on the other side of the park on the next Thursday night at eight.

It was a place I'd never been, the Marliave, tucked away on a side street near a downtown crossing. The entrance was a narrow doorway that led to a tile-floored bar that looked more like a French bistro than the type of place an ex-cop would like to drink. Marty Kingship was at the long bar, talking to one of the bartenders. He almost looked surprised when I grabbed the seat next to him, as though he'd forgotten arranging our meeting.

"You came?" he said.

"Sure."

"What're you having? I'm having a Miller Lite but Robert here"—he indicated the bartender—"tells me that I have terrible taste."

I ordered a Hefeweizen. Marty got another beer and ordered some food—escargot, and a plate of meatball sliders.

I have never been good at making friends. Sometimes I blame it on the fact that I am an only child, and that neither of my parents, excepting my father when he was drunk, was particularly sociable. But I think it goes deeper than that, to an inability to make genuine connections with people. The longer I interact with someone, the more distant I begin to feel from them. I can feel an enormous amount of affection for an elderly German tourist who visits my store for ten minutes and buys a used copy of a Simon Brett novel, but whenever I begin to truly get to know people, it's as though they begin to dim, as though they are behind a glass partition that gets thicker and thicker. The more I learn about them, the harder they are to see and hear in any meaningful way. There are exceptions. Claire, for one. My best friend in junior high, Lawrence Thibaud, who moved to somewhere in Brazil at the end of eighth grade. And characters in books, of course. And poets. The more I learn about them, the more I like them.

Marty, when I first met him, was looking for friends, and for a while I tried to fill that role. He'd been a police officer in western Mass but had quit shortly after his kids had left the house and his wife had filed for divorce. He'd moved into a one-bedroom condo near Dudley Square and considered himself semiretired, even though he did do the occasional security work, and even though he was outlining a novel that I was pretty sure he would never write. He was a funny guy. Also, he was much smarter than he looked with his crew cut and his broken nose, and his pear-shaped body; he easily read about five books a week. For a while he'd come into the bookstore near closing time, stock up on new titles, then we'd go somewhere for a drink. He always had a story, or a funny anecdote, and there was never any silence when we were together. At first, it worked, but like most of my relationships, after a time, I felt that wall come up between us. It was as though we'd hit the natural plateau of our friendship, and it was never going to expand. These days, we usually only get together for a drink around Christmastime.

I didn't know if Marty could help me, but I thought it was worth a try. He'd have the time, and he'd have the resources to find out information about Norman Chaney. It was a risk, but one that I needed to take. Charlie, whoever he was, had wanted Norman Chaney to die. And I also knew that he wanted someone else to do it, which meant that he would have been a suspect in the killing.

At nine I called Marty.

"Hey, stranger," he said.

"Did I wake you?"

"Nah. Just got out of the shower. Spent about twenty goddamn minutes trying to get the old sliver of soap to stick to my new bar. I must have bought a new brand and they wouldn't keep together at all. It's not like one was green and one was brown or something. They were pretty much the same color and they wanted nothing to do with each other. I'm sure that's why you called, to find out about my shower, right?"

"No, but that was a great story. You got a lot going on in your life, huh?"

"I do, actually. Cindy's coming and staying here for spring break. I'm not deluded—she's interested in some guy at BU. But still, something to look forward to."

Cindy was Marty's daughter, the only member of the family with whom he still had regular contact.

"That's good news, Marty. Look, I actually have a favor to ask from you."

"Oh, yeah?"

"If it's something you can't do, or don't feel right about, just tell me. It's not going to be a big deal."

"You want me to kill someone?" he said and laughed.

"No, but I actually do want some information on someone who was killed. Is that something you can do, as an ex-cop?"

"What kind of information?"

"This has to be just between us," I said. "You can't tell anyone."

"Not a problem. You in trouble?"

"No, no," I said. During the course of the phone conversation, I'd begun to realize that I would need some sort of reason for what

I was asking. I quickly decided on a twisted version of the truth. "The FBI got in contact with me over an old homicide case. A man from New Hampshire who was murdered about four years ago. Norman Chaney. C-H-A-N-E-Y. They didn't tell me everything but, apparently, he had a lot of books from the store, and they think there might be some connection."

"What kind of connection?"

"They wouldn't tell me, exactly. I just . . . I'm feeling thrown by this whole thing, and I was wondering if you could look into it for me, find out something about this guy. I feel like maybe they're not telling me the whole story, that it might have something to do with Claire, or something."

"I can make some calls, sure," Marty said, sounding a little confused. "It's probably nothing, Mal. Periodically someone will be handed a cold case, and they find some avenue that wasn't fully investigated—like where he got his books from—and they decide to check it out. It's grasping at straws. You said it was the FBI came to see you?"

"Yeah. That's strange, isn't it?"

"Don't worry about it. I'll make some calls. I'm sure it's nothing."

"Thanks so much, Marty."

"What else is going on with you?"

"Not too much. Buying books, selling books."

"Let's grab a beer soon. I'll call you when I get information on this Donald Chaney, and we can meet."

"Norman Chaney."

"Right, right. Norman Chaney."

"Yeah, let's do that," I said. "Grab a drink."

I hung up the phone, realizing only after I'd done so that my shoulders were rigid, and my jaw ached. Norman Chaney had been a name I'd been trying to forget for years. Just saying it out loud had physically changed me. Again, I wondered if I'd made a mistake by bringing Marty into this, but I needed to know who wanted Chaney dead. I rolled my shoulders, loosening them, just as Emily came through the door, unwinding a long scarf from around her neck. It was opening time, and I turned all the lights on in the store, went and put the Open sign in the front door. There was a stack of new arrivals in the back that needed to be shelved, and after Emily had shed all her outerwear, the two of us got to work, mostly in silence. When we did talk, I noticed that her voice was slightly hoarse, as though she were coming down with a cold, or else she'd talked too much the night before. I remembered that she had plans. Still, it was hard to imagine Emily talking too much to anyone. It was hard to imagine Emily having plans.

"What's new with you these days?" I asked her.

"What do you mean?" she said.

"Nothing, really. I was curious if anything had changed in your life. You still living in Cambridge? You seeing anyone?"

"Uh," she said, and I waited for more.

"Seen any good movies?" I said, just to give her an out after the silence lasted an uncomfortable level of time.

"I saw *Under the Skin*," she said.

"Oh, yeah. Was that the one with Scarlett Johannson as the alien?"

"Exactly."

"How was it?"

"Really great."

"Good to know," I said and decided to not ask her any more questions. I never had children, so I'll never know what it's like to have a suddenly silent teenager, but sometimes I felt like that was my relationship with Emily.

We went back to shelving books, and I found myself thinking about my conversation with Marty. Maybe it had been a mistake to ask him to look at Norman Chaney, but it felt like something I had to do. Chaney was my link to Charlie. Well, also Elaine Johnson, I suppose, but he must have picked her because he knew I knew her. And if I assumed that the other murders were more or less random, then the murder that would lead me to his identity was Norman Chaney. He wanted Chaney dead, and if I found out why, I'd find Charlie.

Around noon my phone buzzed. It was Gwen, texting to let me know she was on her way. I told Emily that I was leaving early that day, but Brandon was closing up, and I also told her that there was a possibility she would have to open up the store herself the following morning. Both Brandon and Emily had their own keys to Old Devils. If she was curious about where I was going, she didn't show it.

Around one I began to keep an eye on the front door, with its view out to Bury Street. My bag was packed, with enough clothes and toiletries for a possible overnight stay. Despite the anxiety I was feeling about the situation, and about what she might discover, I was looking forward to the trip. I'd been feeling cramped in by Boston this winter. I was looking forward to the highway, to snowy vistas, to visiting a place I'd never been before.

At one thirty I poked my head out the front door and spotted Gwen pulling up in front of a hydrant in a beige Chevy Equinox. I said good-bye to Emily and headed out just as my cell phone began to ring. I saw Gwen's number on the screen, ignored it, and walked across the street to the passenger-side door, knocking on the glass. She glanced in my direction, turned off her phone, and I got inside the car. It smelled new, and I wondered if it were a company car. I buckled up and put my small bag on the floor between my feet.

"Hi," she said. "I *did* book us two rooms in Rockland, just in case. You have everything you need?"

"I do," I said.

She continued down Bury Street toward Storrow Drive. We were both quiet, and I decided to not speak first, not knowing if she was trying to concentrate on getting out of Boston. Once we hit 93 North, however, she thanked me for coming.

"It'll be nice to get out of the city," I said. I turned and looked at her for the first time since I'd gotten into the car. She'd taken her coat off to drive and was wearing a cable-knit sweater and a pair of dark jeans. Her hands were correctly positioned on the steering wheel (ten to two) and she was studying the road as though she needed glasses. She was so intent that I was able to study her face a little; it was easier for me to see in profile, more distinctive, with her slightly upturned nose, her dominant forehead, and smooth, pale skin, dusted here and there with a flush of red. Whenever I really look at people, I can't stop myself from picturing them as either very young or very old. With Gwen I saw her as a five-year-old, wide eyed, chewing at her bottom lip, tucked in behind a parent's leg. Then I pictured her as an old woman, gray hair knotted down her back, her skin with that papery quality some old people get, but pretty with her large, intelligent eyes. There was something familiar about her, as well, about the pale oval of her face, but I couldn't quite place it.

"We're meeting Detective Cifelli at Elaine Johnson's house at six o'clock. Have you eaten lunch?"

I told her I'd had a late breakfast, and we ended up stopping at a rest area around Kennebunk in Maine. There was a Burger King and a Popeyes. We each got burgers and coffee and ate quickly at a booth near a window. It was so bright outside, the sky cloudless, and the ground covered with recently fallen snow, that we both squinted as we ate.

After eating her burger, then popping the tab on the lid of her coffee, she said, "They arrested someone for the murder of Daniel Gonzalez," she said. "Last night."

"Oh," I said. "The guy who was shot while walking his dog?"

"Yeah. Turns out he was also dealing MDMA to his students at the college he was working at, and he was shot by a rival drug dealer. I guess we got that wrong."

"Still," I said.

"Right. We've got many definites. *The A.B.C. Murders* are definite, the *Double Indemnity* murder is definite. And I feel pretty sure about what we're going to find at Elaine Johnson's house in Rockland."

"Pretty sure we'll find what?" I said.

"Something. He'll have left something. He's theatrical, Charlie. Like it wasn't just enough for him to murder three people who had a connection between his names, he had to send a feather."

"What feather?" I said.

"Oh, I forgot I didn't tell you. That's what arrived at the police stations after Robin Callahan and Ethan Byrd and Jay Bradshaw all were killed. The police received an envelope containing a single bird feather. I shouldn't really have told you that, since it's being withheld from the press, but I guess I trust you now."

"That's good, I guess," I said.

"And now you know what I mean by theatrical. That's why I think we'll find something at the scene of the crime. That, and because you knew her. Because whoever is following your list knows you. I don't mean that *you* know *them* . . . I mean, you might. But they know you. Charlie knows you. And I think we'll find something there . . . something to connect the crime to the list. Something solid. I feel good about it. You still eating?"

I realized that I'd been holding my half of a burger for the past two minutes. "Oh, sorry," I said and took a large bite, even though I was no longer hungry. I knew everything Gwen was saying was correct, but it was still spooky to hear it from somewhere besides my own head.

"You can take it with you if you want but we need to get back on the road. It's another two hours at least to Rockland."

CHAPTER 15

The inside of Elaine Johnson's house was pretty much as I'd imagined it, cluttered and dusty, books everywhere.

The house was a Cape with chipped gray paint on the outside. It was on a street about half a mile from Route 1, dwarfed by pine trees, and almost unreachable because of the recent snowfall. Gwen parked the Equinox on the rutted street, just behind the police car that was waiting for us, along with its occupant, Detective Laura Cifelli, a middle-aged woman with a round, pretty face mostly obscured by the fur-lined hood of an enormous coat. It was dusk, a pale sun low in the horizon, our breath billowing in the sub-zero air. All three of us quickly said our hellos, then tramped through the snow to the front door, where we stood for what felt like five minutes while Detective Cifelli retrieved the key from one of her pockets. There was a car in the driveway, one of those old boxy Lincolns, probably too big for the attached single-car garage. The detective told us, once we were inside the house, that the last she'd heard, the house was unclaimed property at this point since Elaine Johnson had died without a will, and with no immediate relatives.

"Are there lights?" Gwen asked, and Detective Cifelli answered by hitting the nearest switch, which flooded the kitchen with harsh overhead lighting.

"Utilities haven't been switched off, yet," she said. "And I guess they're keeping the heat on low, so the pipes won't freeze."

I looked around the kitchen, surprised to see an open peanut butter jar on the tiled island, a knife stuck inside of it. I hadn't liked Elaine Johnson, but that didn't mean I rejoiced in her dying a lonely death.

"Did any scene-of-crime officers file a report?" Gwen asked.

"No. Just the coroner. It was ruled a natural death. Heart attack. Since the body was taken out of here no one's been back, far as I know."

"Were you here?"

"I was. I got the call. The body was in the bedroom, halfway between her closet and the bed. I can show you if you like? Corpse was here alone for over a week. I knew it was a dead body as soon as I got this far into the kitchen."

"Ugh, sorry," Gwen said. "Who reported it?"

"Neighbor across the street let us know her mail was piling up. Their mailboxes are side by side. When I came to check, the front door was unlocked, so I entered. Knew it was bad news right away."

"Did the neighbor report anything else? Any suspicious activity in the neighborhood?"

"Not that I know of. We didn't consider this a suspicious death, though, so she was never asked. You're more than welcome to ask the neighbor yourself. Maybe tomorrow? You're spending the night?"

"We are," she said. "I might want to talk with the coroner, as well. It depends on what we find here in the house."

I'd been watching the two have this conversation, but I had begun to look around the kitchen, as well. There were two shelving units above the back wall of the kitchen, probably meant for cooking supplies, or food items, but Elaine had filled them with hardcover novels. I studied the spines, a lot of Elizabeth George novels, and Anne Perry's, two of her favorites, but there were also a few books that I'd categorize as being in the romantic suspense category, veering toward romance, something Elaine Johnson had claimed to despise.

"That would be fine," Detective Cifelli said, then added, "So, I'm happy to stay here with both of you, help you look around. I'm equally happy to leave you the key and let you have at it, just so long as you return it back to us in the morning."

"You don't need to stay," Gwen said. "You've done enough."

"Great, then. I'll leave you here, and you can swing by the police station any time in the morning."

"Sounds good." We both said our good-byes and watched as the detective trudged back through the snow.

Gwen turned toward me. "Ready?" she said.

"Sure. Should we have a plan of attack or just look around?"

"I thought you could focus on the books, and I'd look at everything else."

"Sure," I said.

We stepped through into what had probably been intended as a dining room, and Gwen found the light switch that turned on a flickering chandelier. Every surface was covered with books, most just stacked haphazardly on the floor or on the rectangular dining room table. "Maybe I'll need some help on the books," I said.

"You don't need to study them, but just look for anything out of the ordinary. I'm going to head upstairs to the bedroom."

I stayed in the dining room. It was hard not to look at Elaine Johnson's collection of mystery novels without thinking about what they were worth. She had plenty of worthless books—stacks of mass markets in questionable condition—but I quickly identified a first edition of Patricia Cornwell's *Postmortem*, and one of Michael Connelly's *The Black Echo*. I wondered what would happen to these books, then reminded myself that I wasn't here on business.

"Malcolm." It was Gwen, shouting down from the second floor.

"Hey," I shouted back.

"Can you come up here?"

I went up the stairs, also stacked with books along the edge of each step, and found Gwen in the bedroom, staring at a pair of handcuffs, hanging from a nail. I pointed at them.

"Don't touch anything," Gwen quickly said. "I think we should get fingerprints."

"There's a handcuff on the wall in *Deathtrap*. It plays a crucial role in the play."

"I know," she said. "I watched the movie again last night. And look on the floor."

There was a framed print—a photograph of a lighthouse—that was leaning up against the wall. "You think Charlie brought the handcuffs, took down that print, and hung them up, just so we'd be sure it was an homage to *Deathtrap*?"

"I do," Gwen said, then turned to look toward the closet. "He's hiding, probably in that closet, maybe with a mask, and then he jumps out and scares her to death."

"It's strange," I said. "As far as we know it's the first time he's staged something to point specifically to the list."

"It's also the first time he's killed someone that you knew."

We were both standing, looking toward the closet. Gwen said, "I've seen enough, honestly. I just want these handcuffs photographed, and fingerprinted."

"He probably wore gloves."

"We won't know until we look, but, yes, he probably wore gloves."

I looked around the rest of the room while Gwen pulled out her phone and stared at what looked like a text message she'd just received. There was an old four-poster bed, loosely made up, and covered with a pink chenille bedspread. The hardwood floors had woven throw rugs on them that had faded over the years. The one at the foot of the bed was covered with fur.

"Did she have a pet?" I said.

"I don't remember reading about one in the report," Gwen said.

I tried to remember back to when Elaine Johnson used to come in to Old Devils, and I didn't remember her ever paying attention to Nero. My guess is her sister had a dog or a cat, and she just had never cleaned the rug. In fact, nothing was clean in the house. I went and looked at a framed photograph on the wall above the bureau. The frame was white, and its top edge had turned a shiny black with all the grime. The photograph in the frame was of a family on vacation, a father in a golf shirt, a mother in a short, plaid dress and horn-rimmed glasses. There were four children, two older boys and two younger girls. They were posed in front of an enormous tree, a redwood probably, somewhere in California. I leaned in trying to pick out which one of the preadolescent girls was Elaine, but the photograph was slightly blurry, and had faded with age. I assumed, however, that Elaine was the younger of the two, the one with glasses, holding a doll by her side. She was the only child not smiling.

"Ready?" Gwen said.

"Sure."

When we got to the bottom of the stairs, I peered into the living room, lined with shelves. "Can I look at the books in here real quick?" I said, and Gwen shrugged and nodded.

It was clear that Elaine's sister had been a reader, as well, and that most of the books that filled the living room shelves had belonged to her. There was a lot of nonfiction, and historical fiction. One entire shelf was devoted to James Michener. But there was also a tall bookcase crammed into a corner that looked as though it had been brought by Elaine. One of its shelves was filled with a dusty collection of vintage glass paperweights. The rest were crammed with more mystery novels, arranged by author. I was surprised to see the collected works of Thomas Harris, a writer that Elaine had once told me was an "overrated pervert." I was also surprised to see a copy of *The Drowner* until I saw that it was sitting between *Strangers on a Train*, and a copy of *Deathtrap*. A little shiver went through me. All the books were there—all eight from my list—in order. I brought Gwen over, and her eyes went big. She took a photograph with her phone.

"Do you think he brought these here himself or were the books already here?" she said.

"I think he brought them, probably. Elaine might have had all these books, but I doubt it."

"Think we'll be able to tell anything from these copies?" she said.

"Maybe," I said. "He bought them somewhere. Maybe from my store, or maybe from somewhere else. Usually, when you buy a used book there's a penciled price inside the front cover, and sometimes there's a sticker with the name of the dealer."

"I don't want you to touch them, but can you tell anything by looking at the spines?"

I studied them, all eight books from my list, sitting together like an accusation. The only spine that jumped out was the one for *Malice Aforethought*. I recognized at as a UK paperback edition released as a tie-in with a TV miniseries from about ten years ago. It was a copy that had definitely come through the store, because I remembered how much I disliked that edition. In general, I hate all tie-in book covers. I told Gwen that I thought I recognized one of the books as one I had had in the store.

"Okay, good," she said. I could hear the excitement in her voice. "After I get them checked for fingerprints, I'll have them photographed and we can look at them together. Let's go check in to the hotel."

SHE'D BOOKED US TWO rooms at a Hampton Inn & Suites about a mile out of Rockland's town center. It was across the street from a McDonald's and I was worried that was where we'd end up eating dinner, but she mentioned a place she liked on Main Street. "I made reservations for two but . . . if you'd rather go someplace else . . ."

"No," I said. "I'm happy to follow your lead."

We checked in then met back in the lobby an hour later and drove into town. It was off-season, so I was surprised that several restaurants seemed to be open. We parked right in front of a two-story brick building, only a few steps away from the entrance to the Town Tavern, advertising itself as an "ale and oyster house." It was a Sunday night and predictably empty, although two couples sat at the bar. The hostess, a youngish woman wearing a Bruins sweatshirt, took us to a booth.

"This okay?" Gwen said.

"Sure. You said you've been here before?"

"My parents have a house on Megunticook Lake, which is not far from here. I come up to the midcoast at least two weeks every summer. Honestly, it's my dad who reveres this place because they do baked oysters the way he likes them."

The waitress came. I ordered a Gritty McDuff's English-style bitter and a lobster roll. Gwen ordered a Harpoon and a haddock Rueben.

"No baked oysters?" I said.

She turned to the waitress. "Can we get six oysters to start?"

After the waitress left, Gwen said, "For my dad. I'll let him know."

"Where do they live the rest of the year?" I asked.

"Upstate New York, where I grew up, although they keep talking about moving here year-round. But they'd have to buy a new house. The lake place isn't winterized. Have you been to this part of Maine before?"

"I've been to Camden. Once. That's close to here, right?"

"Next town, yeah. When was that?"

"I don't know, exactly. Ten years ago. Just a vacation." I'd gone with Claire, of course, back when we frequently took road trips all over New England.

Our beers arrived, along with a basket of bread. We each took sips, then Gwen said, "Can I ask you about your wife? Do you mind?"

"I don't mind, no," I said and tried to look normal. But I was aware that we'd lost eye contact across the table.

"When did she die?"

"Five years ago, now, although it doesn't feel that long."

"I'm sure," Gwen said, wiping some foam off her upper lip with a knuckle. "That must have been terrible. Her dying so young. The way she died."

"You've done some checking up."

"Yes. A little bit. When I first got your name, when I found the list, I ran a check on you."

"Did you see that I'd been questioned in the murder investigation into Eric Atwell?"

"I did see that."

"I would have killed him, if I had a chance. But it wasn't me."

"I know that."

"It's okay if you don't. I know you're doing your job, and I know you're wondering what connection I have with all these murders. Truth is, I don't have any, or at least not that I know of. After my wife died, I told myself that I would just go on living by myself, doing my job, reading books. I want a quiet life."

"I believe you," she said, and she looked at me with an emotion I couldn't quite read. It seemed like affection. Or maybe it was pity.

"You sure?"

"Well, this crime scene, Elaine Johnson's murder, does change things. It's different from the others. It's pointing directly at you, directly at the list."

"I know it is. It's giving me a very strange feeling."

"Tell me more about Brian Murray. Would he have known Elaine Johnson?"

"He did, actually," I said. "Well, I don't know if he'd spoken to her, but he definitely knew her because Brian comes to all our readings, and Elaine comes, as well. Used to come."

"How did the two of you end up buying the store together?"

"We were friends, not close, but he was in the store a lot, and we'd occasionally get a drink. When the previous owner decided to sell, I must have told Brian about it, about how I'd buy it if I had the money. I think he offered to come in right away. He had his lawyer write up a deal in which he provided the majority of the capital and I'd manage the business. It was a perfect arrangement. It still is. He doesn't have anything to do with these murders."

"How do you know that?"

I sipped my beer. "He's an alcoholic, a functioning one, but barely. He writes his yearly book in about two months and takes the rest of the year off to drink. He's sixty years old but looks seventy, and every time we hang out together he tells me the exact same stories. I just don't see it. Even if for some reason he had murderous intentions, there's just no way he could pull it off. He doesn't even drive. He takes taxis everywhere."

"Okay."

"You believe me?"

"I'll look into him, but, yes, I believe you. I used to read his books, actually, when I was a teenager. Ellis Fitzgerald was one of the reasons I wanted to go into law enforcement."

"The early books were good."

"I loved them. I remember that I could read an entire book in a day."

Our oysters came, and the rest of our food shortly afterward. We didn't talk anymore about the crime scene, or Brian Murray, or anything remotely personal. We ate, and Gwen went over her plan for the next day. She was going to go in to the local FBI office and arrange for a scene-of-crime officer to conduct an investigation at Elaine Johnson's house. She also wanted to talk with neighbors who might have seen a stranger, or at least a strange car, around the time of Elaine's death.

"I can look into a bus that will take you back to Boston," she said. "Otherwise you can come back with me, but it might not be until late in the afternoon."

"I'll wait," I said, "unless you think it's going to be another night. I brought a book."

"Another one from the list?" she said.

"I did. I brought *Malice Aforethought*."

After dinner, we drove back in silence to the hotel, then stood together in the harsh light of the empty lobby. "Thanks for coming on this trip," she said. "I realize it's probably an inconvenience."

"It's actually nice," I said. "Get out of the city . . ."

"Visit the scene of a murder . . ."

"Yes," I said.

We stood awkwardly for a moment. I did briefly wonder if

Gwen had some romantic interest in me. I was only about ten years older than she was, and I knew that I was not unhandsome. My hair was completely gray now, more of a silver, really, but I'd kept all of it. I was slim and had a decent jawline. My eyes were blue. I took a step backward. I felt that shimmery glass wall between us, the one that kept me from becoming close to anyone except for ghosts. She must have felt it as well, because she said good night.

I went back to my hotel room and began to read.

CHAPTER 16

What impressed me about *Malice Aforethought*, back when I'd first encountered it just after college, was the cold determination of the murderer.

Dr. Bickleigh, we discover on the first page of the novel, has decided that he wants to kill his domineering, vindictive wife. He's also a doctor, with access to an array of drugs. Over the course of the first half of the book, he slowly turns his wife into a morphine addict. He does this by spiking her tea with a drug that gives her blinding headaches, then cures them with the opiate. Then he cuts her off from the morphine, enough so that she begins to fake his signature on prescriptions so that she can procure it herself. It becomes clear to the other residents of their country village that she is an addict. The rest is easy; one evening he simply gives her an overdose. There is no way he can be fingered for the crime.

I read most of the book that night, then finished it the following morning. It was hard to concentrate but there are times in the novel—it's actually quite funny—that I was swept up in the story. As always, I thought back to the last time I'd read the book, how young I'd been, how differently I had reacted to the same words. When I'd first started at Redline Bookstore in Harvard Square after my time at college, Sharon Abrams, the owner's wife, had given me a handwritten list of her favorite books, all mysteries but one. I've long since lost that list, but I have it memorized. Besides *Malice Aforethought*, she'd listed *Gaudy Night* and *The Nine Tailors* by

Dorothy L. Sayers, *The Daughter of Time* by Josephine Tey, *Rebecca* by Daphne DuMaurier, the first two Sue Grafton books, *The Ritual Bath* by Faye Kellerman, and *The Name of the Rose* by Umberto Eco, even though she said she'd never finished it ("I just love the beginning so much"). Her other favorite book was *Bleak House* by Charles Dickens; I guess you could say that it has mystery elements, as well.

I remember being so touched by the fact that she'd written this list for me that in the space of about two weeks I read everything on it, even rereading the books I was familiar with. And reading *Malice Aforethought* back then I remember feeling buoyed by its grim outlook on humanity. It's satire, essentially, ripping the idea of romance to shreds. Reading the book at the Hampton Inn in Rockland, it felt more like a horror story this time. Bickleigh, obsessed by a life he cannot have, kills his wife in a brutal fashion, and it destroys his life. He is infected forever by the act of killing.

Just before noon Gwen texted to tell me that she'd be ready to leave Maine no later than four. I texted back that she should take all the time she needed. I had decided to walk into town. It was a sunny day, the temperatures a little higher than they'd recently been, and I'd memorized the way into town the night before.

I checked out of the hotel, asked the front desk if they could stow my backpack for the day, then walked to Rockland's town center. I visited a small used bookstore, where I bought a copy of *The Hawk in the Rain* by Ted Hughes. I took the book with me to the same restaurant where Gwen and I had dinner the night before and sat at the bar. I got a beer and a bowl of clam chowder that came with soft white rolls. I read the poetry and tried to empty my mind of the preoccupations of the past few days. Not only was I worried that Gwen was going to eventually zero in on my role in Eric Atwell's and Norman Chaney's deaths, but this investigation had churned up memories of Claire, and of the year after her death, that I thought I'd put away for good. After I finished the chowder, I ordered another beer. The lone television soundlessly showed an old episode of *Cheers*, one of the early ones with Coach and Diane.

My phone buzzed in my pocket and I assumed it was Gwen, calling to say she was ready to leave. But it turned out to be Marty Kingship.

"Hey," I said.

"Gotta minute?"

"Sure," I said, and thought about stepping outside of the restaurant, but I was the only one at the bar, and the bartender was unpacking boxes of wine far from where I was seated.

"I looked into your guy Chaney for you. He was a piece of work, let me tell you."

"What does that mean?"

"I mean, if you're looking for who wanted him dead, you'd be better off making a list of who didn't want him dead. He most likely killed his wife."

"What do you mean most likely?"

"There was a house fire, one that *he* managed to escape, while *she* didn't. Chaney's brother-in-law, the brother of the wife, filed a complaint saying he was sure that Chaney had set it, trapping his wife in the bedroom. He told the investigating officers at the time that Margaret, his sister, Chaney's wife, was planning on leaving Norman, and that Norman knew it. He'd been a serial adulterer and she had proof, so she was going to get at least half of the money if not more."

"Were they rich?"

"They had some money, for sure. He owned two service stations, but he'd also been investigated for money laundering. It went nowhere, though."

"Who was he money laundering for?"

"Oh, some local drug outfit. He must have stepped out of line at some point because one of his service stations got held up, and an employee got shot. Only no one thought it was a regular holdup. It was probably revenge. This was only about six months before his wife died. Like I said, there was a whole slew of people wanting to get rid of Norman Chaney. He was a bad apple."

"What happened to him after the house burned down?"

"He sold off his service stations and bought a house up in some minuscule town in New Hampshire. Up near the ski resorts. But someone found him there and killed him. Maybe the brother-in-law."

"Why do you say that?"

"I'm not saying it, but the cop I talked to is. He was beaten to death in his own house, and there'd been a struggle. Chances are this had nothing to do with drugs. If he'd been targeted by a dealer, then someone would have just gone up there and shot him. It was an amateur, which means it was probably the brother-in-law."

"But he was never arrested?"

"I guess he had an alibi."

"What was his name?"

"Nicholas Pruitt. He's an English professor at New Essex University. I know, right . . . Doesn't exactly sound like a murderer."

"Depends on the type of book you like to read."

Marty laughed. "Exactly. Definitely a murderer in an Inspector Morse book. In real life, not so much."

"Thanks for doing this, Marty," I said.

"You kidding me? This was the most fun I've had since that shower I took yesterday. And this is just the start. I'll keep looking for you."

"Will you? That would be great," I said.

Marty coughed, then said, "I don't mean to pry, but you're not in any kind of trouble, or anything?"

"No, it's just like I said. The FBI questioned me about this guy who I'd never heard about, told me he had a collection of used mystery novels, a lot with a bunch of bookmarks from Old Devils."

"You believed them about that?"

I lowered my voice and tried to sound calm. "I don't know, Marty. Not really. Before she died, Claire was back into drugs . . . you know all about that. Maybe she knew Norman Chaney and they think that I might have gone after him because he provided drugs to her, or something. That's what I'm guessing. I should never have asked you to—"

"No, no, no," Marty quickly said. "Fuck them. I know you'd have nothing to do with that, but I had to ask."

"Honestly, I wouldn't have worried about it, but when I started to think it had something to do with Claire, I just couldn't stop turning it over in my mind again and again."

"I'll keep looking into this guy, but nothing about Claire has come up. It won't, either, Mal. I'm sure of it."

"Thanks, Marty," I said. "What you got is great. I owe you a drink."

"Let's do it sometime soon. I'll do a little more snooping for you and deliver my report. How about Wednesday?"

"That works," I said, and we made it official. Six o'clock at Jack Crow's.

After I'd stopped talking on the phone, the bartender floated over to check on my beer. I asked for a pen, instead, then wrote down the name Nicholas Pruitt on a bar napkin. My body was buzzing with excitement. Nicholas Pruitt seemed so right, somehow. If Norman Chaney had killed Pruitt's sister, then he'd have a definite motive. And he was an English professor, which meant he'd most likely be familiar with *Strangers on a Train*. I felt like I had found him. I had found Charlie.

I decided that when I got together for a drink with Marty I'd need to tell him to stop looking into Chaney. He was a retired police detective. Asking him to look into an unsolved crime was a little like dangling a piece of meat in front of a starving dog. I needed to make sure he stopped looking.

It wasn't yet two o'clock, but I didn't feel like sitting at the bar any longer. I went back outside and wandered up and down Rockland's main street, brick buildings filled with shuttered gift shops, and a few open restaurants. I tightened the scarf around my neck and went and looked out toward the harbor, protected by a mile-long jetty that jutted out into the ocean. It had been so cold that chunks of milky ice floated in the seawater. Farther out the water sparkled in the sunlight. I was standing there, the breeze off the ocean cutting right through the layers of my clothing, when my phone buzzed again. This time it was a text from Gwen, saying that she was back at the hotel, ready to leave. I told her I'd be there in half an hour and began the walk back.

ON THE DRIVE BACK to Boston, Gwen told me about her day spent wrangling with the local police department, who didn't seem to consider the death of Elaine Johnson a priority. Still, she'd managed to get a team of forensic investigators to go over the house, in particular focusing on the handcuffs and the ten books in the bookcase downstairs.

I asked her if I'd get a chance to look at the books, maybe see where they'd come from.

"They bagged them as evidence, but I'll have the photographs sent to you. Would you know if they came from Old Devils?"

"Maybe, if I looked at them. All the books that wind up on the shelf are given a price by me, or by one of my employees, in the upper right-hand corner of the first page. But some books never make the shelves; they get sold online directly, and unless I remember a specific copy of a specific book, then I'm not going to recognize them."

"But if Charlie came into your store, and bought the books, or some of them, then . . ."

"It would mean he's a customer."

"Right," Gwen said.

We had just crossed over from Maine into New Hampshire, and it had gotten dark. Gwen's face was periodically illuminated by passing cars.

"I forgot to ask, were there any witnesses?"

"What do you mean?" she said.

"I mean, did you find a witness who saw someone, or someone's car, outside of Elaine Johnson's house around the time of the murder?"

"Oh, that. No. I questioned the neighbor across the street who reported that Elaine's mail hadn't been picked up, but she hadn't seen anything. She's old, and I doubt she could even see anyone on the street."

"So, no luck there," I said.

"I'm not surprised. If there's one other connection between all these murders—besides your list—it's that there have been no witnesses. No clues at all, really. No mistakes."

"There must have been something."

"There was a murder weapon left behind at the site of Jay Bradshaw's homicide."

"He was one of the A.B.C. murders?"

"Yes, he was beaten to death in his garage. In some ways his murder is a bit of an outlier. It was messy, for one; he fought back, and there was a lot of blood. His garage was full of tools, all of which could have been the murder weapon, but it turned out that the weapon that was used, at least initially, was a baseball bat."

"How do they know it didn't come from the garage, that it was brought there?"

"They don't know, not for a fact, but there was no other sports equipment at Bradshaw's house. And all the tools in his garage were carpentry tools. That's what he was—a carpenter—although he'd been charged ten years earlier with attempted rape while putting up bookshelves for a divorced woman. Since then he'd done very little work. He kept a sign up in front of his house at all times, advertising 'used tools for sale,' and according to his only friend, he spent most of the day in his garage. He would have been easy to target. The baseball bat was the only piece of evidence found that seemed as though it didn't belong in his garage."

"Was it special?"

"What, the bat?"

"Yeah, was there something unusual about it? Was it from 1950s or anything? Signed by Mickey Mantle?"

"No, it was new, and it was a brand that's sold at just about every sporting goods store. It didn't go anywhere. Also, it didn't actually deliver the killing blow. Bradshaw was hit by the baseball bat, but he'd been killed with a sledgehammer, directly to his head. Sorry for the image."

When Gwen pulled up in front of the bookstore, she said, "Here you go," then quickly added, "Oh, maybe you wanted to go to your home. I didn't even ask."

"This is fine," I said. "I should probably check in here anyway, and I only live a few blocks away."

"Thanks for coming. As soon as I get those photographs of the books, can I send them to you?"

"Sure," I said.

The store was open for another fifteen minutes and I could see Brandon behind the front desk, a book splayed open in front of him. I swung through the front door and he looked up. "Boss," he said.

"Hey, Brandon."

He tilted the book he was reading so I could see the cover. It was *The Cuckoo's Calling* by Robert Galbraith, who not so long ago had been revealed to actually be J. K. Rowling. "Good," he said, and went back to reading.

"I'm just popping in. Anything happen while I was away?"

He told me how yesterday afternoon a woman in a fur coat came in and bought two hundred dollars' worth of new hardcovers and arranged to have them shipped to her address in Malibu. And he told me that he thought he'd finally fixed the faucet in the employee bathroom that was always leaking.

"Thanks," I said.

I heard Nero's plaintive meow and bent down to greet him.

"He misses you, I think, when you're not here," Brandon said, and something about those words caused me to have one of those periodic waves of deep sadness that suddenly infect me from time to time. I stood suddenly, and the light swam in front of my eyes. I was hungry, I realized. It was late, and I hadn't eaten since lunch in Rockland.

I walked home and got my car, then drove over the river to Somerville, the town I'd lived in with Claire. I sat at the bar at R.F. O'Sullivan's, a place I hadn't been for years, drinking Guinness and eating one of their softball-sized burgers. Afterward I drove to the Somerville Public Library, pleased to see it was still open. I went to the second floor and found a computer with an open internet browser, punched in the name that Marty had given me earlier,

"Nicholas Pruitt."

Not only was he an English professor at New Essex University, he had published a book of short stories called *Little Fish*. There were two pictures of him I could find online, an author photograph, plus a candid from a faculty cocktail party. He was about what you'd expect a college English professor to look like, tall and stoop shouldered, with a slight paunch and hair that stuck up at the front as though he constantly ran his fingers through it. His hair was a brownish black, but his closely trimmed beard was salted with gray. In his author photograph he was turned to a three-quarters profile and was staring toward the camera with an expression that seemed to be asking for validation. *Take me seriously*, it said. *I just might be a genius.* Maybe I'm being harsh, but that was what I saw. I've always been suspicious of literary writers, with their attempts at immortality. That is why I much prefer thriller writers, and poets. I like the writers who know they are fighting a losing battle.

While there was plenty of online information about Nicholas Pruitt, who went by Nick, it seemed, there was very little information about his personal life. If he was married, or had kids, I couldn't find any confirmation of that fact. The most telling thing I read about him was on a site that enabled students to anonymously grade their professors. The bulk of his reviews pointed to a decent professor who was sometimes a hard grader, but one user wrote: To be honest, Professor Pruitt gave me the creeps. He was FAR too into Lady Macbeth to be honest. I don't know why he insisted on acting out all her parts.

It wasn't much, but it was something. I had already constructed an entire fantasy of what might have turned Nicholas Pruitt into Charlie. The way I imagined it was that Pruitt's sister Margaret marries Norman Chaney, who turns out to not only be a creep, but a criminal, and a man who murders Pruitt's sister and gets away with it. Pruitt decides to kill Norman Chaney, but knows that if he does it, he will be the prime suspect. So, thinking he might be able to hire someone to kill Chaney, he goes onto Duckburg and finds my message about *Strangers on a Train*. He's an English professor and knows that book well; he knows what I'm suggesting, and we exchange names and addresses. He kills Eric Atwell. It goes well, not just because he gets away with it, but because he actually enjoys it. It gives him the power he has always craved. When Norman Chaney dies, while Pruitt is away somewhere, establishing an alibi, he feels further empowered. Killing feels good. He decides he has to find out who he swapped with, who murdered Chaney for him. It wouldn't have been hard. A little snooping and he'd discover that Eric Atwell had been questioned by police in regard to a motor vehicle accident that took the wife of Malcolm Kershaw. Not only that, but Malcolm Kershaw works at a mystery bookstore. He'd even once posted a list of eight perfect murders in fiction. It included *Strangers on a Train*.

Years go by, and Pruitt can't forget how alive he felt when he'd taken a life. Every semester when he teaches *Macbeth*, he feels the bloodlust in him grow a little more. He decides that he needs to do it again, commit murder. Inspired by the list of eight perfect murders he begins to look for victims. Maybe he'll even make it obvious; that way Malcolm Kershaw and he might finally meet.

It made perfect sense, and I was filled with excitement mixed with dread. I needed to meet Nick Pruitt and see how he'd react. But first I wanted to read his book of short stories. I logged on to the Minuteman Library Network to see where the book was available, hoping it was here at Somerville, but it wasn't. There was, however, a copy listed as Available at Newton Public Library. They weren't open now but would be the following morning at ten.

CHAPTER 17

I began rereading *The Secret History* the next morning at the store. I was tired of waiting. Waiting for Newton Public Library to open so I could go get a copy of Nicholas Pruitt's *Little Fish*, waiting to hear from Gwen, waiting for more information from Marty Kingship on the murder of Norman Chaney.

I read the prologue and the first chapter and was instantly swept up in the narrator's obsession with the small coterie of classics students at the fictional college of Hampden. Like Richard Papen, I have always been fascinated by intimate groups, by close-knit families, by sibling bonds. But unlike Richard I never found a group to join, the closest being my fellow antiquarian booksellers, but more often than not, when we gather, I feel like an impostor in their midst.

The temperature had risen that day and snow was melting all over the city. Puddles were forming, and gutters were overflowing, and the pedestrians were out in droves. It was a busy morning, a steady stream of browsers dripping on the hardwood floor.

At just before noon I told Emily that I was going home for lunch and could she cover the register. I'd parked out front at a meter, so I got into my car and took Storrow Drive to Newton, then cut through some back roads to get to the main library, an enormous brick structure close to Commonwealth Avenue. I found *Little Fish* on the library's second floor and took the slim paperback volume to a cushy leather chair in a corner of the library near the poetry section. I quickly perused the list of story titles on the contents page, looking, I suppose, for something that might indicate a crime story, something with a murder in it, or some malice, but most of the titles felt either generic or self-consciously literary. "The Garden Party." "What Was Left After It Happened." "Hence the Pyramids." "A Platonic Kiss." Nothing jumped out, so I decided to read the title story, "Little Fish." I was only halfway through it when I realized that it was not particularly helpful. In the story a college senior at a thinly disguised Bowdoin College remembers how his father took him on a fishing trip in Upstate New York when he was ten. The lessons of the trip—throwing the little fish back being the most obvious one—reverberate with the narrator's current relationship. The story was not impressive. At least not to me, and I gave up on it halfway through. Then I scanned the remaining stories in the collection, not finding much. Honestly, I don't know exactly what I was looking for, but maybe just one story that pointed toward an unhealthy attitude toward revenge or justice. I flipped to the front of the book to see if there was a dedication, and there was, a simple one: "To Jillian." I got up and wandered until I found an unmanned computer, then opened a browser window and put in "Jillian" then "New Essex University." The name that most frequently came up was Jillian Nguyen, who had been an English professor at New Essex before getting a job at Emerson College, here in Boston. I memorized her name, deciding I'd contact her, but not until I found out some more about Nick Pruitt.

Then I flipped to the back of the book and saw that there was an author photograph, different from the one I'd seen online. It was also a three-quarters profile—clearly Pruitt thought he had a good side—but in this one he was wearing a hat, a felt fedora, the type of hat that detectives wore in old movies. As soon as I saw it,

I thought of the man at the end of my street I'd seen on Saturday night, the man I thought was following me. He was wearing a hat similar to this one.

Before leaving I ruffled through the pages of the book to see if it had one of those security tags. I didn't find one, and I considered going to the bathroom and hiding the book under my shirt. But the library was busy, people coming and going, and I simply decided to walk out with the paperback in my hand, as though I'd already checked it out. I didn't think they'd miss it, and it seemed prudent that there was no record on my library card of me having borrowed a Nicholas Pruitt book.

I walked through the sensors—no alarms sounded—and out into the warm afternoon.

Back at the store I emailed Gwen to find out if she'd gotten photographs yet of the books we'd seen in Elaine Johnson's house. Then I tried to read some more of *The Secret History* but couldn't concentrate. I ended up pacing through the store, trying to figure out what to do next, straightening shelves.

After Brandon came in for his afternoon shift, I decided that I could probably go home. It was Tuesday, and quiet, and I was waiting to speak with Gwen, something that I'd rather not do in a place where people might hear me. I put *The Secret History* in my messenger bag and asked Brandon if he minded being alone.

He frowned, and said, "Nah, I'm good."

"Okay, then. Call me if anything comes up."

"Will do."

The temperature had dipped, so that all the melted snow had now transformed into ice, the sidewalks littered with dirt and salt. The afternoon was bright, and I was reminded that the days were already getting longer, even though winter would continue unabated for at least two more months. I didn't mind it, personally, but I could read the faces of the passersby on my walk home. Pale and grim, resigned to this gray city, and to the long, wet slog toward springtime.

Out of habit I peered through the plateglass windows of the Beacon Hill Hotel and into their snug bar, always wondering if my co-owner, Brian, would be in residence. He was in today, wearing one of his familiar Harris tweed jackets, anchoring the far side of the oval bar. I hesitated on the street, deciding whether I should join him when I saw his large shaggy head lift up and notice me through the glass.

"Hey, Brian," I said, sliding onto the stool next to him, curious about the half-filled martini on the bar with the lipstick imprint on its rim.

"Tess is here," he said, and just as he said it, I turned to see Tess Murray, his wife for the past ten years, returning, I assumed, from the bathroom, fresh lipstick on her lips.

"Oh, sorry, Tess," I said, stepping back to let her retake her seat.

"No, sit there. We're always thrilled to have a buffer between us, aren't we, Bri?" She slid her martini over, and I sat down between them. I saw Tess far less than I saw Brian, and it was very unusual that she was out for a drink with him, especially early on a Tuesday afternoon. She was his second wife and had to be at least twenty years younger than he was. Everyone said that she'd been his publicist and that was how they met, but I knew that it wasn't true. She *was* a publicist, or had been, back when she worked full-time, but not for him. They'd met the only year he'd attended Bouchercon, the annual crime writers' conference. He didn't usually go, but they'd made him guest of honor about seven years ago and that had forced his hand.

Brian had told me many times that the only way their marriage worked was that Tess spent six months at their house on Longboat

Key without him, and that he spent the other six months at their cabin in downeast Maine without her. They occasionally ran into each other in Boston.

"How are you not in Florida right now, Tess?" I said.

"You didn't hear? Brian, show him your arm."

I turned, and Brian lifted his left arm, ensconced in a device that looked vaguely bionic. "Oh, no."

"It's not a big deal," he said. "I fell a week ago stepping down from this very same barstool. Didn't feel a thing except the remainder of my pride leaving my body. But, apparently, it's broken in two places, and you'd be surprised how hard it is to be a one-handed drunk at my age."

"Are you writing right now?"

"Turned in the new one just before Christmas but I've got copyedits to do, and cans of soup to open up, so Tess is making the sacrifice."

"I tried to talk him into coming down to Florida, but you know what that's like," Tess said. "We've been meaning to call you, Mal, ask you for a drink. And now here you are."

"He knows where to find me," Brian said, then finished his drink, almost always a scotch and soda in a lowball glass with two cubes of ice.

I ordered a Left Hand Stout and managed to talk Brian and Tess into letting me buy them each a drink. Another scotch for Brian and a Grey Goose martini for Tess.

"How's business?" Tess said. "I'd ask Brian but he never knows."

"It's the same," I said. "Not bad at all."

"What's selling?"

Even though she no longer worked as a publicist—last I heard she owned a boutique jewelry store in Florida—she still loved to hear about the business. I liked Tess and had defended her on a number of occasions to other people in the industry, some who saw her as a gold digger who didn't even have the decency to spend much time with her older, rich husband. But she was always nice to me, and Brian had told me several times how much he valued their marriage, how she understood how important solitude was to him. How she loved him in her own way.

I stayed for two beers, aware the whole time that my phone might ring, or buzz, with a message from Gwen. When they ordered dinner, I said that I'd leave, that I had food at home to cook, which was a lie, but Brian was starting to slur a little and I wanted to get out before the monologues started.

Before I left, I said, "Did you hear about Elaine Johnson?"

"Who?" Brian said.

"Elaine Johnson. She used to come into the store every day before she moved to Maine. Coke bottle glasses."

"Sure," Brian said, and I was surprised that Tess, to my right, was nodding along as well.

"She died. Of a heart attack."

"How'd you hear about that?"

I almost told him, told the two of them, I guess, about Agent Mulvey, and the list, but stopped myself, for some reason.

"Another customer told me," I lied. "Just thought you might be interested."

"Good riddance to her," Tess said, and I turned toward her, surprised.

"You knew her?" I said.

"Sure. She cornered me at one of Brian's readings to tell me what a hack he was. I told her I was his wife, and she burst out laughing, asked me if I read his books before I married him. I'll never forget it."

Brian was smiling. "She was all right, actually. I remember her now. Told me once her favorite writer was James Crumley, so I figured she couldn't be all bad. She moved to Rockland, in Maine, didn't she?"

"How'd you know that?"

"Emily, probably, last time I did a shift at Old Devils. She keeps track of all the problem customers for me."

"Huh," I said, slightly annoyed that Brian, who saw Emily probably every three months, seemed to have a better relationship with her than I did.

Tess walked me out. I wondered why, but when we got to the sidewalk, she said, "This stupid accident has changed him completely. He's terrified of everything now. Walking. Getting out of bed. Doing anything. I can stay with him but not forever. I've got the store in Florida and I just can't deal with him all the time, and I'm not sure he can deal with me."

"Maybe you should get some help?"

"Exactly. That's what I've told him a hundred times, but he doesn't want to hear it. Look, if we have you over for dinner some night, will you bring it up for me? Maybe if he hears it from someone else . . ."

"Sure," I said.

"Thanks, Mal. I appreciate it. Don't get me wrong, I'd do absolutely anything for Brian, and he'd do absolutely anything for me, but helping him get out of a bathtub was not part of the deal." She pushed a strand of her long dark hair behind one of her ears, then leaned in and kissed me on the lips before pulling me in for a hug. She'd done this before, even in front of Brian, who never seemed to mind.

Tess shivered in my arms as we hugged. "How do you stand this weather?" she said as she released me. Walking home I could smell her on my skin. A lemony perfume and the smell of olives from her martini.

I ate cereal for dinner that night, read some more of *The Secret History*, and waited for Gwen to get in touch. I sent her one more text before going to sleep, saying that I hoped everything was all right. And it was her face I thought of as I lay in bed, not my wife's.

CHAPTER 18

T he door buzzer went off at just past eight the following morning. I was up already and dressed, starting to brew some coffee.

I pressed the intercom and a male voice came over, saying that his name was Agent Berry and asking if he could come up. In the time it took for the two sets of footsteps to loudly climb the stairs I had enough time to think about what to do when the questions came. I made several quick assumptions. They were here either to arrest me, or to question me about the death of Eric Atwell or Norman Chaney or both. The reason Gwen hadn't returned my messages the day before was because I had become a suspect in a homicide.

I went to my door and opened it. Agent Berry was tall and stoop shouldered, dressed in a pin-striped suit. He showed his FBI identification, reintroduced himself, and said he had come up from the New Haven office and had a few questions. Behind him stood a much shorter woman, also in a suit. He introduced her as Agent Perez from the Boston office. I invited them both in, said that I was about to make coffee, and asked if they wanted some. Agent Berry said he wouldn't mind. Agent Perez, who was now looking out the window, said nothing.

I started the coffee and felt surprisingly calm. All the adrenaline that had flooded through me after the buzzer sounded had dissipated with their arrival. I was light, almost spacey, as I walked the short distance to the chair and directed them to the sofa.

Agent Berry adjusted his suit pants above the knees before sitting down. He had enormous hands, spotted with age, and a large, elongated head with heavy jowls. He cleared his throat, and said, "I was hoping you'd be able to shed some light on your relationship with Gwen Mulvey."

"Okay," I said.

"Can you tell us when you first met her?"

"Sure," I said. "She called me at the bookstore—at Old Devils, where I work—last Thursday and asked if she could come in and ask some questions. Is she all right?"

"What were the questions she wanted to ask you?" he said. Agent Perez still hadn't spoken, but she had pulled out a small spiral-bound notebook and had uncapped a pen.

"She had questions about a list I'd made, a blog post from several years ago."

Berry pulled out his own notebook and peered down at it. "Called 'Eight Perfect Murders'?" I could hear what sounded like disdain in his voice.

"That's right," I said.

"And what were her questions related to?"

I was under the impression that they already knew all about the conversation Gwen and I had had but decided to tell them anything they wanted to know. Well, anything that I'd already told Gwen. So, I began, explaining how Agent Mulvey had noticed a connection between the list I'd written in 2004 and several recent crimes. I mentioned how at first, I'd considered the connection to be dubious, probably coincidental, but how we'd found the eight books from my list at Elaine Johnson's house in Rockland.

"Did it strike you as odd that Agent Mulvey asked you to accompany her on official FBI business? To visit the scene of a possible crime?" This question came from Agent Perez, the first words

I'd heard her speak. She leaned forward as she spoke them, the buttons of her suit jacket straining a little as though she'd recently gained weight. She couldn't have been much older than thirty, with short black hair and a round face dominated by large eyes and thick brows.

"I didn't," I said. "I think she honestly believed that since I'd written the list, since I'd read all the books on it, that I was the expert. She thought I might be able to notice something in Elaine Johnson's house. Also, I knew her. I mean, I'd known Elaine Johnson."

"So what did you find out? From your visit to her house?"

"What I found out—what we found out, Agent Mulvey and myself—was confirmation that someone really is using my list to commit murders, and that quite possibly it has something to do with me—"

"Quite possibly?" Agent Berry said, his jowls quivering.

"Elaine Johnson was someone I knew, someone who used to come into my bookstore all the time. It's clear that her death signifies my involvement. Not my immediate involvement, but the fact that whoever is doing this either knows me, or wanted me to find out about this, or is somehow framing me."

"You discussed all this with Agent Mulvey?"

"Yes, we talked about all the possibilities."

Agent Berry looked down at his notebook. "Just to confirm, you discussed the murders of Robin Callahan, Jay Bradshaw, and Ethan Byrd?"

"Yes," I said.

"And you discussed the murder of Bill Manso?"

"The man killed near the train tracks? . . . Yes, we did."

"What about Eric Atwell?" he said, looking up at me.

"We talked about Eric Atwell a little bit, because of his

relationship to me. But we didn't discuss him as a victim in this particular series of crimes."

"And what was his relationship to you?"

"Eric Atwell's?"

"Yes."

"It's clear that she wrote all this down," I said. "I don't know why you can't just speak with her or consult her notes."

"We just want to hear it from you," said Agent Perez. I'd noticed that any time she spoke Agent Berry would shift on my sofa, uncomfortably, as though he had an itch he was too embarrassed to scratch.

"Eric Atwell had been involved with my wife at the time of her death. He'd gotten her hooked on drugs, and the night she died in a car accident she'd been driving back from his house."

"And Eric Atwell was murdered, correct?"

"He was shot, yes. It was my understanding that the police thought it was a robbery. And it was pretty clear that Agent Mulvey didn't think it had anything to do with the 'Perfect Murders' list."

"Okay, one more," Agent Berry said. "Did you two discuss the death of Steven Clifton?"

I paused, stunned for a moment. Steven Clifton was the name of the science teacher who had molested Claire Mallory back when she was in middle school. I had never heard Gwen mention him. I shook my head and said, "No, I don't know that name."

"No?"

"It's not familiar," I said.

"Okay," Agent Berry said and flipped a page in his notebook. He didn't seem concerned that I hadn't heard of Steven Clifton. He asked, "Did Agent Mulvey ever confide in you her suspicions about who might be responsible for these murders?"

"No," I said. "I mean, that was why she had come to me. She

was trying to find out if there was anyone in my life—any customers, any ex-employees—whom I might suspect."

"And was there anyone?"

"There wasn't," I said. "Isn't. At least not that I could think of. Elaine Johnson was probably the oddest customer who used to come into the store, but she's obviously not guilty."

"You told Agent Mulvey that you currently have two employees working for you?"

"That's right. Brandon Weeks and Emily Barsamian. The only other person who occasionally works in the store is my co-owner, Brian Murray."

Both agents wrote in their notebook. Wind buffeted the window of my apartment. "Is she okay?" I asked, the words coming out spontaneously.

Agent Berry looked up, his lower lip between his teeth. He said, "Agent Mulvey has been suspended from the agency. I need to let you know that she has been informed that she can no longer make any contact with you."

"Oh," I said. "Why?"

The agents glanced at each other, then Agent Perez said, "I'm afraid we can't talk about that. And any information you can provide from here on in should be provided only to me or to Agent Berry."

I nodded. They looked at each other again, and Perez said, "Would you be willing to come back with me to the office and give a full statement?"

I followed Agent Perez to Chelsea in her car, and she was the one who questioned me, in a plush, small room with a recording device plus two cameras mounted high in the ceiling. We started at the beginning: the origin of the list, the books I'd chosen, Gwen Mulvey and the questions that she'd asked. She wanted to know everything about our interaction, all the details we'd talked about. Agent Perez didn't ask about Eric Atwell again, or about Steven Clifton, and I was relieved, although it had occurred to me that she was maybe holding some cards close to her chest. The interview took the entire morning, and I felt strangely guilty, as though I were cheating on Gwen Mulvey with this new agent, telling her everything that we had talked about. I kept wondering why she'd been suspended from the agency, and what it had to do with my list, and what was happening. Toward the end of the interview I did ask Agent Perez one last time if she could tell me anything more about Agent Mulvey.

"There are procedures that we have to follow in the course of an investigation, and Agent Mulvey didn't comply with those procedures. That's all I can really say."

"Okay," I said.

"Before you go, I should ask you if you feel the need for police protection for yourself?" She twisted at what looked like a wedding band.

"No, I guess I don't," I said, pretending like I was thinking about it. "But I will be careful."

"One last thing before I let you go," she said. "I know that you provided an alibi to Gwen Mulvey for the date of the death of Elaine Johnson, but I was hoping you could do the same, or attempt to do the same, for the other murders."

"I can try," I said.

She sent me home with a list of exact dates for the murders of Robin Callahan, Jay Bradshaw, Ethan Byrd, and Bill Manso. I went onto my computer to look at my calendar but was suddenly exhausted, unable to deal with it at that moment. I stood up, was instantly light-headed, and realized that the only thing I'd eaten all day had been a plastic-wrapped raspberry Danish during my morning interview. I went to my kitchen and made myself two peanut butter and jelly sandwiches, ate them both with two large glasses of milk. It was one thirty. The good news was that I was getting a drink with Marty Kingship at Jack Crow's Tavern at six that evening. I knew he'd have more information for me on Norman Chaney's death, probably more information on Nicholas Pruitt. In the meantime, I needed to figure out what to do between now and that meeting at six. It wasn't worth contacting Pruitt, myself. Not yet, anyway. Then I remembered the dedication in his book of short stories: *To Jillian.* I got online and looked some more at Jillian Nguyen, the possible dedicatee. She'd been an adjunct professor at New Essex, primarily teaching survey courses for incoming freshmen; at Emerson College, where she was now, she was teaching some literature classes, but was also teaching poetry in the creative writing department. I googled some of her poetry. As was often the case with contemporary poets, I barely understood what I was reading, although there was one poem, published in a journal called *Undivider*, called "Sunday Afternoon at the PEM." The PEM was the Peabody Essex Museum, located in Salem, Massachusetts, a town adjacent to New Essex. The poem itself was largely about an exhibit related to Vietnamese folk art, although there was a "he" in the poem, a companion of the speaker, who "only saw the negative space, the bent flesh." I wondered if the companion was Nicholas Pruitt, and if he was, then I doubted Pruitt and Jillian Nguyen were still together. Even I could decipher the line from the poem as being critical.

There was a phone number listed for Professor Nguyen on the Emerson faculty page, and I called it, not really expecting her to pick up, but she did, after two rings.

"Hello?"

"Is this Professor Nguyen?" I asked, hoping I was pronouncing it correctly.

"Uh-huh."

"Hi, this is John Haley," I said, spontaneously using the name of the previous owner of Old Devils. "I was wondering if I could speak with you about Nicholas Pruitt."

There was a pause, and for a moment I thought she might have hung up the phone, but then she said. "How'd you get my name?"

"I'm afraid that I can't be overly specific about my reasons for wanting to speak with you, except to say that Mr. Pruitt is being considered for a prestigious job, and it's very important that we fully vet him." Even as I said the words, I knew they weren't entirely convincing.

"Fully vet him for what?"

"Look, I'm right here in Boston, and time is of the essence. Is there any possible way that I could meet with you this afternoon? Either in your office or maybe we could meet for coffee."

"Did Nick list me as a reference?" she said.

"I believe he mentioned you, but you wouldn't be giving an official reference. Anything you told me about him would be in total confidence."

She laughed a little. "I'd be very surprised if I were asked to give some kind of reference. Well, you've piqued my interest."

"You'd be doing me a huge favor if you'd meet with me."

"Okay," she said. "I can meet you this afternoon if you don't mind coming to me."

"Not at all," I said.

"There's a coffee shop in Downtown Crossing. Ladder Café. Do you know it?"

"No, but I'll find it."

"I have office hours until three. Will three thirty work?"

CHAPTER 19

The section of Boston known as Downtown Crossing is on the other side of the Boston Common. It used to be anchored by the large department stores, notably Filene's and Macy's, although both those buildings are currently empty. What remains is a mishmash of sneaker stores, and hot dog vendors, plus a few hip bars and restaurants hoping that the city will successfully be able to rebrand the area as the Ladder District, something they'd been trying to do for a few years now.

Clearly, the Ladder Café was on board with the rebranding. Sandwiched between a fabric shop and a sports bar, the Ladder was a narrow, high-ceilinged room with tattooed baristas and minimalist art on the walls. I got there early, procured a large café au lait, and sat with a view toward the front doors. I suspected that Jillian Nguyen, when she arrived, would have many questions about why I was asking her about her former boyfriend. I decided that I would tell her as little as possible, except that he was being considered as the editor for a forthcoming anthology from a major publisher, and that there'd been some questions about his personal life. If pressed, I'd tell her I was working for a private detective firm doing a background check. I was hoping she wouldn't ask me for my card.

At exactly three thirty a woman I recognized as Jillian came through the doors. She was small, enveloped in a puffy jacket with a hood. She must have caught me looking at her because she immediately came over, and I introduced myself.

"I only have about twenty minutes," she said, and I wondered if she'd gotten more wary since our phone call.

I offered to buy her a coffee and she asked for an herbal tea. I stood in line again and got her one. It was impossible for me to not think of Claire, who always used to get herbal tea at coffee shops, and how it used to drive me crazy to pay three dollars or more for what amounted to a teabag and some hot water.

Back at the table I said, "Thanks so much again for meeting with me. I know this must seem very strange, but I've been asked to do a background check and it has to happen very quickly because the publishers want to make a decision right away."

She perked up at the word *publishers*, which I knew she would. "Oh," she said. "What's the . . ."

"I can't actually tell you the publishing house but he's being considered as an editor for a big anthology, and, apparently, someone somewhere expressed concern about his personal life, that it might inhibit him from doing the work."

Jillian was about to take a sip of her tea but set the mug back down on its saucer. "You said that this conversation would be entirely confidential."

"Oh, absolutely," I said. "One hundred percent. I'll never even file a written report."

"I haven't seen or spoken to Nick for over three years, not since I left New Essex. Clearly, you already know I filed a restraining order against him, otherwise why would you be talking with me, right?"

"Right," I said, then added, "How long were you involved with him?"

She looked toward the ceiling. "Less than a year. I mean, less than a year that we were actually involved. I knew him for a year before we started going out, and after I finally broke it off, I was still in New Essex for another six months or so."

"And can you tell me what prompted you to file the restraining order?"

She sighed. "He never actually hurt me, or threatened me with physical violence, but after we broke up, he called me all the time, showed up wherever I was going to be, and once—it was only the once, but it was what caused me to get the restraining order—he got very drunk and broke into my house."

"Jeez," I said.

"The thing is . . . I do think he's actually a decent man, but he's a drunk. Do you know . . . is he still drinking? The last time I spoke with him he told me he'd been sober for over a month."

"I'll be sure to find out. So he was never actually violent with you?"

"No. Definitely no. Just persistent, really. He considered me the love of his life."

"He dedicated his book to you," I said.

"Oh, God." She covered her face as though she was embarrassed. "I know. And it was after we'd broken up. Look, I don't want to stop Nick from getting a job that he probably needs. I had a bad experience with him, but if he's stopped drinking, then maybe he'll be a good fit. He's very well read."

"So, from your time knowing him, you don't think he'd be capable of any kind of violence? You never felt as though he'd be vengeful after you broke up?"

She looked a little confused at the question, and I wondered if I'd taken it too far. She started to speak, stopped, then said, "I never saw a violent side of him, but he did . . . he was very interested in violence from a literary point of view. He was attracted to stories of revenge. But that . . . that was just professional interest, as far as

I knew. He's a pretty typical English professor, really. Bookish."

I wanted to ask her if she knew anything about what had happened to his sister, or subsequently, his sister's ex-husband, Norman Chaney. But I already felt like I was treading on thin ice. Jillian Nguyen was studying me the way someone studies a person they might have to describe at a later time. "I know these questions sound odd," I said. "Apparently, and this is just between you and me, someone came forward to the publishing house and accused Nicholas Pruitt of a violent act."

"Oh," Jillian said and took a sip from her tea.

"The publishers did not believe the accusation, or the accuser, was trustworthy, but just to make sure—"

"Oh my God, you think it's me," Jillian said, straightening up in her chair.

"Oh, no, no," I said. "Not at all. We have the accuser's name. We're just looking for any kind of corroboration."

"Okay," she said and put her mug down. "Look, I do need to go. Besides, I don't really have anything else to add."

She stood, and I did as well. "Thank you, you've been very helpful." It was clear that I'd lost her trust, but I decided to test my luck. "Just one last thing. As far as you knew did Nick Pruitt own a gun?"

She was sliding on her huge coat, and she shook her head. "I mean, no," she said. "Besides the antique guns, but I don't even think those work."

"The antique guns?"

"He collects guns. Not to shoot, but old revolvers. Anything that was in an old crime film. It's his hobby."

OUR WAITRESS PUT DOWN our beers, a Stella for Marty and a Belhaven for me. We were in a back booth at Jack Crow's Tavern that felt like its own tiny room, reminding me of the pews at the Old South Church. We each sipped our beer.

"Good to see you, Marty," I said. I'd seen him fairly recently, but he looked older to me. His white crew cut was sparser than ever, the skin underneath speckled with dark spots. And the large-knuckled fingers of his hands were bent in a way that suggested arthritis.

"I'd forgotten about this place," he said, leaning out from our booth to look at the busy bar. "Last time we came here we got nachos that had brussels sprouts on them."

"Really?" I said. "I don't remember that."

"I'll never forget it. Who puts brussels sprouts on nachos?"

"Now I remember," I said. "Let's stick to beer tonight." We touched glasses.

"You find out anything new?" I said. I'd been debating whether I should tell him I'd gotten my own information on Nick Pruitt, especially what I'd heard about the gun collection, but I hadn't decided yet.

"Found out a little bit," Marty said. "Don't know if it will help you, but he's no saint, Nick Pruitt."

"No?"

"He's been arrested twice, once for DUI, and once for drunk and disorderly after, get this, a Christmas Eve service. He got caught trying to steal a box of those little white candles they hand out. Also, he's had two restraining orders filed against him. Hold on." He reached into the pocket of his wool blazer and pulled out a spiral-bound notebook plus a pair of reading glasses. "The first was Jodie Blackberry. This was in Michigan, when he was a graduate student. She said she caught him peering through her window and following her around campus. The other one was much more re-cent. Just three years ago, filed by a Jillian N-G-U-Y-E-N. I won't do her the indignity of trying to pronounce it. Kind of the same type of thing. Ex-girlfriend who claimed he wouldn't leave her alone. He'd broken into her house."

"So, nothing violent on his record? Nothing gun related?"

"Nope. But that fits, doesn't it? If Nick Pruitt was the one who wanted Chaney dead, then he'd get someone else to do it. He's not really a killer even though he's clearly a peeper and a guy who can't hold his liquor. Besides, I looked into the alibi and it's rock solid."

"His alibi for when Norman Chaney was killed?"

"Yep." Marty looked down at his notebook again. "It was March of 2011. Nick Pruitt was in California at a family reunion. It checked out. But like I said, I don't think he'd be the type who would beat his own brother-in-law to death, but he very well might be the type to have someone do it for him. Or maybe he asked someone to just rough Norman Chaney up and it went too far. Either way, he got away with it. My guess is, if you really want to know, it would be possible to shake it out of him, get him to make some sort of confession. I know his type, and if you bent him a little, I think he'd give it up. I'm not suggesting, just saying."

"Got it," I said. "No, all I needed was the information. It's helpful, Marty, thanks."

"No, *thank* you. I actually felt useful this week. First time in what feels like forever. The FBI still questioning you about this Chaney homicide?"

I took a long sip of my beer, wondering, once again, how much to tell Marty. "They haven't, no," I said. "Apparently it all had something to do with a list I made on the Old Devils blog about a hundred years ago."

"Oh, yeah?"

"Yeah. You ever go to our blog?"

"I don't know what the fuck a blog even is," Marty said.

"I don't do it anymore, but when I started at Old Devils, it was an online place where I wrote little articles. Reviews of new books. Lists of my favorite authors. That type of thing. I wrote a piece once about my eight favorite perfect murders in books, and someone in the FBI saw a connection between my list and a couple of recent unsolved homicides. They were pretty thin connections, though, so I don't think they'll follow up."

"What else did they ask you about?" he said, clearly interested.

"A death down in Connecticut, someone who was found near the tracks of a commuter train. And they asked me about that newscaster, Robin—"

"Robin Callahan, sure," he said, jumping in. "Her husband did it. I can't believe they haven't made an arrest yet."

"You know that?" I said.

"I don't know it, but, yeah, she was the one who wrote the book about how adultery was good for marriages. I think I'm safe in saying they ought to take a hard look at the husband."

I laughed. "Yeah, so, I think I overreacted."

"I don't know if *you* overreacted. It sounds like *they* overreacted. They asked you about all these cases?"

I could tell he was getting more and more interested, and I just didn't want to involve him. He reminded me of a dog with a bone, and if I told him all about the copycat murders, he'd start looking into it. Not to mention that I'd actually given him the name of Norman Chaney.

"They just asked me if I had any relationship with them, with Norman Chaney, or this guy down in Connecticut, or Robin Callahan. And I said no. I asked you about Norman Chaney because for whatever reason they seemed more interested in that. Honestly, though, it was nothing. At least I hope it was nothing. Your daughter still coming to visit?"

"What books did you put on that list?" he asked, ignoring my question about Cindy.

I told him, pretending I was having a hard time remembering. I left off *Strangers on a Train*, however. Marty, who was always looking for book recommendations, wrote some of the titles down in his little notebook.

"*The A.B.C. Murders*," he said. "I like the sound of that. These days I think I like reading Agatha Christie more than I like reading James Ellroy. Don't know what it is, but maybe I'm getting soft."

"You've been reading Agatha Christie?"

"Yeah, like you told me to, remember? I just read *Ten Little Indians*."

"*And Then There Were None*," I said, almost automatically. It was the less offensive title that the book was now sold under.

"Right, that one. Now that was a perfect crime. Too bad more murderers don't copy that book."

"Kill yourself after you commit the murders, you mean?" I said. I didn't remember telling him to read Agatha Christie, but I'm sure I did. It sounded like me.

We ordered another beer, and talked about books, and a little about his family. He asked if I wanted to stay for a third beer, but I decided to bow out. As always with Marty I liked spending time with him but after a while we'd run out of things to say, and I would feel sad and lonely. I've always felt that being with people, as opposed to being alone, can make you feel loneliness more acutely.

"You gonna do anything about Nick Pruitt?" he asked, as I was pulling on my jacket.

"No," I said. "Not unless the FBI decides to talk with me again. If they do, then I guess I could mention him, say that I had an ex-cop look into the Norman Chaney murder and how Pruitt looked like a suspect."

"I wouldn't mention my name," Marty said. "If you don't mind."

"No, of course not. In fact, I won't mention it at all. I think I was just curious, was all. I was baffled that they'd made some connection between me and these crimes."

"I figured you were going to tell me it had to do with Nero," Marty said, then finished off his beer.

"Huh?" I said.

"Oh. I figured that the FBI came calling to you with questions about Norman Chaney because of your cat. Nero. In the store."

"Why?" I said, trying to sound relatively calm.

"I was reading the police reports and Norman Chaney had a cat, a ginger one like Nero, that went missing after the homicide. I read that . . . then I thought that might be the connection."

"That's funny," I said.

"He's a little bit of a celebrity, that Nero, you know?"

"I know he is. Half the people come to our store come to see him. Emily tells me he has his own Instagram page, although I've never seen it. No, they didn't ask me anything about my cat. And he doesn't come from Vermont, anyway." I laughed, and it sounded fake in my own head.

"I might stay here for one more," Marty said.

I thanked him again and went out into the night. The temperature had dropped in the time I'd spent with Marty, and I walked home carefully, avoiding patches of black ice on the narrow sidewalks. When I reached my street, I didn't immediately see her, waiting in the shadow of the dead linden tree in front of my house, but I did sense her. It was the feeling I'd been experiencing lately, that feeling that I was being watched.

At my stairwell, she stepped out of the shadows, and said, "Hi, Mal."

CHAPTER 20

H i, Gwen," I said.

"You don't seem surprised to see me."

"I guess not. I spoke with two other FBI agents today, and they told me that you'd been suspended."

"Who did you talk to?" she said, stepping forward so that she was now in the light from the street. Her breath was billowing in the cold night, but I wasn't sure I wanted to invite her in.

"One agent from New Haven—"

"Berry, right?"

"Look," I said. "I'm just not sure I should really be talking to you."

"No, I totally understand. I don't want anything from you, but I was hoping to at least talk, just for a little while, explain what happened. I would have called you, but I couldn't do that. Can I come up? Or could we grab a drink somewhere? Anywhere but where we're standing right now."

We walked down my street to Charles, and got a booth at the Sevens, where we each ordered a Newcastle Brown Ale. Gwen removed her coat but kept a thick woolen scarf wrapped around her neck. Her cheeks and the tip of her nose were still red from being outside.

"What do you want to know?" she said.

"You've been suspended?"

"Yes, pending a review."

"How come?"

She took a sip from her bottle of beer, then licked foam from her upper lip. "When I presented what I'd learned to my supervisors . . . well, not what I'd learned so much, but what I suspected, that there was a connection between several unsolved crimes in the New England area, I was told not to pursue the case. I made the mistake of telling them what had initially led me to you. The thing is . . . I knew who you were, already. I'd heard your name, anyway, because once upon a time I knew your wife. I knew Claire."

Her eyes were looking at me but not looking at me, landing somewhere around my chin. "How did you know Claire?" I said.

"I knew her because my father was one of her teachers, in middle school. Steve Clifton."

I needed to make a decision. I needed to decide whether I was going to play dumb, or if I was going to tell her the truth, most of it, anyway. I think the look on her face was what made me decide that I needed to be truthful. She looked terrified, and I realized that if she'd made a decision to be honest with me, I should return the favor.

"Yes, I know all about him."

"What do you know?"

"I know that he molested Claire over the course of two years while she was in middle school. He screwed up her life."

"She told you about it?"

"Yes."

"What did she say about it? If you don't mind my asking. I understand if you feel . . ." She broke off, and I realized how hard this was for her.

I said, "To tell the truth, we didn't talk much about the details. She brought it up early on in our relationship, said it was important for me to know, but she always downplayed it. At least to me."

Gwen was nodding. "You don't have to tell me exactly what she told you. I understand."

"Why don't you have his last name?" I said. "Why aren't you Gwen Clifton?"

"I was, of course, for years, but I had my name legally changed. Mulvey is my mother's maiden name."

"That makes sense," I said. Then added, "Did you actually know Claire?"

"Yes, I remember her. I was younger than she was, by about five years, but she used to come to the house—several of my father's students used to come to the house—and I remember her because she played Boggle with me a bunch of times. And then, later, when I was in high school my father confessed to me what he'd done, and hers was one of the names he told me."

"He told you what he'd done?"

Gwen pursed her lips and breathed out. "At this point Claire had already graduated, but another student, or two students, maybe, had come forward and accused him of inappropriate touching. Everyone knew. We lived in the same town that he taught in. It was one of those already awkward situations where he was a teacher at the same middle school I attended, although he was never *my* teacher. He resigned—he was forced to resign—and there must have been some kind of legal settlement because it never went to court. Or else there wasn't enough evidence. One night, he came to my room . . ." She stopped speaking and pressed her index finger against her left eye for a moment.

"You don't have to tell me all this," I said.

"He came to my room and told me the names of the girls he'd molested, including Claire's name, and he said he did it to protect me. That he never wanted to do anything to *me*, so he did it to other girls." She shrugged and pressed her lips together into something that looked like a half smile.

"Jesus," I said.

"Yeah," she said. "So I never forgot Claire's name, and I remembered later hearing how she died, and looking up her obituary and finding your name. So I knew about you, as well."

"What about you and your dad?"

"That time he came and talked to me was the last time we ever talked. He left the house, after that, and my parents divorced, and I never saw him again. He was killed, you know."

"He was murdered?"

"Not officially, no. But, yes, I believe he was."

"How?"

"Don't you know?" she said.

I was drinking from my bottle of beer even though it was empty. "You think I killed him?" I said.

She shrugged again and gave me that odd smile. The color had disappeared from her cheeks and from her nose, and, as usual, I found it hard to read her face, the paleness of it, the flatness of her eyes. "I don't really know, Mal, but at this point I don't know what to believe. Do you really want to hear what I think?"

"I do."

"Okay. Eric Atwell was murdered, and I know that you weren't in the country, but that doesn't mean you couldn't have arranged it. My father was run down by a car when he was on his bicycle. It was a hit-and-run, but I always assumed someone had killed him for what he'd done. It would make sense. Both of those killings would make sense, would be justified, really, especially for the husband of Claire Mallory."

"I will admit that I don't feel bad for either of them," I said and tried on my own smile that I'm sure looked as awkward as hers.

"But that's all you'll admit?"

"What does either Eric Atwell or your father have to do with my list, and the other murders?"

"I don't know. Maybe nothing. After my father was killed, I did think about you again. I'd also heard about Eric Atwell's death, and I figured you might have something to do with that, as well. I didn't care, even though I was training at the time to be an FBI agent. I knew someone had killed my father, and I actually hoped that it was someone with a reason for doing it, not someone who just accidentally ran him over, and then took off. I wanted his death to be revenge. And I assumed that it was. Honestly, it's something that helps me sleep at night. And in my mind, I thought that it was probably you. There were other girls my father victimized but Claire is the one I always remember, probably because she was kind to me and I'll never forget that.

"And while I was learning about you I discovered the list. I've had it memorized, I think, for many years, and I thought of it right away—I thought of *The A.B.C. Murders*—after hearing about the feathers that were sent to the police station."

"You thought I committed all those murders?"

She shifted forward on her wooden seat. "No, no. I didn't. I don't know what I thought, really, except that something was going on, something that might have to do with my father, and with you. I got obsessed with it, even thought that maybe my father's death was related to *The Secret History*."

"How?" I said.

"Because, in a way, he picked the circumstances of his death."

"Because he biked a lot?"

"Uh-huh. He biked all the time, especially after the divorce, after he'd moved to Upstate New York. Not that I knew this from personal experience, but I read the police report on his death. He always biked alone, hills mainly, on quiet roads. He was hit by a car going the other way. So, yeah, I did think about *Secret History*. If someone wanted to kill him, then running him down while he biked would be the easiest thing to do. It would look like an accident, well, an accident that someone fled from, but it wouldn't necessarily look like a homicide."

"You told your boss all this?"

"Not at first. When I first brought it to him, I told him about your list, and how it connected with the bird murders, and with Bill Manso in Connecticut, and how I wanted to follow it up, but he didn't bite. I made the mistake of mentioning that there was also a connection to my father's death, and that was when I was told that I was barred from investigating any further, that it would be handed off to other agents if they saw fit. I was on vacation last week, when I questioned you, and when we went up to Rockland. Someone at the coroner's office got in touch with my office instead of me directly, and that's how I got busted, and that's why I'm suspended. If they knew I was here now, I'd be fired for sure."

"So why are you here?"

"I think . . ." she said, then paused. "I think I felt I owed you the truth. And maybe I'm warning you, as well. They know everything I know. You are a suspect."

"You must think I'm a suspect, as well."

"I don't know what to think anymore. Do I think you killed Elaine Johnson up in Maine, or Bill Manso, or Robin Callahan or Ethan Byrd? I don't really think so. But that's just a feeling. I know you're not telling me the whole truth. If I had to come up with a theory, and I know it'll sound ridiculous, but I think that maybe you talked someone into doing something to Eric Atwell, and maybe even my father, and now this person . . . whoever they are—"

"Charlie, remember," I said.

"Right, Charlie. Look, I haven't slept in days. I wanted to talk with you, and we've talked. I can't have anything more to do with this investigation, not if I want to keep my job. Can I ask you to keep this meeting secret?"

"Of course."

She took a sip of her beer, still three-quarters full. "And if you did have anything to do with the death of my father . . ."

"I didn't."

"But if you did . . . know that there is no one alive who mourned his death."

She stood up suddenly, banging her thighs against the table be-tween us.

"You okay?" I said.

"I'm fine. I'm just exhausted. I don't think I've slept in days."

"What are you going to do now?"

"I'm going to drive home, and I'm going to try and forget about all this."

I walked her to her car, wondering if I should offer her my couch for the night but decided that was a bad idea for multiple reasons. Besides which, I don't think she would have accepted. And I wasn't sure I wanted her there, myself. She had not been honest with me, and I wasn't convinced she was being entirely honest now.

At her Equinox, parked near the Flat of the Hill Hotel, we stood for a moment in the whistling wind. Gwen had begun to shiver. "Are you still rereading the books?" she said.

"I've been reading *The Secret History*," I said.

"Suddenly, that title takes on a whole new significance."

I laughed. "It does, I suppose."

"Any new insights?"

"From the books?"

"From anything."

"Can I tell you something that you won't share unless you have to?"

"I'm not even supposed to be here talking with you, so, yeah, I wouldn't worry about it."

"Okay," I said. "It's just a name that came up. I won't say how. But if anything does happen to me, maybe take a look at someone named Nicholas Pruitt."

She repeated the name back to me, and I spelled it for her.

"Who is he?"

"He's an English professor. It's probably nothing, but . . ."

"Okay," she said. "Hopefully you'll be fine, and I won't have to look into his name."

We said good-bye, neither of us offering a handshake or a hug. Then I walked back to my apartment, thinking about everything we'd just said to each other.

I'd been home for twenty minutes, wide awake, when I considered leaving again, driving to New Essex, and confronting Nick Pruitt that night. I had gotten his address online from Zillow, a place that posted real estate transactions. He lived in a single-family home on the outskirts of New Essex, in a neighborhood near the university. I could just show up at his door and knock on it. If Nick was Charlie, and I felt almost positive that he was, then he'd know me on sight. Maybe I could just talk with him, find out what he wanted, ask him to stop. But if I went to his house that night, who knew how he would act. Who knew if he'd even be alone.

I decided to drive to New Essex early the next morning, stake out his house, watch him for a while. It might give me an advantage.

CHAPTER 21

E   arly the next morning, before driving to New Essex, I went
       to Old Devils. Nero came up through his cat door from the
       basement to greet me, walking with purpose, his head up.
I picked him up and cradled him in my arms, scratching under his
chin. I'd asked myself before whether it had been worth it to save
him, and I believe it had. I don't know if there really is a way to rate
an animal's happiness, but I believe he loves his life in the bookstore. I put him down, picking one of his hairs off my wool coat.
Would they have collected his hairs from Norman Chaney's house
in Tickhill during the investigation of his murder? Would they
have considered them important or irrelevant? I didn't really know.

I left a note, with a list of things to do, for Emily and Brandon,
then went back out into the cold morning.

I was in New Essex a little over an hour later, idling along the
curb across from where Nick Pruitt lived, a small square house
with a mansard roof. It was eight in the morning, and I felt con-
spicuous. Corning Street was almost entirely residential, and all
the houses had driveways. Mine was the only car parked along the
curb. There was a corner store back about a hundred yards. I U-
turned and parked in front of it, turned off my engine. I still had a
view of Pruitt's house, and if anyone questioned why I was sitting
in my car, I could say I was about to go into the store.

The car began to steam up, and I cleared a small patch on the
bottom right of the windshield so that I could still watch the house

while slumped in my seat. I took small sips from my thermos of coffee. There was a car parked in front of his house—something sporty that might be a Porsche—but that didn't necessarily mean that he was still home. He worked at the university, only a few blocks away. If he was teaching a morning class, he could easily walk there.

While waiting, I went over my list of books in my mind, connecting them with the murders. Unless Gwen Mulvey hadn't spotted one of them, then Charlie had committed murders described in four of the eight books on my list, possibly five. The first one, of course, was done with me. Eric Atwell and Norman Chaney. The swapped murders from *Strangers on a Train*. Then Charlie had recreated the plot from *The A.B.C. Murders*, substituting people with birds in their names. Bill Manso had been killed using the idea from *Double Indemnity*. Elaine Johnson had been killed the same way that the playwright's wife had been killed in *Deathtrap*. And was it possible that Steven Clifton had been murdered by using the method in *The Secret History*? How had Charlie even have known about Clifton? But, of course, he might have. He knew about me, and my wife. How hard would it have been to discover that Claire Mallory had gone to a middle school where a teacher had been accused of improper behavior with his students. It was unlikely, but not impossible. That left three books, three murders to go. *The Red House Mystery*, *Malice Aforethought*, and *The Drowner*. For all I knew, one or more of these had already happened, but somehow, I doubted it.

At about eleven I got out of the car, stretched, then went into the convenience store. It was one of those places that sells milk and basic groceries, but only exists because of lottery tickets and cigarettes. I bought a granola bar and a dusty bottle of water from the man behind the register and paid in cash. As I walked back toward my car, I saw a young woman in jeans and knee-high boots striding toward Pruitt's front door. She pressed the doorbell as I got back into the driver's seat. I swiped a hand across the inside of my windshield to watch the woman as she waited, rocking slightly on her heels. She rang the bell again, then tried knocking, then peered through one of the rectangular panes of glass that lined the side of the door. Finally, she gave up, looked at her phone, and turned around and walked back down the street.

I got out of the car and began to follow her. I figured that if she was looking for Nick Pruitt, she'd eventually find him, and if I was following her, then I'd find him as well.

She was walking fast, almost jogging at times, so I picked up my pace. At the end of Pruitt's street, she turned left onto Gloucester Road, climbing a short hill toward New Essex University, and eventually entering a two-story brick building on the edge of the campus. A sign above the awning read Proctor Hall. I raced to the double glass doors, and pushed through into a lobby-style entrance, catching the retreating figure of the woman, her boots rapping down a long hall to the left. A bearded man behind an information desk looked up at me, and I smiled and nodded like I'd seen him a hundred times, then followed the woman down the fluorescent-lit hallway. She was pushing through the third door at the left. A small placard told me she was in Classroom 1C, and I peered through an inset window of wire-reinforced glass. All I could see was the curved back row of stadium-style seating, about twelve students sprawled at their desks. I pushed through the door and slipped inside, seating myself at the end of the back row. It was a large room that sloped down toward the front. It probably had room for about a hundred students, and I guessed that 60 percent of the seats were taken. The woman I'd followed had removed her black parka and her wool hat and was now standing at the front of the room, looking nervous.

"Unfortunately," she said. "Professor Pruitt won't be able to make today's class. I'll be here for the remainder of the time in case anyone has any questions, but unless you hear otherwise, Friday morning's class is the same as scheduled, and the reading assignment hasn't changed."

Halfway through her announcement all the students had begun to slide their laptops back into their backpacks and put their coats back on. I got up, as well, and quickly left the room, walking back down the hallway, then outside, hoping my presence hadn't been too noteworthy to anyone. I wandered toward a bench, with a view out toward the Atlantic, dark gray under a leaden sky. I sat for a moment, angling my body so that I could see the front of Proctor Hall, students now streaming out, moving quickly out of fear that their professor would suddenly show up and they wouldn't get the morning off.

It was clear what had happened. Pruitt hadn't shown up to his class, hadn't responded to texts or calls to his cell phone. His teaching assistant had resorted to running down to his nearby house and seeing if he was home. I had a bad feeling but tamped it down. Pruitt was a drunk of some kind, at least that is what Jillian Nguyen had reported. Maybe he was hungover. Maybe this sort of thing happened all the time, and his TA would sometimes be able to rouse him by banging on his door.

I kept my eye on Proctor Hall, curious to see what the TA might do when she departed the building, wondering if she might go back down to Pruitt's house. Then I remembered her saying that she would stick around the classroom for the duration of the canceled class. I stood up, began to walk down the hill toward Pruitt's street. My body was telling me to get back in my car and drive home. Something had happened. A line of poetry went through my mind—*someone is dead, even the trees know it*—and it took me a moment to remember that it was an Anne Sexton line, a poem about one of her parents dying, I thought. As I approached Pruitt's house, I studied the line of trees along Corning Street. They were all leafless, of course, and against the dark sky they were just black shapes, pencil scratches. It was hard to imagine them full of leaves on a summer day. Yes, *someone is dead*. But it wasn't enough just to know it.

When I got to Pruitt's house, I cut down his driveway, passing his car. I was wearing gloves and I unlatched the wooden door that led to his fenced-in backyard. Drifts of crusted snow filled the square yard. There was a grill under a tarp, but nothing else. Unraked leaves, black now, were banked up against the far fence.

I climbed three steps that got me to a small deck and a back door. Through the windowpane I could see a kitchen with a checkered linoleum floor; beyond it was what looked like a dining room with a long table. The door was locked, and I knocked on the glass. I was about to punch through the window, but there was a row of old plant pots on the deck. Crouching, I lifted each one. Under a pot with rosemary in it was a single silver key. I pinched it between my gloved fingers; it fit the back door, and I was inside. I shouted "Hello" into the empty house, then waited for an answer. I walked through the uncluttered kitchen into the dining room, going slow, allowing my eyes to adjust to the dim interior. All the curtains were pulled. From the dining room I could see through into the front room of the house, to a long sofa. Pruitt was sitting there on one end of the sofa, his feet flat on the floor, his hands on either side of his thighs, and his head tilted back all the way, resting against the sofa cushion. He was dead. I knew that much just by looking at him, at how still he was, how exposed his neck was with his head at that uncomfortable angle.

As shocked as I was by the sight of his body, I was equally shocked because it meant that Pruitt wasn't Charlie. I'd been so sure that he was, and clearly, I'd been wrong. There was, I suppose, a minuscule possibility that maybe Pruitt really was Charlie, and the guilt of what he'd done had caused him to drink himself to death. But I knew, in my gut, that that wasn't the case. Pruitt had been killed by Charlie, who was many steps ahead of me.

There was a very strong smell of whiskey coming from the room, and I saw the bottle on the floor, tipped on its side on the thin Persian rug. It caught what little light there was in the room, glinting from a line of wire that encased its triangular shape. I recognized the brand—it was a scotch—but couldn't remember exactly what it was called. There was also another smell, one that made me think of hospitals. I moved in a little closer so that I was standing in the doorframe. And from there I could see that there was dried vomit down the front of Pruitt's sweater.

Knowing I wasn't going to go any farther into the room with Pruitt's body there, I glanced around. Not surprisingly there were many bookshelves. In one corner was a large flat-screen television and what looked like an old stereo system. On the wall above the sofa was a large framed theater poster advertising a production of Shakespeare's *The Winter's Tale*; it included a line drawing of a bear with a crown on its head. I did notice that except for the bottle on the floor in front of the sofa I'd seen no other signs of liquor in the house.

I slowly backed away into the dining room, and then the kitchen. I looked around there for liquor, as well, but didn't see any. I opened his refrigerator. It was sparse inside, but there was a six-pack of beer on the top shelf, although looking at it closely I realized that it was nonalcoholic. I shut the refrigerator door, wondering if it would be worth it to look around the house some more, or if it would be foolish to stay any longer. I knew what had happened here, of course, although I hadn't completely processed it yet. It was *Malice Aforethought*. In that book a woman who is a drug addict is killed with a drug overdose, making it look like an accident. Pruitt was an obvious recovering alcoholic, but Charlie had somehow gotten him to drink again, gotten him to drink a fatal amount. Or at least to make it look like he had.

Chirping sounds, like crickets, suddenly filled the kitchen and I jumped, my heart ratcheting up to full speed. It was Pruitt's phone, charging by the toaster on the kitchen counter. I went and looked at the screen. The person calling him was named Tamara Strahovski. I guessed that it was the TA, checking in once more. How soon before she called the police, asking for a wellness check? I had no idea of knowing. I made a quick decision to briefly look through the house—a five-minute search.

The kitchen had two doors and I went through the other one. It led to a back hallway, a half bathroom, and a room that was Pruitt's office. There was a standing desk, a laptop propped open on it, and more shelves, most of these filled with endless copies of his own book, *Little Fish*. I knew from visiting Brian Murray's home that authors got a number of their own editions, but not as many as there were in here. *Little Fish* filled two bookshelves and there were stacks along the floor. It looked to be in the hundreds. I wondered if he'd bought copies of his own books, maybe to boost sales. From the office I worked quickly down a side hall that led to the stairs. At the top of the landing I peered into Pruitt's bedroom, messier than any of the rooms downstairs. And sparser, as well. There was a pile of clothes on the floor, an unmade bed, and another hand-drawn theater poster framed on the wall. This time for *Twelfth Night*. I was able to get a better look at this poster. It was a production of the New Essex Community Playhouse, and the director was Nicholas Pruitt. Before leaving the bedroom, I glanced at the top of his bureau, cluttered with framed photographs, most of them old family shots, although I recognized a picture of Jillian Nguyen, posing with Pruitt in front of what looked like the reconstruction of the Globe Theatre in London.

I let myself out the back door and returned the key underneath the potted rosemary. Then I got back into my car and drove home to Boston.

CHAPTER 22

I hadn't gone back onto Duckburg since 2010, when I'd arranged the murder swap. But I was thinking I needed to revisit the site now, just in case I could get in contact with Charlie. As far as I knew I still had the site bookmarked on my work computer. It was early afternoon, and I walked from home to the Old Devils. Every time I blinked, I could see Nick Pruitt's lifeless body sitting placidly on his sofa, his head tipped back, and his mouth hanging open.

I pushed through the door. Emily was behind the register ringing up a sale, and I heard Brandon before I saw him. "The gang's all here," he said in his loud voice. He was crouched to my left, hunting one of the lower shelves, probably trying to find a book for an online order.

"Just for a while," I said. "Sorry I've left you two alone so much lately."

"What's going on with you?" Brandon said, standing now, holding a copy of John le Carré's *The Spy Who Came in from the Cold*.

"Honestly," I said, "I haven't been feeling too well." It was the first lie that popped into my head. "Just extra tired and a little achy. Don't know what it is."

"Well, don't come here and spread it all around," Brandon said. "E and I have got it covered, don't we, E?"

She didn't respond but I saw Emily look up from behind the desk. The customer she'd been helping, a semiregular whose name

I could never remember, but who always bought the new Michael Connelly from us, was now shuffling toward the exit.

"I have some work to do in my office, then I'm going to head back home, I promise," I said, and made my way there as Brandon started to tell Emily how his mother had had a cold for an entire year once.

Nero was in my desk chair, curled into a circle, but he perked up when I came in, stretched his back, then leapt to the ground. I sat and turned on my computer. I was suddenly worried that I'd deleted the Duckburg bookmark—the smart thing to do, in all honesty—but once I'd gone online, there it was. I logged on, went to the section called Swaps, and did a quick perusal of the last fifty or so entries. It was the usual stuff—offers of work with the payment of either sexual favor or drugs. There were outliers, of course, a man looking to trade his wife's entire shoe collection ("at least eight jimmy choos") for a ticket to a sold-out Springsteen concert. I didn't see anything that referenced *Strangers on a Train*. I wasn't surprised. Charlie didn't need to get in touch with me because he already had, in a way. He knew exactly who I was. Still, it was worth a shot to send him a message on the off chance he was watching this site.

I created a new fake identity, calling myself Farley Walker, and posted a message. Dear Strangers on a Train fan, I'd like to propose another swap. You know who you are. I stared at the message for about five minutes after I'd posted it, wondering if a reply would come through instantly, but nothing did. I logged off Duckburg and did a quick search of New Essex University to see if anything had popped up in the news. I wasn't surprised to find nothing. Even if Scott Pruitt's body had already been discovered, and it probably hadn't yet, then it would hardly be newsworthy. It would look like an accidental overdose from an alcoholic who fell off the wagon. Unless Charlie had screwed up, it was a perfect murder. No one would suspect a homicide.

I did wonder how he'd done it. My best guess was that he'd gone to Pruitt's door with the bottle of whiskey and a gun and forced him to drink. Maybe he'd drugged the whiskey, as well.

The bigger question I had was how had Charlie targeted Pruitt in the first place. The only people who knew I was interested in him were Marty Kingship and Jillian Nguyen. Of course, Pruitt was related to Norman Chaney. And if Charlie had arranged for Chaney's death, then he'd have a connection with Pruitt as well. I suddenly remembered the book, *Little Fish*, and that I'd left it here at the store. Emily was now back at her own desk, dealing with on-line orders probably, so I went to the register. *Little Fish* was there, where I'd left it. I realized how incriminating it was that I had a library copy of this book and decided that the least I could do was not leave it where it was.

"You had a visitor last night," Brandon said.

I looked up. "Oh, yeah."

"Brian Murray's wife—is it Tess?—was here looking for you."

"Oh," I said. "Did she say what she wanted?"

"Nah. She said she was just dropping by because she hadn't been for a while, but I could tell she was a little disappointed you weren't here. She's not usually in Boston, is she? Not when it's freezing cold like this, right?"

"Brian broke his arm," I said. "I saw them two nights ago, and apparently she now has to be here to help him with everything."

"Oh, man, that's hilarious," Brandon said, although I wasn't sure it really was.

I wasn't too surprised that Tess had stopped by the store. She had been in the book business, after all, as a publicist. And I was sure she was tired of babysitting her husband. Still, I couldn't help thinking about the way she'd hugged me good-bye after we had drinks at the Beacon Hill Hotel.

"She buy anything?" I asked.

"Nah. But she rearranged all the Brian Murrays for us."

"I'm not surprised," I said.

Before leaving I copied the complicated link for the Duckburg site onto a piece of paper, so I could check the site from my laptop at home. Then I grabbed *Little Fish*, told Brandon and Emily they might be on their own for a while, and headed home. Outside, tiny ice flakes of snow had begun to swirl in the air. Another storm—not a very big one—was threatening to arrive that night. I kept thinking of Tess Murray, how she'd come into the store. Had she seen my copy of Nick Pruitt's book? And if she had, so what. Still, it bugged me.

I unlocked the outside door and climbed the stairs to my attic apartment. Inside, it was surprisingly cold, and I realized that I'd left the windows cracked, not something that I remembered doing at all. I shut them, then went immediately to my computer to check the Duckburg site. There was no response. I looked up Tess Murray. It occurred to me that I knew hardly anything about her besides the fact that she was the much younger wife of my business partner, and that she'd been a publicist when they first met. I found who I thought was her on a LinkedIn page, although there was no photograph. It listed one of the big publishing houses as a place of former employment, plus a business called Snyman Publicity, and I remembered that Snyman was her name before she changed it to Murray. Her current place of employment was the Treasure Chest on Longboat Key in Florida, the small jewelry store she now ran. I wondered if she'd quit the book business because of her association with Brian Murray. It had been a minor scandal when they'd gotten married, mostly because she'd broken up his marriage, but also because she was so much younger. And so much more attractive. The fact that they had been married for over ten years hadn't changed anyone's opinion that she was a gold digger.

I remembered a story I'd heard about her, probably from another local crime writer. This had been when Tess was still working as a publicist but had just started seeing Brian. She'd been at a cocktail party at Thrillerfest in New York City when someone made a disparaging remark about Brian, how he'd been mailing in his increasingly flimsy thrillers for years. It was not an untrue accusation, in my opinion, but apparently Tess slapped the person who had said it out loud, then stormed away. I remember that whoever had told me that story seemed to be telling it to show what a lunatic Tess was, but I'd heard it as a story that confirmed her essential love for Brian. I believed they had a good marriage.

I checked my phone to see if I had Tess Murray's information on it. I did: both her email address and her cell number. I sent her a message:

> Hey Tess, Malcolm here in case you don't recognize the number. Heard you were in the store and asked after me. Let's have dinner soon—the three of us. I'd love to catch up some more.

I turned my phone off after sending the message, but as soon as I set it down it buzzed, and there was a message from Tess: Yes!!! Come for dinner tomorrow night!!!

I wrote back telling her I'd love to come and asked her what time and what could I bring.

Seven and yourself!!! came the reply, so instantaneously that I wondered how she had time to even type the words. After the exclamation marks, she'd included a single red heart.

I went to the refrigerator to get a beer. I had some eggs and cheese and decided to make an omelet for dinner, even though I hadn't felt any kind of hunger since seeing Pruitt's body in the morning. I put a bunch of Michael Nyman CDs in my old CD player and listened to his score for *The End of the Affair* first. I made the omelet and ate half of it, then opened another beer. I went to my bookshelf and found the section where I kept my Brian Murray books. I had almost all of them. Definitely all the recent ones because Brian had his book launch parties at Old Devils and he always inscribed a book for me. But I also had most of the old paperbacks, the early Ellis Fitzgerald novels that I'd started reading when I was about ten years old. I didn't have to get those particular books from Annie's Book Swap because my mom was an Ellis Fitzgerald fan and bought all the books herself. The early ones were really good, like funnier Ross MacDonald novels. And it was a fairly big deal back then that the detective was a female, and a tough, uncompromising one at that. Brian had told me several times that in the first draft of the first Ellis Fitzgerald novel, *The Poison Tree*, that Ellis had been a man. His agent told him that the book was good but that it was a little familiar. He made Ellis a woman without changing anything else, and the book sold.

I pulled out the paperback edition of *The Sticking Place*. It was the fifth Ellis Fitzgerald book and the one that won the Edgar Award. For fans, it was either their favorite book in the series, or their least favorite book. For me, it was my favorite, at least it had been when I'd first read it as an adolescent. At the end of the previous book in the series, *Temperate Blood*, Ellis's on-again, off-again boyfriend, Peter Appleman, is killed by a member of the Boston Mafia. In *The Sticking Place*, Ellis gets her revenge, carefully and brutally murdering everyone who had been remotely involved in Appleman's death. The book has very little in common with the other books in the series. There are no buffoonish clients, or Ellis witticisms; it has more in common with one of Richard Stark's Parker novels.

I took *The Sticking Place*, along with a fresh bottle of beer, with me to my sofa. The book had been read so many times that some of the pages were slipping away from the cracked binding. The creased cover was black, with an image of a revolver, its cylinder cracked open to reveal six empty spaces where the bullets had been. I opened to the title page, not surprised to see my mother's name, in her handwriting, in the top right corner. Margaret Kershaw, and the date she'd bought the book. It had been July of 1988. So, I'd been thirteen years old, and it was almost certain that I'd read this book as soon as I could get my grubby hands on it, probably immediately after she'd finished. I think I remember her telling me it was very violent. I'm sure that made me all the more eager to read it for myself.

The book was dedicated to Brian Murray's first wife, Mary. I'd never known her, but Brian told me once that the reason he dedicated almost all his books to her was because she'd sulk for days if he didn't. He told me that divorcing her was good for many reasons, but mostly because he was now free to dedicate books to other people in his life.

I began reading the book and was instantly hooked. It opens with Ellis meeting with the head of the Boston Mafia at the bar at the Ritz and handing him a list of names. "Either you'll punish them, or I will. It's up to you." He scoffs at her, tells her that she needs to forget it and move on. The rest of the book is her single-minded pursuit of those responsible for her boyfriend's death. It's suspenseful and violent, and Ellis comes across as slightly psychotic. After each killing, she applies lipstick and kisses the dead man on the cheek, leaving an imprint. The book ends with her at the Ritz again, drinking chardonnay with the Mafia head, who apologizes for underestimating her, and together they agree that balance has been restored. She's gotten her revenge. He does ask her about the lipstick. "I thought it would give the police a kick," she said. "Nothing they like more than some killer with a trademark. Makes them think they're in a Clint Eastwood movie."

I finished the book at just past midnight, kept thinking about trademarks. Ultimately, that was what Charlie's murders were about, leaving a mark of a kind, a signifier that told the world that the murderer was more important than the victim. Charlie might have been inspired by a sense of revenge, or justice, when he'd asked me to kill Norman Chaney. But now it was about him. And about my list. And about me, too, I guess. What kind of person puts himself above his victims? What kind of person becomes obsessed with a list of books?

One of Brian's writer's tips he shares is that when you can't figure something out in the plot of your book, go to bed, and let your subconscious pick at it. I decided to do that, to try and finally get some sleep, and maybe even some answers.

CHAPTER 23

I spent the next morning flipping through all my Brian Murray books. I even sped-read his latest novel, *Die a Little*, in which Ellis Fitzgerald solves a gang murder at a local high school. The novel was so dated that it was a little embarrassing. Brian hated research, and I got the feeling that all he did to prepare for writing his latest book was watch a double feature of *Boyz in the Hood* and whatever that Michelle Pfeiffer movie was where she taught inner-city kids.

At just past noon I got a phone call from Agent Perez reminding me that I hadn't yet provided my whereabouts and movement for the times of the murders.

"Sorry," I said to her. "I got busy. Can we do them right now? Give me the dates and I'll see if I knew where I was when they occurred?"

"That's fine," she said.

I opened up my calendar on my laptop and we started going over dates; first, she asked me about Elaine Johnson.

"I sent that information to Agent Mulvey," I said. "I was in London when she died. September thirteen, right?"

"That's right," Agent Perez said. Then she asked me about Robin Callahan, who had been shot on August 16 of last year. My calendar had nothing that week except for the fact that I would have been at work that day. I told Agent Perez that, and she asked if anyone could vouch for me. August 16 had been a Saturday, so I told her that both of my employees had probably worked that day, and that she was more than welcome to question them. Next, she asked me about Jay Bradshaw, the man who was beaten to death in his garage in Dennis on the Cape. It turned out that that had happened on August 31.

"I flew to London on that Sunday," I said.

"What time?"

"The flight was at six-twenty so I probably left for the airport at three."

"That's pretty early," she said.

"I know," I said. "I like to get there early if I can. I'd rather have extra time there than be running late."

For the two other cases she asked me about—Bill Manso and Ethan Byrd—I had no solid alibi, even though they were probably days when I was at Old Devils.

"Sorry I can't help you more," I said.

"You've been helpful, Mr. Kershaw. I would like you to send me the exact flight numbers for your trip to London if you have them."

"Sure," I said, deciding not to remind her that I'd already sent those to Agent Mulvey.

"And just so we're being thorough, and I know this is a long time ago, but can you tell me where you were on August twenty-seventh of 2011?"

"I'll look. What was it that happened on that date?" I said.

"That was the date that Steven Clifton was killed in a bike accident near Saratoga Springs."

"You mentioned his name before. I don't know who he is. Agent Mulvey never said anything about him."

"His homicide was in her notes," Perez said.

I had flipped backward through my online calendars. I thought of making something up, but said, instead, "I was probably working that day, but, honestly, it was a long time ago. My calendar has nothing."

"That's fine, Mr. Kershaw. Not a problem, but I thought I'd ask."

"Okay, thanks," I said.

I thought that would be the end of the phone call, but Agent Perez coughed, then said, "I know I already asked you this, but when Agent Mulvey came to you, were you convinced right away that there was a connection between your list and the unsolved crimes? I'd like to hear your response again."

"I wasn't convinced, not right away, but maybe that had something to do with me not wanting to admit to a connection. It's a bad feeling, you know, having written some dumb list, and then finding out that someone else is using it to commit actual murders."

"I'm sure it is."

"She told me about the bird murders, first, and how she connected them to *The A.B.C. Murders*—"

"The Agatha Christie book?"

"Right. It seemed a stretch, honestly. But the man killed on the train tracks—Bill Manso—that murder did sound like it was emulating *Double Indemnity*, but, like I said, I didn't really believe it until we found the books at Elaine Johnson's house. Then it was obvious. And it was obvious that the murderer wanted me to know about it. Or wanted it to point to me, I guess. I don't really know. We talked a lot about it, the two of us."

"Who? You and Agent Mulvey?"

"Yes. We thought about what the person, what Charlie—that was the name we gave him—was trying to accomplish with the murders. And we thought that he really was trying to accurately convey the spirit of the original murders from the books."

"Can I ask you about one of her notes? She had written down the three names of what she called the 'bird murders,' and then she'd written: *Who was the actual target?* Do you know what that meant?"

"In *The A.B.C. Murders* a series of murders are committed so it will look like a lunatic is on a crime spree. But the murderer had only one victim in mind that he really wanted dead. The other murders were cover."

"So you think that might be the case with the bird murders?"

"I don't know if I think that, but it's a possibility."

"Maybe it's a possibility that all these crimes—all the ones tied to your list—are just covering for one murder."

"Sure," I said. "It's a possibility, but if that were the case, that's a lot of murders to commit to conceal one."

"Yes." There was a lengthy pause, and I wondered for a moment if our call had been disconnected, or if she were just thinking.

"So, if you had to guess," she finally said, "which one of the three in the bird murders do you think was the intended victim?"

"If you forced me, I'd say Robin Callahan because she's the best known of the three, and she pissed a lot of people off."

"That's what I think," she said, then there was another pause. "Do you mind if I call you back with any other questions I might have?"

"Of course not," I said, and we said our good-byes.

I called Old Devils. Emily answered.

"You still feel sick?"

"Not terrible, but not great."

"Stay home. It's fine here."

I was about to end the call but decided that while I had Emily on the line I could ask her some questions.

"Can I ask you some names and you can tell me if you've heard of them?" I said.

"Uh, sure," she said.

"Ethan Byrd."

She was quiet for a moment, then said, "Haven't heard of him."

"Jay Bradshaw."

"No."

"Robin Callahan."

"Yeah, of course. She was that insane newscaster who got murdered. I'm sure she'll be the subject of an eventual true crime bestseller."

"Why do you say she was insane?"

"I don't know. I guess I heard it. She wrote the book about adultery, right?"

"Right," I said.

After ending the call, I thought some more about Robin Callahan being the intended victim of the three bird murders. And even if there hadn't been an obvious intended victim, there must have been someone that Charlie thought of first. He knew he wanted to emulate the ABC killings, and he knew he wasn't going to use the alphabet. If he decided that he wanted to kill Robin Callahan, then the way to cover it would be to find two more victims with names that suggested a bird. And Robin Callahan was a natural victim in the sense that she'd upset people. She advocated for adultery, and she'd wrecked at least two marriages.

In the afternoon I slept on the sofa. I dreamed I was being chased again, like I always did. Even when I was young, I would have these dreams in which I suddenly found out that my parents, my friends, my teachers were all monsters, and that I needed to run from them. In the worst dreams I found myself powerless to move, my legs heavy, my feet stuck to the earth. That afternoon, in my dream, the only person I wasn't running from was Gwen Mulvey. She was at my side, and together we were trying to escape the murderous horde. When I woke up, I ran to the bathroom thinking I might be sick, but I wasn't.

I dressed for dinner, tucking a blue checked shirt into a pair of dark corduroys, then putting on my favorite sweater, a cashmere rollneck in black, the last gift I'd received from Claire, on the Christmas before she died. I stood in front of a floor-length mirror and, in my mind, I asked Claire how I looked. *You look fine*, she said. *You always look fine.* I imagined her running her fingers through my short gray hairs.

What should I do? I asked her. *About these murders?*

It's your mess, she said. *You need to fix it.*

It was something she used to say, although when she said it, she'd always be referring to herself. It was what she said after confessing to me that she'd gotten involved with drugs again. I told her I could help, and she said, *Ugh, no. It's my fucking mess and I need to fix it myself.* I used to think this trait of hers—the way she owned her failings—was a good thing, but now I'm not so sure. Her life was messy, but the most important thing for her was to avoid confrontation, to not upset people, to take on all the blame herself. Hurting herself was fine, but she would go out of her way to not hurt anyone else.

It was her prime directive, the need to avoid collisions. To avoid letting other people take care of her.

It's my fucking mess.

But she was wrong.

left the house without checking the weather and found that the snow had picked up. It was now coming down in thick clumps, sticking to trees and bushes, but melting on the sidewalks and roads.

Before heading to Brian's house in the South End, I went to a wine shop on Charles Street and bought a bottle of petite sirah. I was halfway out the store when I turned around. I bought a bottle of Zwack, a Hungarian herbal liqueur that I liked. Then I walked to Old Devils, where Brandon and Emily would be getting ready to close up for the night. Before entering the store, I stood outside in the snow for a moment, peering through the window into the warm glow of the bookstore's interior. Brandon was talking to a customer, and even though I couldn't hear the specific words, I could hear the deep boom of his voice all the way out on the street. Emily was in the background moving back and forth behind the checkout desk. Friday nights and Saturdays during the day were the times when the three of us—the Old Devils Bookstore employees—were most likely to all be working, and it felt strange to be outside looking in. The world kept going, I guess.

I pushed through the door and greeted Brandon by offering him the bottle of Zwack.

"What?" he said, his voice high, dragging out the word.

"Peace offering," I said. "I feel bad I've been so absent, lately. You guys have been picking up the slack."

"Yeah, we have," he said and went back to show Emily.

I said hello to the customer, a young woman I recognized as a local mystery author who had given a reading at our store the previous year. Her name had suddenly escaped me.

"How're things?" she said. She had large dark eyes close together in a narrow face. The fact that she parted her straight black hair in the middle made her look like someone Edward Gorey might have drawn.

"Things are fine," I said. "What's new with you?"

Before she could answer, Brandon had pulled Emily out from the back offices and was calling me over. "You, too, Jane," he said. Her full name suddenly came to me: Jane Prendergast. She had written a mystery novel called *The Owl Shall Stoop*. We walked over to where Brandon was pouring out shots into the small water glasses we kept in the back.

"Come in to browse some books, and end up getting a shot," I said to Jane.

"She's part of the family," Brandon said, and Emily, now holding her drink, flushed a deep red. Brandon looked from her to me, and said, "Oh."

Emily said, "Jane and I are seeing each other."

I said, "That explains why you're always putting Jane's books on the front table." And now Jane looked embarrassed, too, and I apologized, and said that I was just kidding. The four of us drank. "To Old Devils," I said.

Emily shuddered and asked me what Zwack was. I said I didn't really know but that it seemed appropriate for the weather, like something a St. Bernard would bring you if you were trapped by an avalanche. I stayed a little longer but turned down a second drink. It was nearing seven, our closing time, and also the time that I was supposed to be in the South End. I suddenly didn't want to go. It felt safe in the store, and I just didn't know what was going to happen at Brian and Tess's house. I texted Tess and told her I'd be there closer to seven thirty, and then I helped Brandon and Emily close up. Jane stuck around, waiting for Emily to get off her shift.

By the time I was walking across Boston Common toward the South End, the temperature had dropped some more, and snow was beginning to stick to the paved pathways. I passed the frog pond, lit up and full of skaters, then walked down Tremont Street, over the Pike, and into the South End. Despite the weather, it was a Friday night and people were out in force, filling the restaurants and bars. The Murrays lived in a bow-fronted brick town house on a residential street. Their front door was painted a dark blue. I pushed the doorbell and heard chimed notes from inside.

"Thank you, Mal," Tess said, as I handed her the bottle of wine, wishing I'd brought them something more interesting. "Come in, get warm. Brian's upstairs making drinks."

I walked up the narrow stairway, the walls adorned with framed covers from the Ellis Fitzgerald series. At the top of the stairs I turned and entered the large second-floor living room. Brian was standing and staring into the fireplace, where it looked as though a fire had just been lit. "Hey, Brian," I said.

He turned. He was holding a glass of whiskey with his good hand. "What can I get you?" he said, and I told him I'd have whatever he was having. From a waist-high cabinet he poured whiskey from a cut-glass decanter into a lowball glass, added a small cube of ice from a bucket, and brought it over to me. On the coffee table between two sofas was a wooden block with cheese and crackers on it. We sat down, and he put down his drink in order to lean over to get himself a cracker.

"How's the arm?" I said.

"If you live as long as me, it turns out you just get used to having two arms. It's not so easy to lose one of them. Even temporarily."

"Tess helps."

"Well, yes, she does help, but she won't let me forget that fact. No, I'm kidding. It's nice to have her here. Tell me about the store. What's selling?"

We talked shop for a while, then Tess came up the stairs and perched on the edge of the sofa that Brian sat on. She wore an apron and her face was red and shiny as though she'd been peering into cooking pots. The Murrays' dog, a speckled hound called Humphrey, had followed Tess into the room, and after briefly sniffing at my outstretched hand, began nosing toward the cheese board.

"Humphrey," Brian and Tess said at the same time, and he sat back on his haunches, his tail slapping the floor.

"What's for dinner?" I said, and I studied the two of them as she replied. Tess's eyes were bright, as though she were excited. Brian watched her the way he might watch a bartender, with slight disinterest, until, of course, you needed another drink.

"Have one more drink, the two of you, then come downstairs for dinner," Tess said before she left. She squeezed my shoulder as she passed me on the way to the stairs, then slapped her thigh and Humphrey followed her out the door.

"I'll get it," I said and took Brian's empty glass and mine to the liquor cabinet. I poured two fingers of scotch in his glass and a little less in mine. I added ice to each of our drinks then brought them back.

"I'll break out the good stuff later," Brian said. "I have a Talisker twenty-five-year-old around here somewhere."

"Don't waste it on me," I said. "This tastes fine."

"Well, we're drinking midweek scotch and unless I'm mistaken, today is Friday, at least that's what Tess said. I'll break out something better later."

"You ever thought of writing a book about drinking?" I said.

"My agent's mentioned it to me a few times. Not because he thinks anyone'll buy it, but because he thinks at least I might profit a little from the time I waste drinking the stuff."

"Before I forget," I said. "I just reread *The Sticking Place*."

"What made you do that?" he said, but I could tell from his face that he was pleased.

"I was going through all my copies of your books, and I just cracked it open and began reading it. Didn't stop until I finished."

"Yeah, I think in retrospect that Ellis should have killed more people. I loved writing that book. You know, I still have readers who send me letters telling me that they pretend that book doesn't exist. And I get letters telling me it's the only good thing I ever wrote."

"Well, can't please everyone all the time."

"That's the truth. I remember when I wrote *Sticking Place* I showed it to my agent first. My agent back then. You remember Bob Drachman? He told me he couldn't put it down, but that they'd never publish it. Ellis wasn't a coldhearted killer, he said. You'll lose half your readers. I told him I might lose half, but I'd get twice as many back. He asked for a second draft, one that wasn't so brutal, so, of course, I added another murder."

"Which one?" I said.

"I can't remember. No, I do. I think it's the guy she locks in the freezer and leaves there. Yeah, that was the one, because Bob admitted he liked that scene when he read the final book. Anyway, I told him to submit the manuscript or I'd look for another agent, and so he sent it in. They published it, and, guess what, the world kept turning."

"And you probably doubled your readers."

"I don't know about that, but I didn't lose many. And I picked up an Edgar, so there was that."

"It's a good book."

"Thanks for that, Mal," he said.

"You never wanted to write another one in the same vein? Another Ellis revenge book?"

"Nah, not really. Thing is, you only need to do it once, and then the reader knows that Ellis has this side to her. But if every time she lost someone she loved, she went on some kind of killing spree, then she'd be someone else. No, it only happens once. She gets broken. She gets her revenge, and she knows she can never let that side of her take over again. I did, however, write a book without her once, did I ever tell you about that?"

He had, of course, but I told him that I didn't think so.

"Yeah, I wrote a standalone. This was a couple of years after *Sticking Place*, I think. It was another revenge book but with a guy this time. South Boston cop whose wife gets raped and murdered by a bunch of Irish thugs. He tracks 'em down and takes them all out. I wrote it in about two weeks, read it over, and realized I'd basically rewritten *Sticking Place*. So I stuck it in my drawer and forgot about it."

"You still have it?"

"Jesus," he said, scratching the side of his rubbery nose. "That's when I was living with Mary out in Newton so who knows if it survived the move. But, yeah, I don't remember throwing it out so it's around here somewhere."

"You talking about Mary?" Tess said, coming into the room. She was no longer wearing the apron, and it looked as though she'd put on some makeup.

"Yeah, the good old days," Brian said. "Dinner ready?"

"Dinner's ready."

We went down to the ground floor and ate by candlelight at the dining room table nestled in front of the bay windows that looked out onto the street. Humphrey the dog had been given some sort of treat and was busy chewing on it from his dog bed in the corner. Tess had made braised short ribs, and between the three of us we went through three bottles of wine before she brought out dessert, a clementine tart.

"Did you make this?" I said.

"God, no. I cook, but I don't bake. Who wants port?"

"We don't," Brian said, looking at me. "Let's have some of that whiskey I was talking about earlier. The Talisker."

"You can have that," Tess said. "I'll have port."

"Can I get it for you?" I said and stood up, banging my thigh a little against the edge of the table.

"Thank you, Mal, that would be lovely. There's port down in our cellar. Bri, tell him which bottle he should grab. And the whiskey's upstairs, I think."

I was given my instructions and went down into the basement first to look for the port. I'd never been down there before; it was semifinished, the walls Sheetrocked, but the floor just poured cement. Along one wall was an enormous bookcase. I went over to look at it and found that it was entirely filled with books by Brian Murray, all the various versions, including foreign editions, of his Ellis Fitzgerald series. I stood, staring at them for a moment, aware that I'd had far too much to drink at dinner. The dim light of the basement made it feel like I was in a dream. Conversation at dinner had been entertaining, Tess and Brian using me as an audience for their slightly hostile, slightly flirty back-and-forth insults. But as I swayed in front of the bookshelf, holding what looked to be a Russian paperback edition of *To Play the Villain*, I kept thinking back to what Brian and I had talked about over drinks, about how much he clearly enjoyed writing his violent, revenge novels. How he'd written one and never published it. I wanted to get back to that conversation.

The other side of the basement was filled with floor-to-ceiling wine racks. Brian had told me to look for a bottle of Taylor Fladgate Tawny Port that should be in the upper right. I pulled several bottles before I found the right one and brought it back upstairs and into the kitchen, where Tess was piling dishes in their enormous sink.

"For you," I said.

I was not entirely surprised when, after she took the bottle, she thanked me, then placed it on the counter and pulled me in for a hug. "So nice to have you here, Mal," she said, "I hope you're having fun, too."

"Of course," I said.

She placed a hand along my jawline and told me how sweet I was. "Go get Brian his whiskey before he sobers up. I'll open the port."

I went up the stairs and into the living room. All that remained of the fire was a few smoldering embers in a pile of ash. The room was still warm. I walked to the liquor cabinet, crouched down, and opened it. Inside there were about a dozen bottles, all whiskey as far as I could tell. I found the Talisker and pulled it out. Behind it was a triangular bottle of whiskey called Dimple Pinch. It was the same scotch that had been lying at the feet of Nick Pruitt. I was sure of it. The shape of the bottle was so unique—three-sided and each side dented in, a little. Thin wire encased the bottle. I dug further into the cabinet and found there were two more bottles of the same scotch, each unopened. This was probably Brian's midweek scotch, the one he put in his decanter on top of the cabinet.

I stood, still holding the Talisker, wishing I was less drunk, wishing I could figure out exactly what to do next. I heard someone enter the room, but it was only Humphrey, breathing heavily, bounding toward the cheese and crackers still on the coffee table.

CHAPTER 25

With the whiskey between us, I listened to Brian tell the story of the weekend he spent getting drunk with Charles Willeford in Miami. Brian knew I was a fan of *The Burnt Orange Heresy*, so he'd told me the Willeford story many times. It changed a little bit every time.

I'm not a connoisseur of scotch but even I could tell that the Talisker was good stuff. Still, I'd bring the glass to my lips, and only sip the tiniest amount. I needed to think about the significance of those bottles of Dimple Pinch I'd seen in the cabinet upstairs. Could Brian Murray be Charlie? My immediate answer was a definitive no. He was one of those men who could talk a good game, but who couldn't actually *do* a whole lot of things. He didn't drive, he couldn't cook. I'm sure he didn't make his own travel arrangements or pay his taxes or figure out his own bills. He could write, he could drink, and he could talk. There'd be no way for him to plan, then execute, actual murders.

But what if he had help?

While we drank, I could see through into the kitchen, where Tess was cleaning up, humming to herself. She seemed happy, relaxed almost. There was a break in Brian's story and I said, "Did you ever read the blog posts that I wrote for the website?"

"What website?" he said.

"Our website. The Old Devils site. The blog that's attached to it."

"Oh, right," he said, remembering. I'd pestered him over the years to write something for it, just an occasional book recommendation, or a list of his favorites, but he never did. "What about it?"

"Do you remember a list I wrote, a few years back, even before you were an owner, called 'Eight Perfect Murders'?"

He scratched at the inside of his eye, and I studied him. "*That* list, I do remember," he finally said. "I think the first time I ever knew your name was from reading that list. And you know what I thought?"

"No."

"I thought: 'I can't believe the prick didn't include one of my books.'"

I laughed. "Is that really what you thought?"

"Sure. You get to a point in your career where every ten-best list or year-end best list is a personal affront if you're not part of it. But the thing is . . . the thing *was*, if I remember correctly, it wasn't that you didn't include one of my books, it's that you hadn't included *The Reaping Season*. I mean, Jesus, Mal, come on." He was smiling now.

"Help me out," I said. "The one with Carl . . ."

"With Carl Boyd, right."

I did remember that one. It was an early book. The villain, Carl Boyd, was a psychopath out to get revenge on everyone who had ever belittled him. And that included a lot of people. If I remembered it correctly, Carl was a pharmacist. He'd kidnap his victims before killing them, give them an injection of sodium pentothal, or something similar, something to make them tell the truth. Then he'd ask them what their worst fear was, ask them to describe the death that terrified them most. Someone would admit that he was claustrophobic, for example, so Carl Boyd would bury him alive in a box.

"How could I forget that one?" I said.

"Apparently, you did."

"It wouldn't have fit in on that list I was doing, anyway. That was specifically for perfect murders. Unsolvable murders."

"What are you two talking about?" It was Tess, coming in from the kitchen, wiping her damp hands down her thighs.

"Murder," I said, at the same time that Brian said, "Disrespect."

"Good times," Tess said. "I was thinking of brewing a pot of coffee and wanted to know how much I should make. Brian, yes, I know you're not interested."

"I'll have some," I said.

"Regular? Decaf?"

"I'll have the real stuff," I said and wondered if I'd slurred a little on the word *stuff*.

She turned back to the kitchen and Brian said, "There's no such thing, really."

"No such thing as what?" I said.

"I'm talking about the list you wrote," he said. "There's no such thing as a perfect murder."

"In fiction, or in real life?"

"In both. Too many variables, always. Let me guess what you had on that list. *Strangers on a Train*, right?"

"Right," I said. Brian was sitting up a little taller now, seemed a little less drunk.

"Of course, you did. I actually remember this list now, and not just because I wasn't on it. *Strangers on a Train*, no disrespect to Pat Highsmith, is a stupid idea for a perfect murder. What makes it clever? That you get some stranger to do your killing for you? And that way you can have a rock-solid alibi? Not a chance. The minute you get some stranger to kill someone for you, you might as well turn yourself into the police. It's too unpredictable. If you're going to kill someone, kill them yourself. You can't trust someone else with a killing."

"What if you knew for a fact that the person would never turn you in?"

Brian made a face, lowering his brow and tightening his mouth. "Look," he said, "I don't pretend to be an expert in psychology, but I do know one thing, and it's the one thing I remind myself over and over when I write a book. No one knows what's going on in another person's mind, or in their heart." He touched his head and his chest. "They just don't. Not even a married couple that have been together for fifty years. You think they know what each other's thinking? They don't. None of us know shit."

"So you don't know what Tess is thinking right now?"

"Well," he said, and raised his eyebrows, shrugging. "I know some of what she's thinking about tonight, but that's only because she told me."

"That doesn't count."

"No, it doesn't. All right, then, what is she thinking, besides trying to remember how many scoops of coffee it takes to make a pot? I don't really know. Well, that's not entirely true. I know a bunch of what she's thinking. For example, she's probably counting my drinks and wondering at what point she'll decide to tell me I've had enough. She's probably already thinking about some pair of three-hundred-dollar jeans she wants to buy. And she's thinking about you, buddy."

"What do you mean?"

"Ever since we ran into you at the bar the other night, she's been talking nonstop about getting you over here for dinner."

"She's got an agenda," I said, remembering what she'd told me about wanting me to convince Brian to get some help into the house.

"Tess always has an agenda."

I could smell the coffee, now, from the kitchen, a dark, bitter smell that made me feel more sober just by smelling it. The shift in conversation to Tess had unnerved me. I'd known Brian a long time, and I'd seen him drunk many, many times, but the way he was acting now, like he had a secret, was something new to me. He'd always been someone who told me what was on his mind.

"What's her agenda tonight?" I said.

"I have an idea, but, like I said earlier, we never really know what's going on inside of someone's head."

I heard the clink of porcelain on porcelain and turned to see Tess coming toward the table, carrying a tray that contained two coffee cups, plus sugar and cream. She placed one of the cups, and its saucer, in front of me, then sat down, sighing as she did so.

"Thank you, thank you," I said, adding some cream to my coffee and taking a sip.

"You want some Irish whiskey for that coffee?" Brian said. "I've got some around here somewhere. Just don't put scotch in it."

"It's perfect as is," I said.

"Really," Tess said. "What *have* you two been talking about out here?" She was adding cream and stirring her coffee. Her lips were slightly stained from the port she'd been drinking, and her hair, that normally hung down on either side of her face, was pushed back behind her ears.

"You tell her," Brian said. "I have to go take a leak." He put his good hand on the table and stood up. Tess and I both watched him, waiting to see how steady he'd be, but he seemed okay as he walked from the room.

"Did you mention anything about him getting some real help in here?" Tess said, after we both heard the bathroom door shut.

"I didn't, no," I said. "I forgot we'd talked about that."

"That's okay," she said. "Anything you mention to him tonight he's not going to remember in the morning, anyway. I am curious, though, what you two were blathering on about in here. Brian sounded almost passionate."

"He was talking about how no one really knows anyone else, how we never know exactly what another person is thinking about."

"You think that's true?" she said, blowing on her coffee. She had little lines around her lips, as though she'd been a smoker for years. I had a vague image of seeing her smoke a cigarette, but not for years.

"I do, actually. I think about it a lot, how we never know the truth of people. But I don't always know if that's just me, or if it's everyone."

"If what's just you?" she said.

"I think I have a hard time getting to know people. Not superficially. I'm fine with that. But when I get close to someone, that's when I feel they disappear. That's when I look at them and I suddenly have no idea what they're really like, or what they're really thinking."

"Was that how you felt about your wife?" she said.

"Claire?" I said, automatically.

Tess laughed. "Unless you've been married more than I know about."

I thought for a moment, trying to remember if I'd ever discussed Claire with Tess in the past. Or even if I'd ever discussed Claire with Brian. "What was the question?" I finally said.

"Ugh, I've made you uncomfortable. I'm sorry."

"No, no. I'm just a little drunk."

"Drink your coffee. It'll help."

I took another sip. Then, without really thinking about it, I let the coffee slide back out of my mouth into the cup. I was being paranoid, I knew, but if Tess or Brian, or both of them, had intentions to harm me, putting drugs in my food or drink would make a lot of sense.

"I felt closer to Claire than I've ever felt to anyone before or since," I said. "But sometimes I didn't know her."

Tess was nodding. "I feel the same way about Brian, close, I mean, then every once in a while, he'll say something, or else I'll read something he wrote, and I wonder if I know anything about him at all. It's universal, that feeling. What got you two talking about that?"

I thought back, worried that my brain was working too slowly. "We were talking about a list I wrote once. About perfect murders. And Brian was saying how you could never trust anyone to commit a murder for you, that you never really knew what they were thinking."

Tess was quiet for a moment, thinking. "I guess if you were going to get someone to commit a murder for you, the best person would be your spouse."

"Yeah," I said. "Would you do that for Brian?"

"I suppose it would depend on who he wanted me to murder. But I'd think about it. It's just the kind of wife I am. People think that Brian broke up with Mary and married me because I was younger, but that wasn't it at all. Even though we spend a lot of time apart, Brian and I, we're very close, you know. Closer than he ever was with anyone. We're loyal. I'd do anything for him, and he'd do anything for me."

She leaned in toward me as she was talking, and I could smell the coffee on her breath, mixed with the wine.

"Speaking of Brian . . ." I said, and she leaned back, cocked her head to listen.

"He's fine, I think," she said. "He's probably just giving you and me some time alone together."

"Are you sure? Maybe we should check on him?" I was suddenly nervous. Maybe it was all the alcohol, but I felt like I was in a stage play, and that the evening had been planned in such a way as to culminate with me alone with Tess over coffee.

She touched my knee with her fingers, then stood. "You're right. I'll go get him and tell him it's time to go to bed. But you should stay, Mal. I mean it. The night is young. Let's move over there and have another drink." She tilted her head to indicate two small couches facing each other by a tall bookcase, forming a cozy nook between the dining room and the open kitchen.

"Okay," I said, and she got up and walked out of the room. I sat for a moment, trying to figure out what to do. There was music playing, from the kitchen, Ella Fitzgerald singing "Moonlight in Vermont." I sniffed at my undrunk coffee, then took another small sip. Then I picked up Tess's coffee and tried that. Like mine, she'd only put cream in it, no sugar, but it tasted noticeably different. I went back and forth between the two, wondering if I was going insane. If she'd wanted to poison me she could have put something in my wine, or even in the food. Still, maybe she'd wanted to wait until the end of the meal. I stood up, walking past the couches, and into the kitchen. I could now hear Tess's voice, speaking to Brian down the hall, but couldn't make out the words. The kitchen was immaculate. I didn't know exactly what I was looking for, just something that would further prove what I was already suspecting. That I'd been brought here for a reason.

I went and looked at the deep, stainless steel sink. It was empty. In the dishrack were a few pots and pans, and I could hear the steady thrum of a dishwasher, although I couldn't see where one was. Beside the coffeepot, its red light on, was a cutting board, and on top of the cutting board was a cylindrical piece of wood, very heavy. I picked it up and it felt like a weapon in my hand. It was probably a rolling pin, although different from any rolling pin I'd ever seen.

"What'cha looking for, Mal?"

Tess stood at the entrance to the kitchen. "Oh, nothing," I said. "Just admiring your kitchen. How's Brian?"

"Asleep in the downstairs guest room. Or, as I like to call it, Brian's bedroom. He's in there more nights than he's upstairs."

I put the roller down on the cutting board. "I'm going to get going," I said.

"You sure?"

"Yes. I'm a little drunk, myself, I think, and I haven't been sleeping well lately. I'm just going to head home."

"I understand," Tess said. "I don't like it, but I understand. Let me get your coat."

I stood in the foyer and waited for what seemed like a long time, then Tess brought me my winter coat, tucked under an arm. She came up close to me, and said, "What if I told you you weren't allowed to leave." Her voice was different. Flatter, quieter.

I grabbed my coat with my left hand and shoved out with my right, hoping to put her off balance long enough for me to get out the door. She stumbled backward, then fell, landing in a sitting position on the hardwood floor. "Oww, what the fuck, Mal?" she said.

"Stay right there." I shook the coat, now in my possession, wondering if she'd hidden a weapon in it. The rolling pin, maybe.

Tess rolled a little onto her side in order to get her legs under her. "What is up with you?" she said.

Doubt flooded me, but I said, "I know what you did to Nick Pruitt," just hoping that saying a name out loud would help confirm it.

She looked up at me, her hair now hanging on either side of her face, and said, "I have no idea who you're talking about. Who's Nick Pruitt?"

"You killed him two nights ago. You saw his book in my store, and you realized that I was investigating him because of his relationship with Norman Chaney. So you got to him first. You got him to drink with you, Dimple Pinch whiskey. Maybe you goaded him into drinking too much."

Tess was staring at me, her eyes confused, and her mouth in a half smile, as though at any moment I was going to reveal the punch line to a joke. "Don't you want me to know about it, to know about you? Isn't that why I'm here?"

Tess now looked concerned. She said, "Mal, I'm going to get up. I have no idea what you're talking about. Is this something between you and Brian? Is this a joke?"

"You know that list I mentioned," I said.

"The list of murders?"

"Someone is using that list to actually kill people. I know I sound crazy. I'm not. The FBI have been talking with me. I thought it might have something to do with you. Or with Brian."

"Why?" she said.

"Why were our coffees different? Why did you just tell me I couldn't leave?"

She lowered her head and laughed a little. "Please, help me up. I promise I won't kill you."

I leaned down, and she took my hand and I helped her to her feet. "Our coffee's tasted different because mine is decaf and yours was regular. And the reason I said you couldn't leave was because I was trying to seduce you."

"Oh," I said.

"Brian knew, or Brian knows, I mean, that I was going to try. He's fine with it. That part of our life is over, and now that I'm here in Boston for a while . . . He likes you." She shrugged. "So did I."

"Sorry," I said.

"Don't be sorry. It's just ridiculous, is all. I'm trying to get you to spend the night, and you think I'm trying to kill you."

"I haven't been getting much sleep," I said, suddenly embarrassed.

"Is it true? About the list?"

"It is," I said. "Someone's using it to kill people. And I'm pretty sure it's someone who knows me."

"Jesus. Are you willing to tell me about it? It really isn't that late."

"Not right now, okay?" I said. "I really do think I should get going. I'm sorry I pushed you. I'm sorry I . . ."

"It's fine," she said and hugged me, squeezing tight. I thought she'd try and kiss me, as well, but I guess that moment had passed. She pulled away and said, "Have a safe walk home. You want me to call you a cab, or anything?"

"No, thanks," I said. "And next time we see each other, I'll tell you more about what's been going on."

"I'll hold you to that."

After the door shut behind me, I stood outside on their landing for a moment. The street was quiet, the snow sticking to everything. I heard the distant sound of music and saw that people were exiting a bar down on the corner. I took the three steps down to the sidewalk and turned left, aware that I was stepping on pristine snow, leaving behind fresh marks. I hadn't gone even half a block when I heard the steps behind me, rushing, and I turned to see Tess moving fast, coatless, something in her hand. I must have flinched because she stopped, three feet away from me, and reached out with a book in her hand.

"I forgot," she said, a little bit breathless. "Brian really wanted you to have this. It's an ARC of his new one. Don't tell him I told you but he's going to dedicate it to you."

CHAPTER 26

I was home an hour later, cold and damp, and out of breath from clambering up my steep street in the accumulating snow.

I shed my coat, and my shoes and socks, and lay down on the sofa in the dark. I needed to think. If nothing else, the long walk home had sobered me up, and images from the farcical night I'd just spent at Brian and Tess's kept repeating in my mind. It now seemed ridiculous that I had accused Tess of murdering Nick Pruitt and the others from the list, but when I'd said it, when I'd been there, convinced my coffee had been poisoned, it made perfect sense. I wondered what Tess was doing right now. Had she woken Brian up, told him the story of how I'd shoved her to the ground and accused her of murder. Did she think I'd gone insane? I decided that I'd call her first thing in the morning, maybe confide in her a little more about what had been going on recently. I also thought a little bit about her offer, about the reason I was brought to their house in the first place. In different circumstances, I might be in bed with Tess Murray right now.

I sat up, and Brian Murray's book fell off my lap and onto the floor. I turned on the lamp, then picked the book up, looking at it for the first time. The title was *The Wild Air*, and the cover art, like the art of so many of his covers, showed the back of Ellis Fitzgerald looking out toward some sort of landscape, or crime scene. On this cover, she was looking at a single tree on the horizon line, a flock of birds taking off from its branches, one of the birds lying on a snow-covered field. Presumably dead.

I turned to the page where the dedication usually was, and all it said was *Dedication TK*, editor-speak for text that wasn't available yet. I wondered if Brian would still dedicate the book to me after he found out I thought his wife was a murderer.

The book began with a line of dialogue: *"What'll you have?" Mitch asked. Ellis hesitated. Her answer was* a glass of wine—*it was always a glass of wine*—*but this time she said, "Soda water and cranberry, thanks."*

I thought about reading the rest, but I decided I needed to get some rest instead. I put the book on the coffee table, turned off the lamp, and turned onto my side on the sofa, closing my eyes. I lasted about five minutes. My mind kept revving, going over and over the events of the past few days. Then I remembered the message I'd left on Duckburg trying to reconnect with Charlie and wondered if I had a response. I went and got my laptop, bringing it back to the sofa, and logged on under Farley Walker, my new alias. A blue dot indicated that I'd received a response to my latest message. I clicked through and read it: Hello, old friend, was all it said.

I wrote back: Are you who I think you are?

There was no timestamp on the message, so I didn't know when I'd gotten it. Still, I waited, staring at the screen. Just when I was about to give up, a new message popped up: Do you even know my name, Malcolm?

I wrote back: I don't. Why don't you tell me?

Maybe I will but we should go to a private chat first.

I checked the box that made the conversation private. My heart was beating, and my jaw was clenched so tight that it was starting to throb.

Why? I wrote.

Why what? Why did I keep going with something that you
started? I think a better question is why did you stop?

I stopped because there was only one person that I wanted
dead. And once he was dead there was no reason to go on
killing.

There was a lengthy pause, and I was suddenly nervous that
Charlie had logged off. I wanted to talk with him more. Also, and
this was ridiculous, but it felt safe, somehow, seeing the words he
was typing on the screen. It meant he wasn't doing anything else,
I suppose.

Sorry for the delay, he eventually wrote. I need to be quiet where
I am.

Where are you?

I'll tell you, but not right now. It will ruin the rest of
this conversation and I'm really happy to be having this
conversation.

Something about his tone was starting to get to me, and I wrote,
You are fucking insane, you know that

A short pause. Then: I thought I was too. After I killed Eric Atwell
for you I felt so incredible good that I was convinced that I was a mon-
ster. It was all I could think about. I shot him five times and it was the
fifth shot that killed him. The first shot went into his stomach. He was in
a lot of pain but after I told him why he was going to die, I saw all that
pain get replaced by fear. I saw the knowledge on his face, the knowledge that he was about to die. Did you see that with chaney?

No, I wrote back.

Did he know why he was dying?

I don't know. I didn't tell him.

Maybe thats why you didn't enjoy it like I did. Maybe if you'd seen it in his eyes, him knowing what was happening to him and why, then you'd understand.

I didn't get any pleasure out of it, I wrote. And you did. That's a big difference between us.

Thats why I think you're the insame one, he wrote. You write a list that celebrates the art of murder and then I decide to actually do what that list proposes, to create actual art, and that doesn't make sense to you?

There's a difference between fiction and reality.

Not as much as you'd think, Charlie wrote. There's beauty in both and I know that you know that.

I wrote out the words There wasn't any beauty when I killed Norman Chaney then deleted them. I needed to think for a moment. I needed to get Charlie to trust me, to tell me either who he was, or where he was.

I wrote, Can we meet?

Oh, we've met came immediately back.

When?

I can see were your going with this. Just to save time I am not going to tell you who I am. Not now, like this. Theres more work to be done. Its amazing how you keep leading me to new perfect victims. You handed me Nick Pruitt on a silver plattter

He wasn't guilty of anything.

He was guilty of something, believe me. I thought it would be harder to get him to drink himself to death but I think he almost enjoyed it. The first drink was the hardest, then he just kept drinking whatever I gave him. He seemed amost happy.

I don't suppose I can get you to turn yourself in before you do anything else.

Only if you go with me, he wrote, like I hoped he would.

Of course, I wrote back. You and I together. We'll tell the whole truth.

There was a long pause, and I thought I'd lost him. Or else I thought he was actually thinking about it. Finally, he wrote:

Its tempting but I'm not done yet. And the thing is that you've provided me with two more victims, one who will die and one who'll go missing, just like red house mystery. You can help ifyou like.

My body went cold.

Let me think about it, I wrote back, already standing. I dressed quickly, pulling my damp socks back on, and putting on my shoes. I was shaking. He would be on his way right now to Brian and Tess's house. Or else he was already there. I grabbed my cell phone and immediately called Tess's number, thinking I could warn her not to let anyone into the house. It went straight to voice mail, and I didn't leave a message. I thought of calling 911, but somehow I knew that if I did make that call, the police would show up to find nothing, and I'd be stuck explaining why I'd made the call in the first place. I told myself I was making the right decision.

OUTSIDE, IT WAS SNOWING harder than it had been all night. I went up the hill to where my car was parked. The roads would be terrible, but I still thought I could get to the South End faster by car than on foot.

I U-turned and drove too fast down the hill, the car sliding at the bottom when I applied the brake, turning almost sideways. I took my foot off the brake and started tapping it, but the car kept going, sliding on its own accord through a red light and onto Charles Street. I braced for an impact, but there were no other drivers on the street. And just a few pedestrians, including a couple that had stopped on the sidewalk to watch my near accident.

When the car finally stopped, it was angled diagonally but pointing more or less in the right direction. I straightened it out and kept driving, going slower this time, telling myself that spinning off the road was the worst thing that could happen. Unless he was just trying to scare me, Charlie had identified his next victims. If I could get there first, I could at least warn them. But I was also wondering if Charlie was already there. He might have been in their house when we were having the conversation on Duckburg, writing from his phone. It would explain the typing errors. I tried to concentrate on driving, and not think about it. The snow was driving now, directly into my windshield. My wipers were working but ice was building up along the edges, and the windshield was fogging. I turned the defrost all the way up, rolled down my window, and stuck my head out, driving along the edge of the Common on Arlington that way. Then I got onto Tremont, and my windshield had cleared a little. I knew that I couldn't turn onto the Murrays' one-way street, so I'd already planned on leaving the car at the corner and walking the rest of the way. But then I passed their street and decided to keep going, to take my next right and see if I could loop back.

My body ached, and I forced myself to loosen my grip on the steering wheel. The side street I was on hadn't been plowed recently, and my wheels were spinning as I whipped along. As soon as I could I turned right then right again, hoping that would put me on the Murrays' side street. It looked right, even though all the residential streets in the South End looked alike to me. I slowed down, moving slowly, peering out my window to see if I could pick out the Murrays' house, with its blue door. I was about three-quarters down the street when I spotted it. Unlike most of the brick town houses, light glowed still from its street-facing windows. I tried not to think what that might mean, what I might find when I entered the house.

I parked in front of a hydrant, killed the engine, and stepped out of the car into three inches of icy slush. As I crossed the street toward the Murrays' house, I heard someone shout out "Can't park there," and turned to see a woman standing under a streetlight with her dog about four houses down. I waved at her and kept going.

I reached the door and suddenly wished that I had some kind of weapon, anything, really, and almost considered going back to my car to get the tire jack from the trunk. But I didn't want to waste any more time. I tried the door and it was locked, then pressed the doorbell while knocking at the same time, wondering what I'd do if no one answered. I was wiping at the octagonal window in the middle of the door when I heard footsteps on the other side. The door swung open.

CHAPTER 27

M al," Tess said in a husky voice, reaching out and taking hold of the inside of my jacket, pulling me inside.

"Is everything okay here?" I said, but she was shutting the door. And then she pushed herself up against me, and we were kissing. I kissed back, part of it relief that she was still here, still alive, and part because it just felt good. I also didn't want to tell her right away that I'd come back because I thought she was in danger. It would sound ludicrous.

We stopped kissing and hugged. She felt heavy in my arms, and I asked her again, "Everything okay here?"

She stepped out of our embrace, backed up, and said, "Why do you keep saying that?" Her voice was thick, and she blinked rapidly.

"You just seem . . . Are you drunk?" I said.

"Maybe," she said. "So what? You're drunk." She turned away from me, and her whole body lurched, as though she were about to fall. I moved quickly and took her by the arm, led her to one of the two facing couches just outside of the entryway to the kitchen. We both sat.

"I feel strange," she said, putting a hand on my shoulder, and leaning in. Her breath was bitter with the smell of coffee.

"Tell me what you've been doing since I left," I said.

"When did you leave?"

"Two hours ago. Maybe less. I'm not sure exactly."

"Oh, right. I licked my wounds, because, you know . . . and had some more coffee, and then I got tired, real tired, and I was going to go upstairs and get ready for bed, but thought I might take a little nap here on this couch, and then I heard the door, and you were here."

"Anyone else come by?"

"Anyone else come by? Here? *No.* Just you. Do you want to kiss again?"

I leaned in and kissed her, hoping to keep it short, but she opened her mouth and pressed hard against me. My eyes were open, but her hair was falling in waves and for a moment I couldn't see anything. I stopped the kiss and brought her head down to my chest.

"That's nice," she said, then mumbled something I couldn't understand.

We were like that for a minute. I could tell she was falling asleep on me, and I let it happen while I looked around at what I could see. It looked just as it had when I left, our coffee cups still on the dining room table in front of the bay windows, a single lamp still on by the table. And what I could see of the kitchen was lit by the under-cabinet lighting. The house was quiet, although I thought I could hear Brian snoring in the downstairs guest room. I wasn't sure. But if it was him, it was a good sign. He was still alive.

I knew that Charlie was in the house.

I'd already constructed a scenario. He'd followed me here tonight, probably waiting outside while I was inside having dinner with Brian and Tess. When I'd left, maybe he'd been planning to follow me, or maybe he'd been planning on breaking into Tess and Brian's house. But then an opportunity had presented itself. Tess had rushed out to give me Brian's book, leaving the door open behind her and unlocked. Charlie snuck inside. And then what? He'd hidden in the house, and somehow, he had managed to put something in Tess's coffee, probably whatever it was that he'd spiked Pruitt's whiskey with. I didn't believe she was drunk, or that she was any more drunk than she'd been when I'd left two hours earlier. No, she'd been drugged. And then I'd arrived before Charlie had done anything else to her. And now here we all were in the house together. Where was Charlie, exactly? Where would I be, if I were him?

I slowly eased Tess off my chest, and onto the couch, then stood up.

"Where you going?" Tess said, but her voice was low and mumbled. She tucked a hand under her cheek and breathed deeply in through her nose, her eyes still closed. I walked as quietly as I could into the kitchen. A side door led to the first-floor hallway; from there you could get to a half bathroom, and to the guest room where Brian was sleeping. There was also a closet, if I remembered correctly. I went to the counter and found the rolling pin I'd noticed earlier, picking it up in my right hand. I thought of getting a knife instead, but I liked how the rolling pin felt. It was a heavy piece of wood, obviously useless if Charlie had a gun. But it was something, and I felt better with it in my hand.

I considered staying in the kitchen, just standing there with my view on both the swinging side door and the large cutout that led to the dining and living room area. I could stand here all night, waiting for Charlie to make a move first. But I was also worried about Tess. Whatever was in her system might be enough to kill her. In what I hoped was my normal voice, I said, "I know you're here," out loud to the empty kitchen.

Nothing.

I waited for what felt like another five minutes and began to wonder if I was just being paranoid. Maybe Tess had just kept drinking after I'd left, and she was simply drunk. And maybe Charlie had been playing with me at this point, trying to manipulate me into rushing over here for nothing. I walked slowly back through into the living area. Tess hadn't moved; she was still curled up on the couch, a hand under her face. I crouched down and could hear her steady breathing. I turned left toward the hallway, aware that the old floor was creaking under every step. After I walked past the stairway, I pushed open the door to the bathroom. There was enough light from a lamp in the hallway for me to see that it was empty.

Then I heard the sound of steps behind me, and I froze.

The steps stopped coming, but I could hear heavy breathing. I turned, tightening my grip on the rolling pin. Humphrey the hound dog stood looking at me quizzically. I put my free hand out, and he came forward, sniffing at it, then losing interest and turning back toward the living room.

I turned again, deciding that I needed to look in on Brian, asleep in the guest room, and to make sure he was alone. Then maybe I could just leave the house? Maybe I didn't need to be here.

"What's the dog's name?"

The voice came from behind me. I recognized it, of course, and turned to see him, standing at the bottom of the stairs, the foyer light behind him so that his face was in shadow.

He held a gun at his side, casually, but when I took a step toward him, toward Marty Kingship, he lifted it and pointed it at my chest.

CHAPTER 28

H umphrey," I said.

"Huh," he said. "Like the actor?"

"I guess so. I don't know."

"Some guard dog."

"Yeah," I said. There was something in Marty's other hand, and it took me a moment to realize it was a cell phone. It looked out of place on Marty. I'd had drinks with him many times, seen him at readings at my store, but somehow, I couldn't recall ever seeing him look at a cell phone. I'd never seen him with a gun, either, but the cell phone looked more foreign on him than the gun.

"How long have you been here?" I said. "Were you typing on that thing? On the Duckburg site?" I jerked my head to indicate the phone.

"Yeah," he said. "Not bad, right? With *my* sausage fingers. Hey, look, let's go sit down." He gestured with the gun. "Maybe around the table. You can put down whatever it is you're holding in your hand, and I won't have to point this at you. Then we can have a nice chat."

"Okay," I said.

He turned and walked toward the table. I pictured myself sprinting and lunging, hitting him just as he turned with the gun, knocking him down on the ground. But all I did was follow him, and together we both sat at the table, in the same seats that Tess and I had been sitting in a few hours earlier. Marty pushed his back a few feet, then rested the gun on his thigh.

"What is that you're holding?"

"It's a rolling pin," I said, setting it down on the table.

"You pick it up here, or bring it with you?"

"No, I picked it up here."

There was a hanging ceiling light above the table that was still on, and I could see Marty's face much better in its light. He looked the way he always looked, sallow skin, disheveled, and like he'd forgotten to get any sleep lately, but there was something a little different about his eyes. I want to say they were more intense, more alive, but that wasn't quite it. It was more that they were happy. He might not be smiling but his eyes were.

"Thought you might come here with more firepower," he said. "Although I realize that's probably not your thing. Did you call the police?"

"Yes," I quickly said. "They'll be on their way right now."

He frowned. "Let's not lie to each other. Let's tell the truth, and then, together, we can figure out where to go next. I know you're thinking that your only chance here is to get the jump on me, but it's not. I'm going to be reasonable. And, honestly, I'm not young, but what is that word they condescendingly use for old people when they can get around on their own two feet?"

"Spry," I said.

"Right, spry. That's what I am. And if you decide to suddenly lunge at me, I'll put a fucking bullet right through your face."

He smiled.

"Okay," I said.

"Just warning you in advance. I don't want you to get any silly ideas."

I held up both my hands. "I'll stay right here," I said.

"Good. I trust you. Now we can talk. I keep thinking about the thing you just wrote me about fiction and reality. How your list of murders was fiction, and that there's some difference. I think you're right about that, Mal, but I think you're seeing it the wrong way. Fiction is so much better than reality. I know. I've been alive a long time. And you know where I learned that from, about fiction. I learned it from you. You got me into reading, and you got me into murder. It changed my life for the better. Hey, do you think they have beer here? I wouldn't mind a cold beer while we talk."

"I'm sure they do," I said.

He looked from the table all the way into the kitchen, where the large refrigerator gleamed in the dim lighting. "Can you go get us a couple? Can I trust you not to try and do something stupid?"

"Sure," I said.

I got up and walked to the kitchen while Marty pointed the gun in my direction. I passed the two couches; Humphrey the dog was now sprawled on the couch opposite from Tess, both of them asleep and oblivious. I opened the refrigerator, hunted around, and spotted two bottles of Heineken buried toward the back, located a bottle opener in one of the drawers, and popped their tops.

"Oh, Heineken," Marty said, smiling when I put it in front of him. "That's a pleasant surprise."

He took a sip, and so did I. My mouth was dry and gluey, and the beer tasted good, despite the circumstances. "Yeah, twice you've changed me, Mal, you know that?" Marty said, as though the conversation we'd started had kept running through his brain while I'd gotten the beers. "You introduced me to killing, and you introduced me to reading. And my life got better."

"I doubt I introduced you to killing," I said.

He laughed. "Oh, you did. I was a cop. That didn't make me a killer."

In all, I think we talked three hours that night. Marty talked the most, his voice getting hoarser the longer he spoke, but, despite this, the years seemed to fall away from him as he told his story. It was clear that doing what he'd done had brought new life to him. But it had not been enough. He also needed to tell someone about it.

He told me how five years earlier, back in 2010, the year that Claire died, he'd still been an officer in the Smithfield Police Department, considering retirement, and living with an unfaithful wife. On at least two separate occasions he'd put a loaded gun into his mouth late at night. He'd even considered taking out his wife first just to ensure she wouldn't enjoy herself anymore after he was gone. The only thing that really stopped him was his two kids, and the fact that they'd have to live with that for the rest of their lives. Still, he thought about it almost every day.

Around this same time, he'd been part of a small task force that had taken down an amateur prostitution ring operating out of a Smithfield laundromat. They'd advertised their services on Craigslist, but also on a shadier website called Duckburg. Marty had started perusing both sites, late at night, wondering if maybe he should have his own affair, wondering if could arrange something like that online, and if it would make a difference. It was where he found me, on Duckburg, looking for a fellow fan of *Strangers on a Train*. He hadn't read the book—Marty wasn't a reader, yet—but he'd seen the movie as a kid and never forgotten it. Robert Walker. Farley Granger. *I do your murder, and you do mine.* He'd responded to my query. He even considered asking me to kill his wife, but realized that he'd never get away with it, not even if he had an alibi. But there *was* someone he wanted dead even more than his cheating spouse. Norman Chaney had been a small-time business owner in Holyoke; he owned three service stations, none of them known for the excellence of their automotive service, but all of them known as being connected to the local drug trade. They'd never pinned anything concrete onto Chaney but it was clear that he was money laundering, at the very least, and possibly even dealing out of his stations. But what had gotten Marty's attention had been when Margaret Chaney, Norman's semi-estranged wife, had died in a house fire. All the local cops knew that Chaney had done it for the insurance money, property for the house and life for the wife, and that he'd subsequently fled to New Hampshire. He'd gotten away with it.

After receiving Eric Atwell's name and address from me via message, he gave me Norman Chaney's name and address in return.

Before shooting Eric Atwell in Southwell, Marty had done some research, just to make sure that he wasn't killing some kind of saint. He'd discovered, of course, that Atwell was a known scumbag. There'd been a few arrests for minor violations: driving while intoxicated; possession of a controlled substance. But there'd also been three separate restraining orders filed against Atwell, from three separate woman, all alleging abuse.

Killing Atwell had not been hard. Marty staked him out for a couple of days, learning that in the late afternoon Atwell would often leave his house and go for long, strenuous walks, wearing headphones, utilizing the multiple isolated walking paths near his farmhouse. Using a gun that Chaney had taken during an abandoned house search two years earlier, he followed him into a wooded section of Southwell and shot him five times.

"You know that scene in *The Wizard of Oz*?" Marty said. "When it goes from black and white to color?"

"Sure," I said.

"That's what it was like for me. The world changed. And I

guess I just assumed the world had changed for you, as well. After I heard what happened to Norman Chaney."

"It didn't," I said. "Well, it did, but it was the reverse. The world drained of color."

He frowned and shrugged. "I guess I was wrong. Still, I figured that maybe you'd felt the same as me, and that I should find out who you were. Maybe even meet you."

As it was, I had been easy to find. Having done his prior research on Atwell, Marty had learned about Atwell's involvement in the death of Claire Mallory, married to a bookstore manager in Boston. Once Chaney had my name, he found my blog, and in particular he found the list I'd written, "Eight Perfect Murders." And there was *Strangers on a Train*, sitting right there in the middle of the list. Marty read the book, then read the remaining recommendations, and the world opened up some more for him. Before all this had happened, he'd been in a broken, loveless marriage. His son was struggling with drug addiction and his daughter would still spend time with him, but he knew, down deep, that it was a chore for her. But now he'd discovered murder, and then, even better, he'd discovered reading. Marty signed the divorce papers, took early retirement, and moved to Boston.

To be near me.

In 2012, he started to come to readings, and eventually we got to know each other. I think he thought it was going to be enough to meet me, to become friends. Maybe we'd even eventually speak about what had happened, about the murders we'd committed for each other. But that didn't happen. Yes, we became friends, but it wasn't enough for him. And as I've already said, we started to spend less time together. And that was when he came up with the idea of finishing off the murders from the list I'd written. It was a way to bond with me because bonding over a couple of beers was not getting it done. In other words, if I'd been better company, a whole bunch of people would never have been murdered. Or maybe that's simply not true. When Marty first killed Eric Atwell, it was like popping a bottle of champagne. The cork was never going to go back into the bottle. And now he had a whole bunch of murder methods to utilize for his new hobby. He just needed a victim.

Before his wife had had an affair, back when Marty Kingship was still living out west in Smithfield, she'd read newscaster Robin Callahan's infamous book about the benefits of adultery. It was called *Life's Too Long* and had been published a year after she'd been caught in a love affair with her married coanchor. It had been tabloid fodder for months, helped along by the fact that Callahan was a striking blonde, and seemingly unrepentant. She cashed in on her notoriety by publishing a book that essentially argued that adultery was more natural than monogamy, that life spans had increased too much to have it make sense for people to stay married forever. She made the talk-show rounds, and the book rocketed up the bestseller charts. Marty Kingship blamed that book for his wife's subsequent fling with the family dentist. I'm sure he wasn't the only man, or woman, with bad feelings about Robin Callahan. But Marty was someone who'd murdered before, gotten away with it, and was itching to try again.

He went through my list of perfect murders, seeing if there were any good ideas for how he could get away with the murder of Robin Callahan. He had particularly loved Agatha Christie's *The A.B.C. Murders*, in which a specific killing was hidden among a string of murders made to look like they'd been done by a madman. What if he could do the same with Robin Callahan. Maybe kill a few people who all had similar names—names of birds, for example. Then he thought he could even leave a single feather at each scene of the crime. Or better yet, mail a single feather to the local police.

And that was what he did. He killed Robin Callahan inside her own home, having gotten inside by showing her his old police identification card. He also killed Ethan Byrd, a local student whom Marty found by searching through police reports looking for bird-related names. Ethan had been arrested at a sports bar in Lowell for threatening the bartender, and for disturbing the peace. He found Jay Bradshaw the same way; he'd been arrested for rape, but never convicted. It turned out Bradshaw spent most of his days on the Cape sitting in his garage, trying to sell used tools. Marty had pulled up in broad daylight, then beat Bradshaw to death with a baseball bat he'd brought and a sledgehammer he'd borrowed.

As soon as he'd begun to plot the *A.B.C. Murders*, Marty knew that he couldn't stop until he'd finished the list. Bill Manso was another name he pulled from browsing police records, a man who had been investigated in a domestic disturbance, but someone who had also been accused by a neighbor of breaking into her house during the daytime, stealing her underwear. This had all happened five years previous, but Marty read up on the case, discovering that Manso had gotten off because he was a regular train commuter into New York City, and that he'd provided evidence that he was commuting at the time of the break-in. The train made him think of *Double Indemnity*, another book on the list. Marty had read it, of course, but he'd also gotten the movie from the local library. He liked the movie better ("It gave me a brand-new appreciation of Fred MacMurray"). He decided to kill Bill Manso, bludgeon him to death, and leave him on the tracks. Then he'd take the commuter rail himself the following morning, bust out a window at just the right time to make it look as though Manso had decided to jump. He knew it wouldn't wash. Scene-of-the-crime investigators would know almost instantly that Manso had been killed elsewhere, and that his body had been staged. But what excited Marty was that someone might start to figure it out, make a connection between the two books, and that it would lead back to me. Maybe they'd even arrest me. Either way, I'd become involved, and that was what he was hoping for.

Marty wasn't sure how to gain access to Bill Manso, but when he got down to Connecticut, it was made easier by the fact that Manso liked to drink at the bar nearest to the train station. Manso would go directly from his commute to the Corridor Bar and Grill at five thirty every day and stumble out of there at about ten at night, to drive the mile and a half to his town house condo. Marty killed him in the parking lot with a telescoping baton ("much better than a baseball bat, let me tell you") and left his body along the tracks. The next day he took the train and punched out a window in between cars using the same steel baton.

Four murders in, Marty got impatient. He didn't say that in so many words, but he decided it was time to get a little more obvious. Time to get me involved.

Like all the regulars at Old Devils, especially anyone who came to our author readings, Marty had known Elaine Johnson. She'd cornered him on numerous occasions to let him know the books he should be reading, and the books that were a waste of time. She told him about that nasty lesbian who owned the apartment she lived in, and about how disgustingly dirty the city of Boston was, and how, without her, the Old Devils Bookstore would have gone out of business years ago. And she told him about her heart condition, how her doctors had told her she should move to a quieter region, make sure that nothing stressed her out.

Knowing she'd moved into her dead sister's house in Rockland, Maine, Marty paid her a visit. He broke into her house when she'd been out—probably terrorizing a staff member at some local bookstore—and hid in her bedroom closet. He wore a clown mask with a large, hideous mouth, full of sharp teeth, and when Elaine Johnson came home, he waited patiently. He could hear her puttering around downstairs, oblivious to his presence. Eventually, she came upstairs to the bedroom, and went straight to the closet, opening it up. All he had to do was stand there, then take a step toward her. She turned white, then pawed at her chest, then did exactly what he'd been hoping she'd do. She died of a heart attack.

"Why'd you leave the books?" I said.

"I wanted them to come to you, at some point at least. I knew that the murder of Elaine Johnson was absolutely foolproof. There'd be no way any coroner would consider it a suspicious death. So I left the books, just hoping to muddy the waters. Hoping someone in law enforcement somewhere would be smart enough to put it all together."

"Someone did," I said.

"And you panicked and came running to me for help. I never thought that would happen, but I was thrilled when it did. It was good to hear your voice, asking me for a favor."

"You could have ended it there. You'd gotten what you wanted."

"No. What I wanted was to complete the project, but I wanted you along for the ride. And that's what we have, now, the two of us. Do you want to hear the rest?"

CHAPTER 29

After you told me that the FBI had paid you a visit, I knew that someone had finally noticed. I knew that the closer things got to you, the faster you'd try and figure out who I was. So, just to delay the inevitable, I handed you Nick Pruitt on a silver platter."

Marty told me that it was true that Pruitt had made a formal complaint against Norman Chaney after the house fire that killed Chaney's wife, Pruitt's sister. And for that reason, Marty had already checked Pruitt out before I ever asked him for information on Chaney's death. Pruitt was a recovering alcoholic with a few arrests on his record, someone Marty thought was the perfect candidate for the murder based on *Malice Aforethought*. If Pruitt suddenly died of alcohol poisoning, who would suspect it was a murder? He had a verifiable past as someone who abused alcohol.

After Marty and I had drinks at Jack Crow's Tavern on that Wednesday night, Marty went to a liquor store and bought a bottle of scotch to take to Pruitt in New Essex. "He just let me in. I'd shown him my gun, of course. Told him I needed him to take a few drinks. Once he started, he actually couldn't stop. It wasn't that hard to convince him to drink almost the whole bottle. I'd laced it with liquid benzos, just to be sure."

He smiled. "After Pruitt was a dead end, I figured I could push you toward thinking Brian Murray, or even Tess, was involved. Did it work? Did you actually notice the brand of scotch?"

"I did," I said.

"That pleases me," Marty said, as though I'd just complimented him on his sweater.

"How well do you know Brian and Tess Murray?" I said.

"Tess I just met tonight. Played a little hide-and-seek with her around the house before you got here. I know Brian pretty well, just through the store, but over the past few years I've gotten into the habit of stopping by that hotel bar he likes and having a few with him. I actually saw you with the two of them on Tuesday night. I knew Tess was back because of Brian's broken arm. And now it's all set up. Police'll find Brian's dead body in his home—I'm thinking a pillow over the face with a gun fired into it—and Tess will have disappeared. We can even pack a suitcase for her. It will be just like *Red House Mystery*. One dead body, one fleeing murderer. All we need is a good place to hide her body."

"What's wrong with her, with Tess?" I said, glancing toward where she was still sleeping curled up on the sofa. She hadn't moved.

"I slipped some of that benzodiazepine into the coffee she was drinking. Put it in her port, as well, and I think she had some of that. There's a good chance she took enough to put her over, but if not, I don't think it'll be a problem finishing her off. Something gentle like a plastic bag over the head should do it."

I think we'd both gotten used to hearing the steady snoring coming from Brian in the downstairs bedroom, but suddenly we both heard a loud grunting snore, so violent that we both looked at each other. Marty picked the gun up off his thigh and turned his attention in that direction. "Sleep apnea," he said. "I doubt he'll wake himself up, but let's go have a look."

He stood up and I could hear his knees pop. "You, too," he said, pointing the gun toward me. I stood, as well.

Together we walked to the guest bedroom at the end of the

hall, me first, with Marty behind me. The door had been left open a crack, and I pushed it open. It was dark inside, but a small amount of light came through a window so that I could see Brian, lying on his back above the sheets of the bed. Tess had left his clothes on, but his pants were unbuttoned, his belt hanging loose. I watched as his chest fluttered a little, rising and falling fast, then he let out another explosive snore. I didn't know how it hadn't woken him.

"Jesus," Marty said from behind me. "Let's put the mother-fucker out of his misery."

I turned, just as Marty flicked the wall switch, and the bedroom was suddenly flooded with light from a floor lamp. Above the bed that Brian was sleeping on was a large abstract painting, chunky blocks of red and black.

"You can quit right now, Marty," I said.

"And do what?"

"Turn yourself in. We'll both do it. We'll go together." I knew it was a long shot, but Marty seemed tired, and it occurred to me that he was at the end of this particular game. Maybe, down deep, he wanted to get caught.

He shook his head. "It sounds exhausting, having to talk to all those cops, and then the lawyers and the psychiatrists. It's easier to keep going. We're almost done here. Eight perfect murders. Your favorite murders, Mal."

"They were my favorites in books, not in real life."

Marty was quiet for a moment, and I thought that he was maybe breathing a little heavy. For a moment, I fantasized that he might just keel over dead from a sudden heart attack. He looked up, though, and said, "I'll admit that the thought of it all being over is not unpleasant. I tell you what I will do for you. I'll let you have this one—have Brian—because, frankly, I've been doing all the heavy lifting since you took care of Norman Chaney. I'll give you this gun, and all you have to do is go put a pillow over his face and fire the gun into it. I don't think the neighbors will hear it, and if they do, they'll just figure they heard something else. A car backfiring, or something."

"Sure," I said and held out my hand.

"I know what you're thinking, Mal. If I give you the gun, then you can keep me at gunpoint and call the cops, but I'm not going to let that happen. I'll come after you and you'll have to shoot me. So, either way, you're going to have to shoot someone. It's either Brian, here, or me. I'm giving you that choice. And if it's me, that's okay. I've got a prostate the size of a whiffle ball. I've had my go-around. I think these last few years, getting to know you, and playing this little game, it's all been gravy."

"Not for everyone."

"Ha. I suppose so. But, down deep, like me, you know none of this really matters much. If I hand you this gun and you put a bullet through Brian's brain, you'll be doing him a favor, most likely. You just might like it, too. Trust me."

"Okay," I said, extending my hand farther toward him.

He smiled. Whatever I'd seen in his eyes earlier, that happiness, was gone now. I saw what I always used to see in his eyes. I always thought it was kindness.

He put the gun in my hand. It was a revolver, and I pulled the hammer back.

"It's a double action revolver," Marty said. "You don't actually need to cock the hammer."

I looked at Brian Murray, prostrate on the bed, and then I turned back to Marty and shot him in the chest.

CHAPTER 30

The penultimate chapter of *The Murder of Roger Ackroyd* is called "The Whole Truth." It's when the narrator, the country doctor who is secretly the murderer, reveals to the readers exactly what he's done.

I haven't given any of my chapters in this narrative a title. It's an old-fashioned convention, I guess, and it seems a little corny. What would I have called that last chapter? Maybe something like, "Charlie Shows His Face." See what I mean? Corny. But if I had done it, if I had given these chapters a name, then this chapter would definitely have been called, "The Whole Truth."

THE NIGHT MY WIFE died I'd followed her in my car out to Southwell, to Eric Atwell's place. It wasn't the first time I'd been there. After figuring out that Claire had gotten back into drugs, and that she was most likely involved with someone at Black Barn Enterprises, I'd driven past the restored farmhouse a few times. I'd even seen Atwell once, at least I thought it was him. He was jogging along the sidewalk not far from his house, wearing a maroon jogging outfit. As he ran, he performed little boxing moves, punching like he was Rocky Balboa.

On New Year's Eve that year Claire and I had decided to stay home. She told me that there was a small party out at Black Barn but now that she'd stopped taking drugs (at least that's what she'd told me), there was no reason for her to go. We roasted a chicken together that night. I made some mashed potatoes, and she steamed some brussels sprouts. We drank a bottle of Vermentino while we ate, then opened a second bottle after we'd cleaned up. We were settling in to watch a movie, *Eternal Sunshine of the Spotless Mind*, one of Claire's favorites. I liked it, too. At least I did back then. Now, the very thought of it makes me nauseated.

I must have fallen asleep because when I woke up the film was over, the screen showing the menu options of the DVD. On the coffee table was a note from Claire.

I'll be back soon. I promise, and I'm sorry. Love, C

I knew where she'd gone, of course. Outside, her Subaru was no longer parked on our street. I got into my Chevy Impala and drove out to Southwell.

There was some kind of small party going on at Atwell's house when I got there. Five cars were in the driveway and two more along the street, including Claire's. I parked about two hundred yards away, just pulling my car tight against the side of the road. This part of Southwell was sparsely populated. It was mostly gently rolling old farmland, crisscrossed by stone walls and dotted here and there by million-dollar homes.

I left my car, stepping out into the cold, clear night. I'd departed my house so suddenly that I wasn't properly dressed, just wearing an old jean jacket over a sweater and jeans. I buttoned the jacket up to my throat, tucked my hands into my pockets, and walked along the road to Atwell's place. A small, discreet sign with the words BLACK BARN ENTERPRISES was posted next to the mailbox. I stood there for a moment, studying the house from a distance. There was the farmhouse, painted white, and looming beside it was an enormous barn. I'd seen it in the daytime, of course, and it wasn't even painted black. It was more of a dark gray, but it had been modernized into a stylized workspace, its front doors replaced by solid glass, and the inside converted into an open-concept work studio, with modular desks and Ping-Pong tables.

Skirting along the edge of the property, I got close enough to the barn to see that even though it was lit by hanging industrial light fixtures, no one was inside. The party was happening inside the house. I went around the back of the barn to approach the house from the rear, and I was stunned for a moment by the view. It was close to a full moon and there were no clouds in the sky. Atwell's property was on a slight ridge, and from where I stood, I could see across the sloping fields, all the way to a line of dark trees, all bathed in silver moonlight. I stared at it for a few moments, shivering in my thin jacket, until suddenly I could hear laughter and could smell cigarette smoke in the air. At the rear corner of the barn I could see the back deck, clearly an add-on to the farmhouse. A couple I didn't recognize smoked cigarettes and laughed uproariously, the specifics of their conversation getting carried away by the bitter wind. I watched them finish their cigarettes then go back inside the house. After approaching the nearest window, I peered inside.

There are many things I'll never forget about the night, but the image that I saw through the window is certainly one of them. About twenty people were milling about a large, well-furnished living room. At its center was an overstuffed leather couch, and that's where I could see Claire, dressed in a short green corduroy skirt and a cream silk blouse I felt as though I'd never seen before. She was next to Atwell, their shoulders touching, and she held a champagne glass in her hand. The room was dimly lit but I could see that there was a small mound of white powder on the glass-topped coffee table, and one of the guests was kneeling on the carpeted floor cutting himself a line. Techno music, the kind you'd hear in a club, pounded from the house, and behind the couch three of the guests were dancing. But what I'll never really forget was how Claire looked; not her clothes, and not even the way she was pressed up against Atwell, one of his hands touching her naked thigh, but the glow of her face. It was the drugs, but it was also something else, a gleam of pure animal joy. She kept laughing, her mouth opened wide in a way that seemed unnatural, her lips wet.

I walked back to my car, turned on the engine, and cranked the heat all the way up. I was shivering but I was also crying. And then I got angry, punching my fist repeatedly against the roof of the car. I was angry at Claire, of course, and Atwell, but I think I was angry at myself most of all. At least right then. Because what I planned on doing was driving back to Somerville and waiting for my wife, hoping she'd return safe and sound, and hoping one day she would return to just me.

The car warmed up, and I calmed down. From where I was parked, I could see Claire's Subaru along the road, and I decided to wait. I knew from past experience that she would not spend the night, that she'd be back before morning came, even though it might be late. And I knew that I would forgive her, that I would do what my mother always did with my father. I'd wait for her to return to me. But the longer I sat in my car, the engine purring, heat pumping from the vents, the more I found myself growing livid at Claire. I knew she was a drug addict, and that on some level she could not help herself, but she'd also looked so happy in Atwell's living room, so alive.

It was two thirty in the morning when I saw the two figures appear next to Claire's car. In the moonlight I saw them come together, and kiss, then Claire opened the door—I could make out the hooded winter coat above the bare legs—and stepped inside while Atwell jogged back to his house. The brake lights came on, then she made a U-turn. Her headlights must have picked up my car in the shadow of a cluster of pine trees, but she must not have paid attention. She sped away down the street toward Route 2.

I followed her. She drove fast on the back roads, but once she was on the highway heading back toward Boston, she slowed down to the exact speed limit. It was New Year's Eve, still, and police were probably out in force looking for drunk drivers. Something about that fact irked me, that despite whatever she'd ingested that night, and whatever she'd done, she was careful enough to avoid getting pulled over. In the same way I knew that when she got back to our shared apartment she'd quietly sneak in the door, not wanting to wake me. And that when we talked about what happened the following morning, she'd cry and say she was a terrible person and beg forgiveness. She wanted the double life, but she didn't want the confrontation. It was the way she was. I remember thinking that I'd have more respect for her if she just left me, if she gave in to the fact that she'd rather be with Eric Atwell, that she'd rather be an addict. Then at least we could have it out.

There were a few other cars along the two-lane highway but not many. I stayed close behind her, not really worried that she'd notice. She hadn't noticed me on the side of the street outside of Atwell's house and she probably wouldn't notice me now. I'd driven this route many times, and we were approaching an over-pass. There was only a low guardrail along the edge. Suddenly I imagined Claire losing control of her car, plunging off the edge, and landing on the road below. Without thinking too much about it, I sped up, overtaking Claire in the passing lane. For a moment we were side by side, and I looked over at her, but all I could see was her profile in darkness. She might have turned toward me, but it was hard to tell. What would she have seen? My face in darkness, as well. Would she have recognized me?

I overtook her but stayed in my lane. The overpass was coming up fast and I was imagining scenarios. What if I nudged her, edging my own car into her lane? Would she let us collide, spin out together, and go over the edge? Down deep, I knew that she wouldn't. My wife avoided collisions. That didn't stop her from wrecking her own life, but I knew that if I pulled into her lane, she'd swerve to avoid me.

I did it. I cut diagonally across in front of her when we were barreling along the overpass, and she did exactly what I thought she'd do. She drove right off the edge.

BACK AT HOME, I waited for the police to arrive. They showed up at eight in the morning to tell me that my wife was dead. It was a relief, of course. I'd been worried that maybe I'd injured her in some horrible way. I'd also been worried that maybe she'd killed someone else when her car had landed on the road below. But she hadn't, and for that I was also grateful.

IT'S A FUNNY THING grieving for someone you've murdered. In the beginning my sadness was coupled with an enormous guilt. I kept wondering if I'd simply let Claire drive home that night what would have happened next. Maybe she'd have asked me to check her into a rehabilitation center, that she'd hit bottom, and wanted to get better. Or maybe she'd have kept returning to Atwell for drugs, and I'd have let her do it. Just waiting around, hoping she might change.

Reading her diary helped. There was such a clear villain in the story of Claire and me, and that villain was Eric Atwell. Finding a way to kill him got me through the worst of my grief, and then time did its trick. I haven't gotten over it, but it did get easier. I bought the store and immersed myself in work. Even though I stopped reading crime novels myself—violent death loomed too large in them—I knew enough to help my customers. I was a bookseller, and I was good at it. That was enough.

CHAPTER 31

The phone rang, and then switched over to voice mail. I hit
end on my cell phone and was about to destroy the phone
when it buzzed. Gwen Mulvey was calling back.

"Hey."

"What's going on?" she said.

"Have you heard anything?"

"Anything about what?"

"There's a dead man in Boston. His name is Marty Kingship, and he's Charlie. He's *our* Charlie. He killed Robin Callahan, Ethan Byrd, and Jay Bradshaw. And he killed Bill Manso and
Elaine Johnson, and one night ago he killed Nicholas Pruitt in
New Essex, Massachusetts."

"Slow down," she said. "Where is he now? You said he's dead?"

"I just called 911 and gave them the address. They should be on
the way."

"Who killed him?"

"I did. I shot him late last night. More like this morning. He
was going to kill Brian and Tess Murray and make it look like the
murder from *The Red House Mystery*."

"Who was he?"

"He'd been a police officer in Smithfield, Massachusetts. He'd
retired and was living in Boston. He also killed Eric Atwell. He
did it for me. I asked him to. That's how this whole thing started.
It's my fault, really. I started it. Marty was insane, but I started it."

"You're going to need to slow down, Mal. Where are you right now? Can I come to you?"

For one brief moment I thought about it. Thought about seeing Gwen again just one more time. But I also knew that there was no way to do that without ending up in a holding cell, and I had decided a long time ago that I would never willingly allow that to happen.

I said, "Sorry, no. And I can't talk long. As soon as we're done here, I'm getting rid of this cell phone. I have five minutes. What do you want to know?"

I heard a sharp intake of breath. "Are you hurt?" she said.

"No, I'm fine."

"Did you know it was him all along?"

"Marty? No, I didn't. We planned it all online, and never gave each other our identities. He figured out who I was, then found my list, and started using it. I only figured out who he was last night. If I'd known earlier, I would have told you."

"You said Nicholas Pruitt is dead. That's the name you gave me, right? Last time we talked?"

"I thought that Pruitt might have been Charlie, but he wasn't. He died from an overdose of alcohol and some kind of drug. Check the house for Kingship's prints. They'll probably be there."

"Good lord."

"Look, when you talk with the investigators on this case, just tell them that I called you with this information. You don't need to say that you came and found me in Boston. I want you to get your job back."

"I'm not sure that'll happen."

"I think it will. You'll get some credit for figuring out that the list and the murders were connected. Give them the information they don't have. He killed Eric Atwell, with a gun he said he took from a crime scene. Tell them we met on a website called Duck-burg. You'll be fine."

"I have a lot more questions."

"I have to go. Sorry, Gwen."

"Can I ask you one more, then?"

"Of course," I said. I knew what it would be.

"What happened to my father? Did Marty kill Steve Clifton?"

I must have hesitated for a few seconds because she added, "Or was it you? I need to know."

"After Claire . . . after my wife died, I have a very hard time remembering the following year. I had terrible dreams, and I was filled with guilt, and maybe I was drinking too much."

"Okay," she said.

"And during that time, I had this recurring dream, and some-times I wonder if it actually happened." It was cold where I was standing, but I could feel sweat beading up at the base of my neck while I talked. "In this dream I hit your father with my car. I got out to see if he was okay, and he wasn't, of course, but he was still alive. His legs were going one way and the top part of his body was going the other. I told him who I was and why I was there, and then I watched him die."

"Okay, thanks," Gwen said in a voice I couldn't read.

"It still feels like a dream," I said. "It all feels like a dream."

"Are you sure you can't meet with me? I could drive to you. I'd come alone."

"No," I said, after a moment. "Sorry, Gwen, I just can't. I just don't think I could take it if I was arrested—"

"I told you I would come alone."

"—and I don't want to answer any more questions. I don't want to relive the past any more than I've had to do these past few days. It's been pure luck that I've had these few years, even though, down deep, I knew it couldn't last. Sorry, I can't see you again. It's impossible."

"You do have a choice in the matter," Gwen said.

"I don't. I really don't. It might not seem like it to you, but the last five years . . . I have terrible dreams every night. I managed to keep going because it was all I knew how to do, but there hasn't been any joy in it. I'm not afraid, anymore, but I am tired."

I thought I heard a sigh on the other end of the line.

"Is there anything else you want to tell me?" Gwen said.

"No."

"Okay. But what you've told me is the truth?"

"Yes," I said. "Everything I've said is true."

CHAPTER 32

Claire Mallory
Eric Atwell
Norman Chaney
Steven Clifton
Robin Callahan
Ethan Byrd
Jay Bradshaw
Bill Manso
Elaine Johnson
Nicholas Pruitt
Marty Kingship

Those are the names of the dead. The real names. All except for Marty Kingship.

I don't know why I changed his name for the purposes of this narrative. Maybe because he has children, and they, like all children, are innocent of their parents' crimes. And maybe it's because he's the only one on the list who deserves blame for what happened. Besides me, of course.

It's funny, I just now realized that Marty Kingship has my initials. Freudian slip, I suppose. I also suppose that astute readers out there will be convinced that there is no Marty Kingship, that there is only Malcolm Kershaw, and that I did all the killings myself. It's not true. I wish it was, in a way. It would make for a clever ending.

What is true is that I am responsible for everything that happened. Marty carried most of the acts out, but I was the architect. It all started with me.

That is the truth. I have committed the sin of omission, but when I said something is true, it is. Believe me.

I AM IN ROCKLAND, Maine.

After shooting Marty Kingship (he looked almost pleased as he touched the blood coming through his sweater, then shuddered and died), I went first to Brian Murray. He'd woken when I'd fired the shot, of course, lifting his head, and muttering something. I sat by his side and told him that it was a champagne bottle he'd heard. He rolled over and began to snore again.

Then I checked on Tess. Humphrey was no longer occupying the sofa across from her. He'd heard the shot and disappeared. As Marty had said, "Some guard dog."

Tess was still breathing, and she was on her side so if she did vomit, I thought she'd be okay. It meant that I didn't need to call 911 right away. I would call them soon enough, but I wanted just a little bit of time.

I returned to my own apartment and packed a bag. Cold weather clothes, some toiletries, my favorite picture of Claire. It was from our honeymoon, two rainy weeks in London, the best weeks of my life. The picture was taken in a pub, Claire sitting across from me, a slight smirk on her face, not sure she really wanted to have her picture taken, but happy nonetheless.

I thought about going to Old Devils one last time, saying goodbye to Nero, but it would take time that I wasn't sure I had. I needed to call the police and let them know that there was a dead body in the residence of Brian and Tess Murray. I wanted to do this soon, of course, because of Tess and the drugs in her system. But

I also didn't want Brian to wake up early in the morning to find a corpse in his bedroom.

The sky was beginning to lighten as I drove into New Hampshire. I pulled off the highway into a twenty-four-hour convenience store, and using cash, I bought enough canned food and bottled beer to last me a week. After loading up the trunk of my car in the parking lot, I called 911 on my cell phone, identified myself, and said there was a dead man at 59 Deering Street in Boston. Then I called Gwen, and when she called me back, we had the conversation that I've already written about. Afterward, I smashed the cell phone with a brick I found in the parking lot, then put the pieces in a trash bin outside of the store. If they decided to trace me, then I guess they'd figure out that I was traveling north. But I wasn't too worried about it.

It had actually snowed a lot less north of the city. There was a scrim of white over everything, more frost than snow, and in the dawn hours the sky was a checkerboard of thin clouds. The world was colorless.

I reached Rockland by midmorning. I considered waiting somewhere until it was dark again but decided to risk it instead. There was only one other house with a view of Elaine Johnson's old property, and I would just have to hope that whoever lived there was not spending the morning looking out the window. From my previous visit to Elaine's house, I'd noticed the single-car garage. Its door had been up, and I remembered it as being empty inside. Elaine's car, a rusty Lincoln, probably too big for the garage, had sat encased in ice in the driveway.

I found the house immediately, not far from Route 1 and turned into the unplowed drive with enough speed so that I didn't get stuck. I pulled into the garage, killed the engine, then got out and yanked down the garage door by its rusted handle. I had briefly looked across the street before I did this, toward a boxy, shingled house, smoke billowing from its chimney. I was happy that the front of the garage wasn't angled toward the street. Hopefully no one would notice that its door was now down.

I popped a single pane of glass from the back door, reached in, and unlocked it. Once I was inside with my food and my duffel bag, I found some cardboard and tape and sealed the door back up.

The heat was still on, although the thermostat was set to the low sixties. It was cold, but bearable. I unpacked my food and put the beer in the fridge next to what remained of Elaine's unclaimed provisions. It was clear that she had been living on cottage cheese and tinned fruit. There was a decent couch in the living room, midcentury style with wooden legs, and a low back. I decided that I would sleep there. I went upstairs to look for clean sheets and a blanket and found them in the master bedroom closet. All I could think about was Marty in his clown mask emerging from this very closet to scare Elaine Johnson to death. She wasn't my favorite person, but she hadn't deserved that. When I got back to the living room, I knew that I would never go upstairs again.

IT'S BEEN FOUR DAYS and I'm still here. I work on this manuscript, and I eat canned beef stew and tomato soup. The beer is gone but I found several gallon bottles of Gallo burgundy in the cellar and I am working steadily through those.

Mostly what I do is read. During the day I sit in a comfortable club chair by a window. At night I read on the couch, using a penlight under a blanket to see. I am reading mysteries again, not just because they are the only books here, but because I don't have much time left and I want to revisit some of my favorites. I find that I am most drawn to books I first read when I was barely a teenager. Agatha Christie novels. Robert Parkers. Gregory Mc-Donald's Fletch novels. I read *When the Sacred Ginmill Closes* by

Lawrence Block in one sitting and cried after finishing the last sentence.

I do wish there were more poetry books in this house—I found an anthology of American poetry that had been published in 1962. But I also managed to write down some of my favorite poems from memory. "Winter Nightfall," of course, by Sir John Squire, "Aubade" by Philip Larkin, "Crossing the Water" by Sylvia Plath, and at least half the stanzas from "Elegy Written in a Country Churchyard" by Thomas Gray.

THERE IS NO INTERNET here, and I don't have a phone.

I am sure they are looking for me, the man who killed Marty Kingship, the man who has the answers to a string of related murders. I don't know how much Gwen has helped them out. I assume that she has told them everything about our phone call. Maybe she hasn't told them how we met in Boston after she'd been suspended. I wonder if she might figure out where I am. So far no one has come knocking on this door.

They'll still have plenty of questions. Gwen, I'm sure, still has questions. That's one of the reasons why I'm writing this memoir. I want to set the record straight. I want to tell the whole truth.

I WROTE THAT I burned Claire's entire diary after reading it. That's not entirely true. I saved one page, probably because I wanted some proof that she had loved me, something in her own handwriting.

The entry was from the spring of 2009, and this is what she wrote:

I don't write enough about Mal in these pages and how happy he can make me. I come home late and he is always on the couch waiting.

More often than not he is asleep, a book cracked open and across his chest. Last night when I woke him up he was so pleased to see me. He said he'd read a poem that he thought I'd like.

I did like it, maybe even loved it. It's a Bill Knott and I'm going to copy it down here so I will never forget. It's called "Goodbye."

If you are still alive when you read this,
close your eyes. I am
under their lids, growing black.

What else have I lied about?

I don't know if this was a lie so much as an omission, but when I killed Norman Chaney up in Tickhill, New Hampshire, I made it sound as though after I strangled him, I left him there on the floor. But in reality, after checking his pulse, I must have panicked, because I picked up the crowbar and hit him in the face and head repeatedly. I won't describe what he looked like when I'd finished but I sat down on the floor and thought that I would never get up again, that I would never be sane again. It was Nero coming across the floor that eventually saved me. He gave me a reason to get up and out of the house. I think I made it sound as though I'd saved Nero, but he was actually the one who saved me. Trite, I know. But the truth sometimes is.

When I told Gwen about my dream of killing Steven Clifton, I was telling the truth, as well. The truth as I know it. I really don't remember a lot of what happened in that year after Claire's death (after I ran Claire off the road, I guess I should say), but I do remember that dream, that vivid dream of hitting Clifton with my car. And there are moments, lucid moments, when I remember everything, when it all falls into place. But those moments never last.

Steven Clifton was terrified. I remember his face. It was pale as milk, almost a blur. It was Gwen's face. I suppose it wasn't a dream, after all.

THERE'S ONE OTHER OMISSION I ought to record. When Marty and I were talking in the Murrays' house, the night he told me everything, I asked him about the comment he left on the Old Devils website, the comment he posted using the name Doctor Sheppard.

He'd looked confused when I asked him about it. "Doctor Sheppard," I said. "He was the killer in *The Murder of Roger Ackroyd*."

Now that I think about it, I think that it was possible I was the one who left that comment. It rings a distant bell. Like I've said, there have been many nights in the past few years when I don't know what is real and what is a dream. Claire, her face in darkness, turning and looking at me from her car right before I nudged her off the overpass. Norman Chaney, what was left of him, on the floor of his house in Tickhill. The jolt of the car as Steven Clifton went flying through the summery air. Beer sometimes helps, and maybe I drank so much that I left myself a message in the comments section for "Eight Perfect Murders."

And if it was me, then it was a premonition of sorts. I am reading *The Murder of Roger Ackroyd* now, again. I found a copy at the bottom of a stack in the corner of Elaine Johnson's dining room. It's the Pocket paperback edition, Ackroyd slumped over in his chair on the cover, a knife protruding from high up on his back. It's a dull book, really, until you get to the last two chapters. I've already mentioned the penultimate one, the chapter titled "The Whole Truth."

Well, the last chapter is called "Apologia" and it is the chapter that makes you realize that all along you've been reading a suicide note.

IT IS SNOWING OUTSIDE, and the wind is battering at the windows of the house. I've taken a huge risk and lit a fire in the fireplace. Still, I don't think anyone will notice a little bit of chimney smoke during a storm like this one.

It's so nice by the fire with a glass of wine. For my last book, I am reading *And Then There Were None*. If it isn't my favorite novel of all time, it's pretty damn close. Appropriate, too, for the circumstances.

I'd like to say something here about how I'll be with Claire again, soon, but I don't believe any of that nonsense. When we die, we become nothing, the same nothing we were before we were born, but, of course, this time that nothingness is forever. But if it's where Claire is, in the black, in the nothing, then that is where I should be as well.

My plan is that when the storm comes to an end, and the plows have done their job, I will fill the pockets of my winter coat with the heavy glass paperweights from the shelf in the living room. At nightfall I will walk from the house into Rockland's center, and from there out to the jetty, the one that extends a mile out to the sea, creating a breakwater for Rockland Harbor. I will walk to the end, and just keep going. I'm not looking forward to the cold water, but I don't suppose I'll feel the cold for very long.

There will be some satisfaction that I'll die by drowning, that in a sense I'll be fulfilling one of the murders from my list. MacDonald's *The Drowner*.

Maybe they'll wonder if it wasn't a suicide, after all. Or maybe my body will never be found.

It's nice to think I'll leave a mystery in my wake.

ACKNOWLEDGMENTS

[TK]